THE WORLD WITHIN

A WEIRDWATER ROMANCE

DANI FINN

DRAGONHEART PRESS

Copyright © 2024 by Dani Finn

Cover design by Dani Finn

All rights reserved.

No portion of this book may be reproduced in any form without written permission from the publisher or author, except as permitted by U.S. copyright law.

CONTENT WARNINGS

The World Within is intended for an adult audience. Content warnings include numerous explicit, consensual sex scenes, occasional dysphoria, societal transphobia, and child peril.

Author's note

The World Within is set in the Weirdwater universe and includes some characters from *The Living Waters* and *Unpainted* but is meant as a standalone.

One detail that may be relevant for some readers: Aven, a side character in this book who was a main character in *Unpainted*, used he/him in *Unpainted* but has shifted to use they/them in the time elapsed between these two stories.

This book is dedicated to other-me, the one I see through the Sooth Mirror.

I hope she's thriving, wherever she is.

1

Lila shared a glance with Aven and Tera, who stood on either side of her with clipboards and huge rings of carefully labeled keys. Aven raised their eyebrows and pushed out a wide smile; Tera blinked softly. Lila blew out a slow breath, turned the knob, and threw open the door.

A gong sounded behind her on cue, and a collective buzz rose from the line of well-heeled attendees stretching through the courtyard gate. Most were painted faces, but not all; the only requirement was the willingness to plunk down a thousand poul to pre-order the new flameglass vibrating olli from the Silver Dock workshop in Rontaia. Lila flashed her biggest smile and twisted her hips so her flowery lavender dress twirled dramatically.

"Welcome to the exclusive pre-opening of The World Within!" She remembered to breathe before continuing. "The price of admission is a pre-order key for the latest in Rontaian interactive pleasureware." She nodded as a number of people raised their silver keys, which had been Aven's idea, and a good one at that. The alchemical vibrating ollis came in locking decorative boxes with silver inlay, and the customers would trade their generic keys for the real ones tonight at the opening. "And while no one is obliged to personally thank the proprietress for bringing such joy into your lives, kisses are an acceptable way to show your appreciation."

The first in line, a sky-blue-painted woman in her thirties who had visited Lila's old shop in the fourth ring, giggled to her husband and strode forward with a smile. She put gentle hands on Lila's shoulders and leaned in for a light kiss, which Lila deepened just a touch. The woman's eyes widened and she covered her smile as she drifted toward her green-and-silver-painted husband, who swooped in and gave Lila a gallant peck on the lips. He pulled away quickly, his eyes narrowing as he flashed a too-sharp smile.

Lila sighed internally as she stretched her smile wider. Even in the most educated circles, not everyone was at ease around the transcendent. She breathed through it and prepared for the next in line.

In the end, she accepted kisses from the majority of those in line, some on the cheek, but most on the lips. Only a few tried to push their luck and get more than a quick peck. She put them in their place firmly but gently. She'd decided to sacrifice her body—and her dignity—to make this an event to remember. From the wide-eyed smiles on their faces once she had finally greeted everyone and joined them inside, she'd succeeded beyond her wildest imaginings. Guests filled the spacious lobby, their excited chatter echoing off the domed ceiling as trays of bubble wine and canapés circulated among them.

Lila excused herself from the conversation she was half engaged in as Tera and Aven approached, comparing clipboards and key rings. Tera's ring was empty, but Aven's still had one key left.

Lila glanced at Aven's clipboard. "I think I'd remember if I'd kissed Sylvan Kirin."

Aven shrugged apologetically.

"He'll be here." Tera put a reassuring hand on Lila's shoulder. "He keeps his own schedule."

"So does the Silver Dock delivery person, apparently," Lila muttered. The new mechanical vibrating ollis were supposed to have been delivered three days ago, and while they weren't strictly necessary for the soft opening, she'd hoped to show them off as a teaser tonight.

"It wouldn't be opening night without a few hiccups," Aven said cheerfully. Their smile faltered when Lila flashed them a withering stare, then re-formed when she relented in the space of half a second. They were far too cute for her to hold a grudge against.

"He's surely on his way," Tera reassured her. "He told me himself how much he was looking forward to it." She frowned, looking up at the cracked ceiling of the lobby, which the rows of waterfall plants had more or less disguised. "He went on and on about the harmonics of the lobby." Lila sensed there was something Tera wasn't saying, but the door banged open abruptly, interrupting her inquiry.

"I said, I've got it!" A short, muscular woman in neat gray overalls and a ponytail eased a dolly with several crates strapped to it through the doorway. She had the reddish-brown coloring common to Rontaia and the Naeili Gulf, which would make sense if she were delivering the order of one hundred hand-powered vibrating ollis from the Silver Dock workshop three days late. Sylvan Kirin hovered just outside the door in a blue and purple robe in the Naeili style, his silvered eyebrows rising above his pale-gray-painted face.

"I should say so, and I apologize for my intrusion. As I said, I'm—"

"Sylvan Kirin, I know. I've delivered to your house before. That glass fountain you had commissioned this spring?" Her voice had a playful sharpness to it; she was getting her dig in without twisting the knife.

Sylvan smacked his forehead dramatically. "Yes, gods, how could I forget? You installed it by yourself, with some sort of..." he wiggled his fingers in the air. "Like a miniature crane, wasn't it?"

"A gantry. Yes, it was a lovely piece, I must say, and as much as I'd love to talk about it, I really must deliver these crates to Ms. Lila Thelkis right away, so if you happen to—"

"That would be me." Lila ran her fingertips across the top crate, which had the dripping S.D. of the Silver Dock logo burned into the lid. "You got here just in time."

The woman's sharp brown eyes softened with contrition. "I am *so* sorry for the delay. There was a flood near Guluch, and the bridge was underwater for four days. Even the ferries couldn't make it upriver."

"And yet you're only three days late."

The corner of her mouth turned up in a proud smile. "My girls run on rails." Her smile faltered a little, and she glanced toward the door. "Speaking of which, if we could check this inventory, I'd love to get my horses squared away. It's been a long day."

"Of course, well..." Lila glanced at the guests, many of whom were watching the exchange with scarcely disguised interest. She eyed Sylvan, then glanced toward the masses of people filling the lobby.

"We could use a little distraction," she whispered.

"I had heard something about guests getting kisses," he said theatrically, drawing oohs and aahs and laughter from the crowd. His eyes sparkled with mirth as he moved in with lips pursed chastely. Lila clasped the back of his neck and kissed him long and slowly, curious to see how he would react. He kissed her back as one might kiss a fellow actor on the stage, playing the part to perfection with friendly warmth, but no more. He winked, then turned and strode into the crowd, which parted to greet him, seeming to forget Lila and the delivery woman for the moment.

"Right this way...I don't believe I caught your name."

"Avisse." She took Lila's outstretched hand, matching her grip and gaze before returning her attention to the cart. "I love your dress, by the way. I always wished I could pull off lavender."

Lila steeled her jaw, wishing for a moment she were painted again to hide her blush. "I'm of the opinion anyone can pull off anything if they want it enough. This way."

She led Avisse to the office, which was not in any shape for company—not that a delivery woman counted as company, but still. Ledgers and bills crowded the usually neat desk, along with the remains of Lila's half-eaten chicken and olive pasta. She scooped the dish to the side and cleared space on the desk while Avisse was getting her paperwork together with precise gestures. She had working hands, strongly veined, with callused fingers, maybe from riding. Lila's throat was suddenly parched, and she was pleased to discover half a flute of bubble wine in her hand. She tipped the glass and almost choked on it as she saw Avisse smirking at her.

"Sorry," she sputtered. "It's been a long night, and it's only just begun. Can I offer you something?"

"I wouldn't say no to a glass of water. It's been a long day for me too."

Lila sighed with relief when she saw half a carafe and a clean glass on the desk. She served Avisse, who drained half of it, then wiped her lips with the back of her hand. She glanced back toward the door, then stood and pulled a small pry bar from her belt.

"If you're ready, I'll just open these up then so we can do the inspection?"

"Of course!" Lila rushed forward, almost tripping in her haste. She'd nearly died from a heart attack inspecting the shipment of alchemical vibrators. Though these only cost a quarter of what those did, they still represented a huge investment.

Avisse pried the lid off with smooth, practiced movements. Lila couldn't help noticing the muscles in her arms flexing with each corner she lifted. She tipped her empty glass, managing only a drop, then set it aside as Avisse removed the lid to reveal layers of thick red velvet. The Silver Dock workshop spared no expense.

Once the velvet had been removed, the rows of glass ollis were a sight to behold, perfectly intact and gleaming, their interior mechanisms hazily visible through the blue and red swirls. One end of each was metal, flush with the glass, connected to the mechanisms on the inside. One sharp strike against the palm would create the vibration, which the oscillators inside the ollis would continue for several minutes before it would need to be struck again.

Avisse lifted the first tray, showing the next layer in similarly flawless condition. Each of the crates showed the same perfect packing and undisturbed contents, and the count was exactly as it should be, except for one unusually shaped piece in a separate tray of the last crate.

This one was opaque black glass with gold swirls and a paddle-shaped arm near one end, like a forked branch made of the same black and gold swirled glass. It had the same metal on the other end as the rest of the ollis, so it had to be a mechanical vibrator as well. Lila picked it up and turned it over in her hands, picturing it in use, until it snapped into focus, and a smile spread from ear to ear. She glanced up at Avisse, whose grin set Lila's neck and cheeks flushing.

"That's the newest mechanical. It's called—" Avisse covered her mouth, but her laughter was evident in the wrinkles around her eyes. "They call it the Satisfy-her." She kept a straight face for almost a second, then barked out a loud laugh, which she quickly covered with her hand.

Lila snort-laughed, covering her face, which was surely beet-red by now. Avisse leaned to the side, shaking with laughter, and soon they were both cackling, no longer bothering to cover up or pretend. Lila flushed with joy, not just at the hilarity of the situation, but at being able to share such a moment. She was often intimidated by immanent women, worried that deep down, no matter how politely they treated her, they would never truly accept a transcendent woman as one of their own.

"I suppose I have to make sure they work before I sign." Lila had handled a test model on her trip to Rontaia when she'd placed the initial order, but she still hesitated as she held the elegant glassware above her palm. She knew flameglass was almost as hard as stone, and the base was steel, so there was no risk of it breaking, but these things cost fifty poul wholesale and sold for two hundred. She braced herself and gave it a hard smack.

The vibration was as impressive as it was instantaneous, sending a renewed flush up her cheeks and a tingle between her legs as she swelled against her gaff. She double-tapped it, and the vibration stopped as suddenly as it had started. She glanced up at Avisse, whose smiling face was flushed as well. Lila quickly turned her eyes back down to the olli as she set it in the velvet indentation in the crate.

"Perfect quality as always." Lila tried to keep the nervous edge from her voice. Once she had composed her face, she turned a smile back up to Avisse, who seemed to have recovered as well, though the way she bit her lip suggested she was holding back a smirk.

"Silver Dock never fails to satisfy." A hint of suppressed laughter hid behind Avisse's words as she held out her ledger.

Lila returned to her desk to sign the paperwork, shifting in her seat, as the swelling between her legs took some time to subside. Lila signed in several places, then studied Avisse's fingers as she signed in turn. Her fingernails were clean and neatly trimmed, and her signature was bold and precise. She blotted the pages, carefully tore out Lila's copy, and slid it across the desk. A roar of laughter echoed in from the lobby. Lila glanced toward the half-open door, wondering what manner of shenanigans Sylvan was using to distract the crowd. Avisse snapped her ledger shut and stood, turning toward the door.

"Are you sure you won't stay for a drink or something to eat after your long day? The caterer is amazing, and there's an ungodly amount of food and bubble wine." She knew it was a long shot, but she couldn't help feeling there was something here.

"Thanks, but..." Avisse eyed the door, her fingers tapping her leg nervously. "I've really got to get back to my horses. I rode them extra hard today, and the stable I use is in the fourth ring."

"No need to go all the way out there! We have a valet contract with a stable just around the corner. They'll take excellent care of your girls."

"It's not just that. My..." Avisse closed her eyes and sighed. "My son is used to the stable there, and he likes his routines. That, and his books." She half-rolled her eyes, but there was a touch of pride in her expression as well.

A light knock sounded on the door, and Aven's head peered through the crack.

"Just a minute!" Lila called, trying to keep the impatience from her voice.

"Your...how old is he?" Lila studied Avisse's face, trying to figure out her age. Thirties, maybe? "My apartment in the carriage house has a nice little library with a comfy couch, if you want to stay just for a bite. And I'm sure he's probably hungry, too."

"Theo's twelve, though sometimes he talks like he's older than me. I'm sure he'd love to have a look at your library, but we really should get going."

"Well, then, it's settled." Lila rose from her seat, emboldened by the hesitation in Avisse's voice and the fatigue evident in her posture. "I'll have the valets get your horses sorted and I'll bring some food out to the carriage house in a bit. You can have a bite and rest up before you move on."

Avisse sighed through her nose as her mouth formed a wry smile.

"You are a kind woman, Lila Thelkis."

The evening passed in a blur of bubble wine, painted faces, and open-mouthed laughter. The demonstration of the alchemically powered olli was a raging success. Everyone sat in a circle, with Lila in the center showing how to insert the pellets and turn it on. Giggles and squeals erupted as it was passed around from hand to hand; most of the painted faces had even removed their gloves for the full experience. They didn't need their gloves at night, of course, and certainly not indoors, but etiquette required they be kept on in most public gatherings.

When Aven wheeled in the cart with all the chests on it, Lila had to raise her voice to prevent a stampede. Tera called out the names one at a time, and eager customers rushed forward with keys in hand to seize their prizes. Lila had asked them to wait until everyone had their chests before they opened them, but the room was soon a chaotic scene of shrieks and sharp intakes of breath as they held the gleaming glass up to the light.

Lila stood amid the chaos, annoyance slowly giving way to euphoria as she saw the joy and excitement on every face.

The World Within was on the map. She'd have customers lining up on opening day for the hundred mechanicals that had just been delivered. She'd have to put in a call to Silver Dock via the Inkwell tomorrow to see how many more of the alchemicals and mechanicals they could get her and how quickly. She was the only purveyor in Anari, and the only one outside of Rontaia besides Tralum, which was two hundred miles downstream. Once word got out, she was going to have a stampede of customers from all over the upper Agra.

Aven and Tera helped a few customers who had trouble with their locks, then drifted toward her, standing on either side of her much as they had when they'd first seen the place, then a moldering ruin. Aven and Tera had invested the proceeds from the sale of Tera's Pureline bars into this venture. After all they'd risked together, taking on Tera's mother and leaving the world of the painted faces behind, it looked like their gamble was going to pay off. She put an arm around each of them and kissed them on their unpainted cheeks.

"Thank you both so much," she said, feeling suddenly maudlin, hoping the almost-tears in her eyes wouldn't erupt for real and ruin her makeup. "I couldn't have done it without you."

"So true," Aven murmured, squeezing her waist tightly. She bumped them with her hip, and they bumped her back. They were so soft, so comfy—if they and Tera weren't still thick as thieves after a year of marriage, she would have—

"Did that delivery woman leave?" Tera asked.

Lila's heart lurched. She'd had food sent out and had meant to go check on her but had gotten swept away by the evening's busy schedule.

"I assume so. What time is it?" Lila glanced at the water clock; it was almost ten. "I should probably go check." She slipped out of their arms, glancing around at the customers, who were smiling and talking excitedly among themselves, comparing their ollis and inspecting the little pellets that powered them. She slipped through a break in the chairs, widening her smile and making a few excuses, then picked up her stride as she headed toward the door. How rude of her to completely neglect her guest, especially one as cute as Avisse, and her son, whom Lila hadn't even had a chance to meet.

A sleek black carriage stood in the courtyard with two freshly combed horses, one a dappled tan and the other black as midnight. It was a bit longer and narrower than a standard carriage, with a windowless segment in the back, presumably for cargo. A valet leaned against the frame, looking bored, but he quickly stood up straight as Lila strode across the courtyard. She flashed him a friendly half-smile as she hurried to the carriage house, pausing before her own door. The light of her kitchen lamp shone through the window above, but no sound filtered down. She knocked lightly and waited. Soft footsteps descended, and the door opened slowly.

"Ms. Thelkis," Avisse said in a low voice, her face drawn with fatigue but her eyes remarkably bright. "Sorry we're still here. Theo fell asleep on your couch, and he doesn't always sleep well, so I wanted to let him get some rest while he could. We'll be out of your hair in just a few minutes."

Lila waved away the concern.

"Stay as long as you like. They'll be here for quite a while anyway." She motioned with her head toward the hulking shadow of The World Within. Avisse slipped through the door and joined her outside. "And call me Lila, please."

"Of course, sorry. Business habits. Thank you, Lila. The food was delicious, and you have a lovely apartment. My son was *very* excited about your library, especially the illustrated river tales book. It's quite beautiful. And signed by the author, I noticed. I can't believe you know him. He seems nice, if a bit of a bumbling fool." Avisse glanced toward the main building with an indulgent smile.

"Sylvan's...amazingly normal, in a completely un-normal way."

"I noticed you kissed him in a not-so-normal way when he arrived." Avisse bit her lip, eyes teasing. Lila's heart thumped against her ribcage.

"Oh gods, no, I mean—" She covered her face for a moment, trying to shake away the embarrassment. "I offered kisses to all the guests, as a stunt, and I needed a distraction. Sylvan just kind of took it and ran with it. He was a perfect gentleman."

Avisse stepped closer, and Lila backed against the post supporting the balcony, her mouth suddenly dry, sweat popping out under her arms.

"I don't want to impinge on your hospitality any further than I already have." Avisse's fingers traced across the backs of Lila's hands and slid up her arms, raising goosebumps as they went. She moved closer, heat radiating into Lila as her hands slid across Lila's bare shoulders. She tiptoed up, pressing Lila against the post, her lips so close Lila could feel her breath on her chin.

"You're no trouble at all," Lila managed.

"It's just that," Avisse whispered, "if you're offering kisses to all your guests, I think technically, I might qualify." Her fingers traced delicate lines along Lila's collarbones. Lila's eyes fluttered closed and her hands came to rest on Avisse's tight hips as their lips met in a moment of soft heat that sent her into a spiral of dizzy ecstasy. Avisse pulled away too quickly, leaving Lila swollen and breathless.

"Mmm." Avisse licked her lips, her eyes running up and down Lila's body, spreading heat in their wake. "Not how I pictured my night going, but I'm sure not complaining."

"I—gods, Avisse, me neither, I just…" Lila touched her lips, wondering for a moment about her lipstick. The kiss had been so gentle, but her whole body was still buzzing.

"Look, I really should go wake up Theo, but I deliver to Anari pretty regularly. Maybe next time…"

"I'll cook you dinner. For you and Theo. And maybe we can have drinks after." Lila kicked herself mentally; she was the worst cook in the seven rings.

Avisse's smile started in one corner of her mouth and spread to the other, and she held out her hand.

"It's a deal."

The warmth and strength of that handshake would keep Lila awake for many a night in the weeks to come.

2

The week leading up to opening day was a draining mix of dread and frenzy. Lila was used to doing everything her way; she was terrible at delegating, but there was too much for one person to do all by herself. Aven and Tera meant well and were generally competent, but neither of them had ever run a business before. It was painful at times to watch them struggle with the simplest tasks. But they each had their strengths. Aven was good with their hands, and they helped build displays and take care of the finicky doors and windows. And though Tera claimed to have missed out on her family's banking genes, she kept the finances organized, Lila's least favorite task, leaving her free to deal with the hundred and one vendors and specialists who needed her attention.

The sex shop should have been the easy part, but she'd decided to open an alchemical wing with all manner of oils, ointments, and creams. Dealing with the alchemists turned out to be almost more trouble than it was worth. Most of them weren't used to selling wholesale, and though her clientele were rich, they wouldn't be willing to pay double the price they'd find at

Alchemist's Row. She haggled and bargained and strong-armed them one by one.

Two days before opening, she stood before the lacquered display Aven had made, backlit by red-tinted brightstone lamps, and knew the painted faces would go wild for it. She even had a special display shaped like a mortar and pestle for products from a transcendent alchemist she was friendly with, including a cream she used on her face to slow hair growth without turning her skin scaly.

On the counseling side, she'd planned to do most of the services herself but had needed a little help. Tera had already scheduled her for four intimacy consultations in the first month, one of which was a little outside her comfort zone. She'd reached out to some colleagues and found a good fit, a quiet androgyne named Tienne known for their ironclad placidity who was willing to take on the occasional client for her.

She'd subcontracted most of the spa work, poaching disgruntled masseurs and a manager from one of the bigger spas in the third ring whose owner had been caught peeping through mirror tubes in the ceiling. It had cost a fortune to get the plumbing sorted, and the mineral baths wouldn't be ready for another month, but they had steam and hot water, which would do for now.

On the day before opening, she drifted from room to room of the huge building, trying to imagine the experience of a customer entering for the first time. The domed ceiling of the lobby was festooned with hanging plants, which drew the eyes away from the many cracks that Aven had assured her were no indication of structural weakness. Light poured in through numerous round windows, most of which had had to be replaced, at considerable expense. Small greenorange trees in oversized pots lined the walls, and a stone fountain that had cost an absurd amount to rehabilitate burbled tranquilly in the center. Whiffs of lavender reached her nose at every turn from the many plants growing at the foot of each of the little trees, masking the occasional musty exhalations of the old temple.

The entrance to the spa was marked by a trellis of jasmine vines. She'd planted them as soon as she'd signed the mortgage, knowing how long it would take for them to grow in, even with alchemical fertilizers. They were blooming nicely, and their scent billowed out well into the lobby, mingling with the lavender. She plucked a few spent blossoms, studying the effect of the soft orange lighting from the brightstones set behind colored paper in sconces in the hallway leading to the spa. It was inviting, comforting, exactly as it should be.

Her smile widened as she turned and saw the flamboyant red and pink flowery fresco around the entrance to the Pleasure Palace, as she'd begrudgingly agreed to call the sex shop on Aven and Tera's insistence. They'd polled some of their painted-faced friends, and this name had consistently come out on top. It felt cheap somehow, but they were partners, and she had to trust them. Besides, she had been out of touch with painted face society for almost a decade, while they'd only been unpainted for a year. She needed their expertise and their contacts.

The door swung open—Lila reminded herself that she really needed to keep it locked when she was here by herself—and Sylvan Kirin slipped through it, wearing a tan robe, his face painted an unassuming medium green. He carried a shoulder bag with a long leather tube sticking out of it.

"Lila!" he called out, crossing the lobby in several long strides and meeting her by the fountain. "The place is looking fantastic!" He stared up at the ceiling, then around the room, then at her, studying her from her feet to her eyes. "As do you, if I may say so without it being taken amiss."

"Welcome words, after the week I've had." She took his shoulders and kissed the air around his cheeks. "To what do I owe the honor? Not that you aren't welcome any time, of course." Lila eyed the tube tucked under his arm. He chuckled, tapping it and looking around for a flat surface. He motioned her toward the reception desk, where he pulled what looked like an architectural plan out of the tube and rolled it flat.

"I took the liberty of doing some research down at the archives, in preparation for my meditation session. We're still on for secondday, yes?"

Sylvan had offered to lead an Endulian erotic meditation session, based on a technique he'd learned on his trip down to Endulai. He was said to have developed powers like those of the Endulian masters, though rumors could never agree as to what those powers might be. Most painted faces claimed not to believe in such things, but that didn't stop them from speculating about Sylvan's supposed magical abilities to an almost obsessive degree. Lila wasn't sure if her own experiences with Endulian meditation counted as magic, but after what she'd seen Tera do to her mother, she knew there was more to the world than she'd been brought up believing. In any case, Sylvan's mystique would make the session quite popular.

"The sixty people who've reserved spots are going to be sorely disappointed if we're not."

"Yes, very good. Very good." He turned to the paper, running his fingers along the circle at the center. "I noticed before that the harmonics were exceptional, and of course with the shape and the windows, I assumed it was Endulian, which, technically it is, but..." He traced a line along the hallway leading to the pools, which were still under repair. "According to the records, these pools here, and this section here, predate the rest of the construction by hundreds of years at least." He pointed to a set of lines leading off beyond the pools, ending in another circle.

But Lila knew the pools were surrounded by stone walls with no second exit.

"What's this?" she asked. "There's no hallway past the pools."

Sylvan looked up from the map, eyes alight with mischief.

"Isn't there indeed?"

The distant sound of construction greeted them as they approached the leathered doors leading to the baths. Once they entered the hallway, dust and chaos filled their eyes, ears, and noses. A half-dozen workers were busy patching the walls of the baths while another group was assembling new pipes in a section of dismantled wall leading from the newly installed furnace to the first bath. The ancient design of the baths was ingenious; they tapped into natural mineral springs deep below the city and somehow used the heat of the furnace to siphon the water up and warm it. A series of pipes would keep each pool at a different temperature, from cave-cool to near-scalding, and bathers would rotate between baths as their needs dictated. Assuming the contractors ever finished the job.

Ash, the forewoman, stood from overseeing the pipe fitting. She shucked her gloves and walked toward Lila, waving up at her from the bottom of the pool.

"We're still on schedule for a week from tomorrow," she said, wiping the sweat from her dirt-covered brow with the back of her hand. "Assuming our last delivery of hardsteel fixtures isn't delayed."

"Highsmith, is it?" Lila asked. Ash nodded, closing her eyes for a moment. Alexander Highsmith had a signed contract with her, and if he didn't want to cut his profits in half, he damned sure better get the parts in on time. "I'll make sure that it isn't. Listen, can we borrow your expertise for a moment?" She tilted her head toward the end of the room indicated on

Sylvan's map. Ash nodded, quickly scaling a ladder and dusting her hands on her overalls.

"Sure thing. What's up?"

"Sylvan, do you want to do the honors?"

Sylvan hurried ahead, dodging the buckets and tools lining the walkway between the pools, then unrolled the map awkwardly on a plank laid over two sawhorses. Ash leaned over the map, apparently unaware of who Sylvan was, or possibly uninterested—her frankness was part of why Lila had given her the contract. Her finger quickly found the passage and the circle before Sylvan had time to point it out. She stared at the wall ahead, then turned her eyes back down to the map.

"Well, I'll be damned," she muttered. "That would explain it."

"Explain what?" Lila's heart fluttered with nervous excitement, though this was the very last thing she needed to be worried about one day before opening.

"The mortar is newer there, and some of the stones are a bit lighter as well." Ash left the two of them behind, walking toward the end of the room. They followed, stopping to examine the wall in the light of her brightstone headlamp. "I guess 'new' is a relative term, since the whole place is a thousand years old or more, but see the coloring of the mortar here?" She pointed to the cracks between the blocks of stone forming the walls. Lila could see a subtle difference in a roughly rectangular area, though she wouldn't have noticed it on her own.

"We figured they'd redone the wall due to structural issues, but it never quite made sense. My guess is they closed it off during renovations at some point long ago." Ash picked at the mortar with an awl she pulled from her belt, and only a few bits came loose. "Did a good job, I'll give them that. This whole place, really, considering how old it is. They don't make them like they used to." She shot Sylvan a glance. "Where'd you get that floor plan? Records like that are usually reserved for registered architects."

Lila bit her knuckle; she'd never seen anyone except Avisse stand up so brazenly to the third-richest man in Anari, but Sylvan just flashed his usual placid smile.

"Since this is a historical site, the records are public, to those who take the trouble to look." Lila gave a start, and Sylvan put a gentle hand on her arm. "Don't worry, it doesn't affect your ownership of the property. But any changes you make to the subterranean structure must be registered with the archives, as I'm sure your forewoman knows."

"I do, and the paperwork is atrocious." Ash smiled, her voice tinged with respect, studying Sylvan with renewed interest. "What do you think is back there anyway?"

He raised his hands and let them fall to his thighs, blowing air out through pursed lips. "I really have no idea! It could be just another part of the bathing facilities that was no longer of use, or it could be something much more interesting. There's only one way to find out. I was wondering, in your professional opinion, how difficult would it be to—"

"Whoa, whoa, let me stop you *right there*, Sylvan." Lila's voice echoed through the wide chamber. The sounds of construction and chatter died in an instant. Sylvan recoiled, and Ash covered her mouth with her hand, laughter apparent in her eyes. "No one is knocking down any walls, or exploring any hidden passageways, or doing anything else except getting these baths ready as soon as humanly possible." She glared at Sylvan, then tried to soften her look without diluting her point as she turned to Ash. Lila's blood rushed in her ears, and she closed her eyes, taking in a deep breath and releasing it before opening them again.

"I apologize," she said in a soft voice. "As you can imagine, it's been a stressful week. As *truly fascinating* as this little discovery is, I simply cannot have any further distractions in my life right now. I'm sure you understand."

Sylvan raised his hands as if in defense, a faint smile on his lips, eyes dancing with merriment. "Quite right, and I understand fully. But if I were to offer to—"

Lila stopped him with a glare, and he closed his mouth promptly. She couldn't believe she'd shut down Sylvan Kirin so harshly. What was he going to offer? He could throw money and influence at any problem and make it go away in an instant. His pull with the painted faces had already guaranteed her opening day success. And despite how pushy he was being, she couldn't help liking him. She took his hands in hers and locked eyes with him as Ash sidled away and rejoined her crew.

"Listen. Tomorrow is the big day, and we don't need any negative energy between us clouding your meditation session the night after. Give me a few days to recover, then come back and make your offer. I promise I'll listen."

"You drive a hard but extremely fair bargain, Ms. Thelkis."

Opening day was pure chaos. It seemed like every painted face from the inner rings was there, and not a few from the middle rings as well. The mechanical vibrators sold out before noon, many to the very same people who'd bought the alchemicals, and the back-order list for both types was close to a hundred. Lila told each of them personally that there was no guarantee when she'd be able to fill the orders, but no one seemed to mind. The excitement on their faces lifted Lila's spirits even as her body groaned beneath the fatigue and stress of the day's work. She knew all too well that behind their paint and their cloistered walls, they longed for something more. She would help them unlock the world within themselves they had been hiding from for all this time.

It wasn't only the painted faces who visited, of course. She clocked most of the non-painted visitors as first or second ring, but some came from farther out. She had expanded her line of pleasure- and comfortwear, including undergarments for the transcendent, who came to the opening in surprising numbers.

She was both proud and disappointed to see that the line of gaffs she'd personally designed for her own comfort and pleasure sold out before the day was done. Her seamstress was going to be busy in the weeks to come. The creams for hair growth and suppression sold particularly well, as did the scented lubes and pleasure enhancers; the alchemical wing was a huge success.

Lila was so busy in the store that she hardly had time to check on the spa. When she did, it was so calm and filled with relaxing smells, it was all she could do not to lie down on one of the leathered tables and have one of the masseurs knead all the stress from her body. Not that there were any tables free; they were booked solid all day. All week, in fact, and most of the week after. She wondered if they'd be able to handle the volume once the baths opened.

By the time the store closed, it was a shambles of half-empty shelves, barren displays, and racks with forlorn hangers. Aven and Tera sat on a bench in the lobby, Tera cradling Aven's head in her lap, gently stroking their curls. Lila lay down on the cool marble floor, knowing it would dirty her dress, knowing her dress was already dirty from the day's work, not caring in the slightest. They'd made more money in one day than she'd made in any *year* her previous shop had been open. And this was just the first day.

"Just think," Aven said without opening their eyes. "We get to get up bright and early tomorrow and do it all again."

3

The second day was controlled chaos; Lila spent most of her time processing deliveries while Tera and Aven ran the store. She'd sent the same delivery girl out with messages to vendors three different times. When she returned the fourth time, Lila offered her a job, and she accepted. Ferdie didn't speak much but paid attention and was swift of foot. Lila sent her off with an ultimatum to Highsmith that if he didn't have the fixtures by the next day, he'd be sending them at cost. It was a risk, she knew, but this was a huge job, and they had a contract. As the proprietor of a spa and bathhouse, she would be an important customer. He needed her as much as she needed him.

In the afternoon, when a ponytailed delivery woman arrived with a dolly loaded with crates, Lila's heart leapt for a moment, though she knew it wasn't Avisse. Lila found herself thinking about her at odd moments, reliving the kiss, the feel of Avisse's fingers on her collarbones, how she'd pushed Lila against the post. Whenever she looked at the door, she wondered when she'd see Avisse come through it again.

It was a two-week journey by carriage between Rontaia and Anari, though maybe less, considering how Avisse had made up time after the flood in Guluch. Lila had sent a message to the Silver Dock workshop through the Inkwell requesting a hundred fifty alchemical vibrators and two hundred mechanicals, along with fifty of the Satisfy-hers, which she hadn't been able to stop giggling about as she wrote it. She had no idea how long it would take, or if they'd even be able to fill such an order, but she had to try.

The waitlists were close to a hundred for the alchemicals and higher for the mechanicals. There was surely a limit to the market for these things, but she hadn't begun to see it. She could practically make the mortgage just on the sales of them alone. She hoped to sell even more if it meant they got delivered by the pint-sized butch who had captured her imagination.

Lila unrolled her mat and set it down near the fountain, hoping a little meditation in the lobby might help settle her mind, enhanced by the echoes of the fountain off the dome. She didn't get very deep, but she washed the thickest of the day's mental grime away. When she was done, she lay on the mat with eyes closed, thinking of Avisse. One day or another, the door would open and she'd roll in a dolly stacked with crates. She'd dust her hands on her gray pants, looking around for Lila, then creep up on soft feet when she saw her lying on the floor. Was Lila asleep, she'd wonder? What was she doing on the floor?

Lila would hear her approach, feel the warmth of Avisse's hand approach her cheek, and try not to smile as her heart hammered in her chest. Soft fingertips and rough calluses caressed her cheek, sending shivers along her neck, spreading across her chest and further down. Lila lay still as a stone as Avisse's fingers slid down, grazing across her bare shoulders, tracing down her chest, feathering across her nipples, which throbbed at the contact. The faintest moan escaped her lips, and a tinkle of laughter filtered in.

"Someone's off to an early start."

Sylvan's voice jarred Lila from her daydream, and she jerked up to sitting, woozy from the sudden return to reality.

"Did I fall asleep?" she murmured, running her fingers through her hair, which felt a right mess.

"For a little while." Sylvan offered her a gloved hand and pulled her up to standing. He wore a plain gray robe, and his face was painted the most neutral tan imaginable. She wondered if that was part of the ceremony.

"I should go get ready. What time is it?"

"It's seven. The guests will be here in half an hour."

It took Lila less than half that to fix her hair and makeup, which she toned down for the erotic meditation. She hadn't been to too many Endulian sessions lately, but they were a plain-dressing lot who didn't wear much if any makeup. Sylvan was just about the only painted face she knew of who practiced; her family would have pulled the rug out from under her sooner if they'd known she was attending sessions on the sly. They'd have feared a taint on the family's reputation, and they wouldn't have been wrong. The painted faces valued tradition above all and discouraged anything that broadened people's horizons too much. Even now that she'd been unpainted for more than a decade, Lila still felt uneasy going into the temple and did most of her practice alone.

She had a few crackers and a bite of cheese and washed it down with a bit of leftover wine, then did a couple of breath cycles until she heard the first guests arrive. This wasn't exactly her event, but she had to put her best face forward at all times. If The World Within was to succeed, it needed to be a home for the soul and the body alike. And it needed the tax break that the weekly Endulian sessions provided.

There were more painted faces than she'd expected, though they were by no means in the majority. She recognized a handful from the Unpainted community as well, and she greeted them with knowing smiles. Refugees from painted face society tended to stick together; she credited the success of her shop in the fourth ring in part to their faithful patronage. There were sure to be some with connections to the painted faces in the crowd, but if there was any animosity between them, they hid it well. That was what the painted faces did best: hide their feelings and judge you with a faint smile.

Tera and Aven helped check everyone in and kept them corralled into the lobby, which soon filled with sixty souls, all whispering as if by common accord. They all dressed plainly, some in gray Endulian robes, but most were just regular folks, albeit mostly rich ones, wearing drab clothing. The painted faces wore muted colors as well; Lila smiled to herself, remembering the whisper networks ahead of events, people arguing and knowing-best over the brightness or color palettes people were going to be wearing. For all its ridiculousness, there were times she missed that world dearly.

Tera moved to the fountain just before eight, scanning the crowd with a beatific smile, and everyone went silent. As charming as she could be among friends, she had a quality of indifference, an almost-aloofness at times that made people respect her, not unlike her bitch-queen of a mother, and she used it to command the room.

"Sylvan will be out shortly. He's asked that we all take our seats on our mats."

Cloaks rustled and sandals scuffed as everyone hurried to the neatly spaced mats in a wide semicircle around the fountain, where Sylvan's mat was laid out. Lila lowered herself down to sit cross-legged with more difficulty than expected; it had been far too long since she'd practiced, and she'd never been the most flexible. She closed her eyes and let the scent of jasmine and lavender flow into her, draining the ache from her body. The burble of the fountain and the occasional sniff or rustle of a cloak were the only sounds until the soft slap of sandaled feet indicated Sylvan's arrival. The footsteps stopped, and Sylvan's voice filled the space, rich, warm, and inviting.

"Greetings."

A muffled gasp rose into the air, followed by another, then several more. Lila opened her eyes and had to cover her mouth to avoid adding to the chorus.

Sylvan stood before them with his remarkably pale face completely unpainted.

Lila sat in stunned silence, absorbing the fact that she'd just seen Sylvan Kirin unpainted. Surely this didn't mean…

"I apologize for any unease my naked face might cause. I always practice unpainted. I find it useful to remove the barriers between the world without and the world within." His gaze turned to Lila for a moment, and though he did not wink, his eye sparkled just a little more than usual. "For that is what we come here to do tonight. To break down the walls that keep us from our inner truth. Our inner pleasure. Close your eyes." He said the last words with gentle force, and Lila obeyed, along with everyone else. Any awkwardness at seeing his face passed as his voice filled her mind.

"At the core of each one of us lies an inexhaustible well of joy."

The fountain's burble intermixed with his words as he continued, draining the worry from her mind and the tension from her body.

"The vagaries of each day weave their webs around it. They layer themselves so thickly, we can hardly hear it calling out to us. Until we almost forget it exists, except in those moments when we ask another person to slice through to the core of us in an instant of raw vulnerability."

Lila's heart clenched as his words cut her deep.

"But as beautiful and important as those moments can be, there are other ways to access this joy. And no, I'm not talking about those wonderful contraptions they make in Rontaia." A ripple of laughter circled the room, then quickly died out. "To find the joy in others, you must learn to find it in yourself."

As Sylvan wove his cocoon of words, Lila teased apart the sticky strands that recent weeks and months had wrapped around her heart. Her vision of The World Within had become so all-consuming that she'd forgotten its most basic premise. She'd neglected her own wellness.

She hadn't dated, and she'd rarely found time for her once-frequent breakfast partner Cyntia. She'd hardly even taken care of her own physical needs, except in brief frantic moments late at night when the pressure got to be too much. And though she got hit on often enough, until the other night with Avisse, hardly anyone looked at her, really *looked* at her, and saw her as more than just a pretty face in a gorgeous dress.

Sylvan was saying something about finding yourself desirable as a person. Lila pictured the look in Avisse's eyes as she closed for a kiss, and something stirred inside her, deeper than mere desire. This woman hardly knew her, but she *liked* Lila. Not just wanted her, which happened plenty; after just a few interactions, Avisse had wanted to see Lila again, to bring her kid to dinner. She *trusted* Lila, based on a first impression. It made her feel desirable in a way she seldom had before, allowing her to tear through the cobwebs of doubt and self-loathing under the guidance of Sylvan's soothing voice.

"Once you have swept away the initial barriers laid by the stress of your daily life, the real work begins. There are layers upon layers, with caves and fissures to explore and exploit before you reach the molten core of joy at the center of your being. It is the work of a lifetime, but tonight, I ask you to probe deep beneath the surface, looking for one single spark. Capture it if you can. Hold it in your heart and let it flow throughout your mind and body."

As Sylvan's voice trailed off, Lila saw herself floating in a great empty space with a dark orb at the center, lined with red cracks that poured rays of warm light in all directions. She willed herself toward it, and her body tingled as she passed through the light, like bubble wine going down her throat and pouring through her veins. Energy radiated from the orb, thick like the heat from a well-laid bed of coals but not hot; rather, an almost uncomfortable sense of being filled, passed through, and surrounded. She grew dizzy as a tingly warmth spread from limb to limb. Her mind flew open, racked with deep pulses she was unable or unwilling to stop. Energy poured from her chest through her head and circled back down over and over. She heard herself gasp, felt her nails dig into her thighs, and let out a shuddering sigh as her eyes opened and her consciousness returned to her body.

A handful of the attendees were in similar states, wide-eyed and slumped on one arm, curled up in fetal position, or splayed out on the floor, staring at the ceiling. Others sat in perfect concentration, while some peeked through half-opened eyelids as if wondering what the fuss was all about.

Sylvan emitted a low hum, which Lila recognized from some of the Endulian practices she'd attended. She regained her position after checking to make sure she hadn't spilled; fortunately, whatever had just happened seemed to have been entirely in her mind. She'd gone deeper into herself under the spell of Sylvan's words than she ever had before. There had to be something to the rumors of the abilities he'd gained from his trip to the Living Waters. She joined in the hum, along with the other attendees, until they were all humming in the same pitch. Sylvan took a breath, and the hum continued, slowly rising in pitch until it reached a certain minor note. He stopped abruptly, and the other voices died out moments later.

"You honor me by joining me in practice this evening. What is inside me is open to you."

He put his hands together at his forehead, and the attendees repeated his gesture.

"The experience is different for everyone, and the first attempt does not always produce the results we imagine, though it seems clear that, for some of you, it did." His eyes sparkled benevolently at Lila as he spoke. "I hope you will join me another time, if Ms. Thelkis will permit further sessions."

"I'm afraid I must insist," Lila said somewhat breathlessly to a round of laughter. "And I hope it's not too untoward of me to offer refreshments to anyone wishing them?" She glanced at Tera, who signaled to the caterer to wheel in the cart.

"The body must be nourished along with the mind," Sylvan said, springing up and heading straight toward the cart. "Are those tri-fries I see?"

"And he's going to pay to have the whole bath area tiled in red sandstone."

Aven's eyes nearly popped out of their head. "But that would cost—"

"He said money was, and I quote, 'Absolutely no object.' So, I took him at his word." Lila shrugged. "He's got his crew working nights, and they're putting in a restored bronze door he got from somewhere. It's gorgeous."

"Gods, I can't wait to see that. I wonder if he sourced it from Anari or Freburr; they have some nice antique pieces there, and—"

"Did he say anything else about the room at the end of the hall?" Tera asked quietly, holding her tea just below her lips. Her hazel eyes locked onto Lila's. Not for the first time, she sensed Tera holding something back about Sylvan.

"No," Lila said softly, staring into her tea. "He's been distracting me with pretty talk of bronze and sandstone, the bastard. What do you think he's after in there? Something Endulian?" She tried to match Tera's cool gaze, but if it had any effect, she couldn't see it.

"Pre-Endulian, I think." Tera took a sip of her tea and glanced into the cup as if mildly displeased. "Something he learned about at Endulai, I believe."

"He told you this?" Sylvan had a reputation as a mystic, and the meditation session had shown him to be a master of Endulian practice.

Tera gave a slight frown, turning her cup in a slow circle by the handle. Lila wondered if Tera had sensed it somehow, in the way Endulian masters were said to be able to read minds or auras. Lila had seen her break out of a locked safe and nearly kill her mother with the power of her mind. Who knew what else she was capable of?

"He spoke about his time at Endulai a while back at one of the meditation workshops at the temple. Something about the movement that gave birth to the Endulians at the dawn of history. The time before the Time Before, if you will."

Lila shook her head. "I'm much more into the here and now, myself. If whatever he's after down there can bring beauty to The World Within and help our clients find what *they* are after, he can do whatever he wants behind that big beautiful antique bronze door."

Tera's eyebrows arched slightly. "What does your contract say about that?"

Lila straightened up. She was especially proud of what she'd made him sign. "It stipulates that I own the property, the tunnel, the room, the door, and everything in it, and that he is leasing it from me, month to month. He's only allowed to come and go during non-business hours, of course; we can't have him walking through a room full of bathers. I will have a copy of the key, and the right to inspect the premises on an hour's notice, day or night."

"I helped write the lease," Aven said proudly. "It's water-tight and very favorable to the landlady." They made a gallant gesture toward Lila. "But fair to the tenant as well." They held up their hands toward Tera as if she'd take offense on Sylvan's behalf.

"And the renovations on the spa are a down payment?" Tera asked.

"Precisely. Baked into the contract. His crews are already installing the stone, and the door goes in tomorrow. And he nudged Highsmith and we got our fittings the next morning. The baths should be ready in four days."

Tera nodded, opening her ledger and picking up her pen. "That's good, because I have a full schedule of seventy-two bathers signed up for each of the first four days. Ferdie would be awfully busy delivering cancellations if they weren't ready."

Lila's heart leapt, fluttering uncomfortably. She was still waiting on a shipment of robes and towels, and she was several attendants short. She had a delivery of bath salts coming that afternoon, and with the rain coming, she had to figure out where to put it. Her stock of binders had been depleted in the first few days. She hadn't heard back from the tailor about when he'd be able to deliver more. And the latch on the front door was sticking again. She stood up, straightened her dress, and took a deep breath.

"We'll be ready. Keep taking reservations. Aven, can you have a look at the latch please?" Lila picked up her lizard skin briefcase, unsure exactly what she was going to do with it, but she needed to move. "I have to go see to a few things."

By the time the baths opened four days later, business in the Pleasure Palace had slowed to a steady but manageable stream, and the spa was a quiet oasis that seemed like it had been there forever. The lobby was big enough that the small groups moving to and from their destinations did not overlap too much. It was lively without being crowded, just as Lila had dreamed.

Many faces were painted, but plenty were not, and no one seemed to mind. Even in the baths, they mingled, pale faces bobbing above the steaming water side by side with the pink and tan shades of the non-painted. When she was painted, Lila had always found it awkward to bathe naked-faced in public, but it was the norm for all but the wealthiest families, the one time it was acceptable to be seen without their paint. In a city with only so many baths, few could afford the luxury of painted-only accommodations, and Lila was certainly not inclined to provide them.

She often dozed in her office chair, surrounded by piles of paperwork. She'd drag her weary bones up the stairs to crash in her apartment, which smelled almost as if no one lived there. She took her morning tea at her breakfast table, but all her meals were eaten in her office or on her feet in the shop. She hadn't exercised in weeks, and though she wasn't gaining weight, she knew she would pay for the time off when she finally hit the bars again. Soon, she promised herself. As soon as this place was well and truly off and running.

4

It was another week before Lila took the time to hit the bars she kept behind the carriage house. A stack of wood too dry to be much good as firewood provided some privacy so she could lift in her cut-off trousers and sweat-stained sleeveless shirt. Her arms burned, then her legs, and finally her back as she went through her routine with one bar, then two, then three. She didn't have the time or energy to go any higher, but it was a start. When she'd wound her way through the routine and set the bars down with a gentle *clang*, she chugged the last of her water, pride swelling in her chest. Two weeks in, and The World Within was a resounding success.

Even Tera, who was inclined to frown at every bill as she carefully scratched it into her ledger, had raised her eyebrows as she'd slid the end-of-week tally across the desk to Lila. They'd cleared fifteen thousand poul in the second week, almost half of what they drew in the first week, which had included the first deliveries of vibrating ollis. The baths had been a huge draw, and they already had regular clients there and at the spa, whose crew had gelled and created an atmosphere that left every customer with half-closed lids and serene smiles.

As her sweat dried and she peeked around the corner of the woodpile to make sure no one was around to see her dart back into her apartment, Lila paused. If everything was going so well, why did she feel like something was missing? She wasn't normally given to introspection outside of her Endulian practice, which she'd been neglecting, but it hovered about her like a ghost. Avisse was part of it, but there was something else there. Something she'd have time to worry about later.

She slipped around the woodpile and up the stairs, giving herself a thorough wash in the basin. She threw on a simple pink dress with thin vines coiling up around the chest, giving a sense of movement. It flared just right at the hips and cinched tight at the waist; she needed more in this style. She redid her makeup with a practiced hand, pressing her lips together to set the lipstick. The clip-clop of hooves and the rattle of wheels on cobbles outside sent her heart racing. She flew down the stairs, almost tripping over her sensibly comfortable but still stylish heels in her haste.

It was the bath salts delivery man. Lila's heart sank, mostly at her own foolishness. It couldn't be Avisse. That delivery wasn't scheduled to arrive for another week and a half, though in Lila's mind, it would arrive in a week. *My girls run on rails,* Avisse had said. Lila felt her smile bloom, and she waved to the delivery man, who tipped his cap and hauled himself out of his seat.

"Good afternoon, Miss Lila." He bowed low in the old-fashioned style. "I hope you won't mind my remarking that you look lovely today." His eyes took in her figure in what felt like an appreciative but not creepy way.

"I won't mind as long as you have the entire delivery this time." Lila batted her eyelashes, and he held up his chubby hands.

"Never fear. Won't happen again. Come on back and we'll do inventory." He pulled the clipboard from under his arm and motioned her to the back of the wagon. She stifled a sigh. The bath manager should really do this, but by the time Lila went inside and found her, she could have already completed the inventory and moved on to something else.

"All right, here's your order, and I've got the manifest." He handed her the order, written in Tera's neat script. "Ready when you are."

Lila counted the days as the time of Avisse's expected arrival approached. She spent more time on the floor of the shop, which she found she missed. It was nice to talk to clients about their needs and help them find just the right tool, ointment, or strap for the job. The clientele was different here than in her old shop, more hesitant, more in need of her help. For whatever reason, the wealthier residents of Anari tended to be more prudish, but also more desperate to break out of their shackles. Or be put in them, as the case often was, and the Pleasure Palace had them covered in either case.

She also consulted with a few painted face marriage clients, which was a nice change of pace, though one of them was a man so utterly clueless about what was expected on his honeymoon that she almost turned him away. She decided on a more diplomatic approach.

"You can't merely 'put it in' unless she's as ready and eager for it as you are," she explained as patiently as she could. "This is why, for the first month at least, I recommend you use your tongue only."

She'd sent him off with a solid pep talk and the most expensive illustrated guide in the shop. Heavens knew if it would be enough, but she'd done her absolute best.

Sylvan started bringing in packages after dark, large crates brought in by the kind of quiet, efficient delivery service only the super-rich could afford. Lila wanted to respect his privacy as a tenant, but her curiosity wouldn't let her. She stepped out from behind a greenorange tree one evening to block his way as he pranced with excitement alongside the gray-clad delivery people wheeling a pair of thin rectangular crates the size of large doors through the lobby.

"Oh! Hello, Lila!" he said nervously, eyeing the delivery people as they wheeled the cart carefully through the door toward the baths. "Just...same place as before!" he called after them. His smile returned, a bright blue curve across his lavender-painted face, but his fingers were wound too tightly together. "And how is business?"

"Fantastic, thank you! Couldn't be better. Having a hard time keeping a few things in stock, but that's to be expected. It seems the painted faces had a pent-up need for what we offer."

Sylvan's laugh bloomed naturally, and his posture relaxed a little.

"We're not all wound so tightly, as you well know." He studied her face, and she wondered what she would register as now, having lived as an Unpainted for eleven years. She'd been a shade six once, but she doubted she'd be more than a three or four anymore. The thought didn't even bother her now, though it had in the first few years. She'd always been horrified by the painted faces' obsession with intermarrying for pale, unblemished skin, especially since they were rarely allowed to show it. But the fear of getting freckles or losing a shade every time she stepped outside unpainted had been one of the hardest habits to break.

"I do indeed. I've had some enlightening conversations in the shop, to be sure."

"Oh, I can only imagine. And we're on for another erotic meditation session tomorrow night?"

"It's on the schedule, fully booked."

"Excellent!" He clasped his hands together, eyes warm and gleaming. "I really am proud of what you're doing here, you know. The way you bring people together. We never got more than twenty for these sessions at the temple. Anari is...I don't want to say prejudiced; maybe skeptical is a better word. It's so different farther south."

"Anari's plenty prejudiced." Lila glanced down at her nails, mad at herself for saying it out loud, but it was true. Societal norms kept prejudices polite, but she was reminded daily that not everyone accepted her as she was. The painted faces were the worst, of course; Lila could still see her mother's waxy smile as she'd watched Lila sign her disinheritance papers. She blinked to keep almost-tears at bay, pulled on a smile, and looked back up into Sylvan's face, which was soft with understanding.

"We can only change one heart at a time." He put a hand on his chest, and Lila instinctively repeated the gesture, though she wasn't sure exactly what it meant. Something Endulian, most likely.

"So." She raised her chin toward the door to the baths. "Any chance you'd want to let me in on what you're cooking up down there?"

Sylvan fixed her with a gaze that was at once spacey and intense, and she felt almost dizzy for an instant. She wondered if he might be reading her aura, but the thought soon fled. He blinked, then gestured toward the door.

"You're familiar with the theory of the Thousand Worlds?" he asked as they walked down the hallway, quiet and dimly lit by the orange-shaded brightstone lamps.

"Of course." Endulian masters were said to be able to communicate through space and even time via special cradles in their temples. It was the same ancient technology that made the Inkwell possible, and which the failed Strongbox company had tried to use to transfer currency. Tera and Aven had foiled that plan, with a little help from Lila. She was still proud of sticking it to Tera's mother, though she was no doubt doing just fine. The painted faces always managed to land on their feet, like cats.

"The Endulians of old discovered how to access the Thousand Worlds, and a few of their cradles are still in use, but..." Sylvan paused as they reached the open bronze door. The delivery crew was busy wheeling the carts down a long hallway, which was lit with numerous small brightstone lights in the ceiling. Its floors and walls were ancient, more so than the rest of the underground complex, and had been patched and reinforced in places. Sylvan's crews had been busy. Sylvan said nothing as they followed the cart to the end of the hall, where another door stood, this one of wood, recently installed.

"Line those up along the wall here, please." The crew unloaded the boxes carefully and set them gently down next to the door. He thanked them, shook the hand of the crew leader, and they wheeled their carts back up the hallway and disappeared, leaving him and Lila alone in the dank but harshly lit stone depths.

"Don't worry, I had it keyed to match the lock of the bronze door, as per our contract." Sylvan produced his key and opened the door to reveal a spherical room with a set of stairs leading down to a level floor, with a round hole filled with stagnant water in the center. There was more evidence of recent patching and support here, but the fundamental structure seemed intact from however many centuries ago it was built. Pieces of corroded metal were lined up on the floor, along with various books and diagrams.

"What is this place?" Lila whispered. *And why is it beneath my shop?*

"This," Sylvan said in a voice tinged with awe, "is the Well of All."

"The what of what now?"

Sylvan's eyes fluttered closed in patient annoyance. "The Endulians call it the Well of All. I was asking if you knew about the Thousand Worlds before. The cradles in the temples allow the mind to travel across distance, even time and…worlds, for lack of a better word. But they require a high level of mastery, not to mention alchemical tinctures not easily procured. This," he said, gesturing toward the room as he stepped down the stairs, "if the theories are correct, would allow not only the mind, but the body as well to travel from one place, one time, one world to another."

Lila grew dizzy once again. "You're talking about…some kind of teleportation device?"

"Much more than that. The Thousand Worlds is a misnomer; the worlds are infinite, limited only by our imagination. Anything you can imagine, and many things you cannot, exist in some hidden corner of the universe of your mind. It's what Endulian practice is all about. But those who created the practice, those who came before the Endulians, were far more advanced than they, just as the Endulians who built the temple in which The World Within sits were more advanced than we. History is often like that, though we tend to see it in the opposite way."

Lila chewed on her lip. The Time Before was said to be the pinnacle of civilization, but she'd always assumed it to be a fairy tale. "And you're trying to rebuild this thing? This Well of..."

"All. As in, you can access *all* of the Thousand Worlds through it."

"And what would you do with it?" Lila's stomach roiled uncomfortably. She wasn't sure if she believed such a thing was possible, but it hardly seemed like something she'd want in the basement of the business she'd devoted her life savings to.

Sylvan's eyes lit up like brightstone. "What couldn't you do with it? What truth could not be uncovered if you had access to all places, all times, all worlds? If you could see into every possible past, every alternate reality, just think of the knowledge, the understanding of the fundamental nature of the universe..." He trailed off, staring at the circle of scummy water. Lila's mind spun with his words. She wasn't quite sure what 'alternate realities' even meant, but it terrified and fascinated her at the same time. They stood in heavy silence, encapsulated by the stone globe of the chamber, until Sylvan kicked a pebble into the water, breaking the spell.

"How can you be sure nothing will come through from...somewhere else?"

He shook his head impatiently. "That's not how it works. Or rather, when you travel through the well, your physical body leaves, but it doesn't manifest physically on the other side. It's...an advanced form of what's called astral projection. You can't affect the physical world wherever, or whenever you go, but you can feel it."

"So, if your physical body leaves, and it's not on the other side, where is it?"

Sylvan spread his arms wide, a mysterious smile on his face. "In the Thousand Worlds."

Lila always dressed to kill, but as Avisse's uncertain arrival date approached, she found herself overthinking each day's outfit. It was silly, she knew; Avisse wasn't the sort to care about things like that, but she *had* complimented Lila's dress the first time they'd met, hadn't she? Was she into how femme Lila was, or was she into her *despite* that? Or was she even into her at all?

Her brain-weasels struck her again as she was at her favorite salon getting a full body wax. Avisse was almost certainly not shaven; only the painted faces shaved themselves entirely, and most non-painted women in Anari shaved only their legs and armpits, if anything. She wasn't sure about Rontaia, but she doubted it was any different. Lila had always shaved, even after becoming unpainted. It was part of how she saw her body, which she wanted to be as smooth as possible, just in case. As for how Avisse would react to what was between Lila's legs if it ever came to that...it made her heart ache too much to even think about it.

Avisse had to know she was transcendent. Lila knew how to dress, wear makeup, and carry herself well enough to pass a casual inspection, but as close as they had been, with the kissing...She pressed her eyes shut, then blinked away the feelings that threatened to surge forth, which would have made things more than a little awkward for the stylist. Avisse knew, and she'd kissed Lila anyway and agreed to come for dinner. She didn't care. Or maybe she was into it, which was a whole other problem, as Lila had no interest in the kind of sex people tended to expect from women with cocks. There was really no way to know until things happened, and by then, it would be too late.

But she was getting way ahead of herself. Avisse had agreed to have dinner with her. Nothing more. Would there be kissing? Probably. But her kid would be there, so how much more could there even be?

She tipped the stylist extra for their trouble, though the only trouble had been in her mind. It was a pleasant day, so she walked back home, enjoying the smooth feel of the skin of her legs and underarms exposed to the air. As a painted face, and especially before she'd found her true self, she'd hated waxing, the idea of it, that the body must be hidden, changed, purified. She saw the power in it now, the ability to control how people saw her, to make them see her for the woman she was rather than the man they wanted her to be.

She could not deny the lift it gave her to feel silky smooth all over, and she loved the sensation of someone's tongue over her freshly waxed skin. Her nipples responded to the thought, and she crossed her arms over her chest, glancing around to see if anyone had noticed, but of course, there was nothing to notice with the frilly dress she wore.

As she approached the gate, her mind spun with the hundred tasks she had ahead of her, the inventory she'd put off to go to the spa, the interviews she had to schedule for two new openings in the baths, and countless other things. All of it vanished in an instant when she saw the gleaming black carriage parked in the courtyard, with Avisse brushing down her horses, muscles rippling under her reddish-brown skin. A thin boy with long, flyaway hair held a bucket of water under one of the horses' mouths. He turned and studied her as she approached, deep brown eyes set in a face a shade lighter than his mother's and more serious than any Endulian master. He said something and set down the bucket, wiping his hands on his pants. Avisse spun around, her ponytail slapping her ear, and a wide smile spread across her face. It was all Lila could do not to dash across the courtyard and wrap her arms around her.

"You're early!" Lila approached, holding out her hand. Avisse grabbed it and pulled her in for a half-hug, which set Lila's heart racing.

"I told you, my girls run on rails. Lila, I'd like you to meet my son Theo. Theo, this is Lila, who was kind enough to let us rest in her apartment last time we were here."

Theo clasped his hands together at his chest and bowed in the Endulian style. Lila repeated his gesture, stifling a giggle when she saw his serious face.

"I saw your Endulian books, so I assumed you practice," he said in a high, cheery voice. "I hope I wasn't being presumptuous. I never know what the protocols are in other cities."

"I do, a little bit, but I don't...I usually just shake hands."

Theo offered his hand, which was small and soft, thin bones just below the surface.

"Theo's a little enthusiastic about these things," Avisse said fondly but apologetically. "It's part of his cultural sensitivity curriculum, but I'm afraid he's misunderstood the fundamental aspect of *watching* and *waiting*." Avisse put a gentle hand on Theo's shoulder. He looked like he wanted to squirm away from her touch but didn't.

"I'm afraid you've misunderstood my dedication to my Endulian practice, Mother. I meditate daily, I go to temple whenever we're in a city, I speak and read the language, and I've studied the foundational texts extensively. I—"

"How about you let Lila and me take care of inventory before you give us the rest of your lecture."

"You're welcome to hang out in my apartment," Lila said, holding out an arm toward the carriage house. "My library is always open to you, and I've still got that book on the river legends."

"Signed by the author, Sylvan Kirin, whom my mother tells me you know personally, is that correct?"

"It is. In fact, he's likely to be here this evening. I could introduce you if you like."

Theo's eyes widened, and he nodded somberly. "It would be an honor to meet a scholar of his repute. I should get reading so I have some pertinent questions to ask him." He glanced at the carriage house.

"Yes, let me just get the door unlocked for you."

Theo followed Lila to the door, thanked her quietly, and disappeared.

"My son," Avisse said, closing her eyes and cocking her head.

"He's amazing!" Lila glanced up at the window, where the light had already gone on.

"He is that." Avisse smiled up at the window. Lila noticed that she was wearing eyeliner. She definitely hadn't been the last time she was here. She turned back to Lila, tucking her hands awkwardly into her pockets, which made her shoulders jut up.

"So, how've you been?" Avisse angled her hip toward Lila as she spoke, not quite looking her in the eyes.

"Busy." Lila's brain swam, trying to think of something better to say. "With the…you know," was all she managed, gesturing toward the hulking shape of the ancient temple that now housed her livelihood.

Avisse barked a laugh. "I bet. Must be doing good, considering…" She tilted her head toward the carriage, which looked freshly cleaned and waxed, certainly not like it had just traveled for two weeks across the continent.

"Yeah, the painted faces can't seem to get enough of them. Which is good, since it means I get to see you again." Lila's face burned as she touched Avisse lightly on the shoulder. When she pulled her hand away, her fingers retained the feel of those hard muscles under warm, soft skin, the fine layer of sweat. Lila's pulse beat in her temple, and the sun's heat bled through her wide-brimmed hat. She faltered for a moment, then steadied herself. She probably should have caught a carriage back from the spa, as sunny as it was out today.

"You want to get out of this sun and get the inventory taken care of?" Avisse's eyes furrowed with concern, and she took Lila's elbow and led her toward the double doors. Lila did not resist, though she was perfectly capable of walking on her own. She'd spent weeks cooped up inside The World Within, and she'd lost track of her time in the sun and pushed too hard. She'd gone unpainted for so long that sometimes she forgot why the painted faces lived the way they did. Unnaturally pale skin and the hot Anari sun did not mix well.

Once they got through the doors and into the cool, dim interior, she felt immediately better. Doubly so when Avisse helped her into her office chair and poured her a glass of water, which she forced herself to drink in small sips, fanning herself with her hat. Avisse sat across from her, watching her with concern.

"I'm *fine*," Lila assured her. "Just took in a bit too much sun today, is all."

Avisse nodded, studying her, tight-lipped. Did she know Lila was an Unpainted? How could she possibly know?

Most non-painted folks didn't even know the word, let alone what it meant to people to leave the cloistered world behind and venture forth into the harsh light of a society and a climate they weren't built for. There were hundreds of Unpainted in Anari who'd left for all sorts of reasons. Many, mostly women and queer folk, fled arranged marriages, though doing so meant losing out on all inheritance and privileges associated with their families' stature. For others, the many-layered fabric of rules and mores that dictated their public lives was simply too heavy to wear day after month after year. Lila's exit had been forced by the greed and prejudice of her family; those memories burned in her gut like cheap liquor, and she preferred to keep them sequestered where they couldn't rise back up to hurt her.

"I said I'm fine. It's just...I'm very sensitive to the sun, and sometimes I forget myself. Especially when I'm talking to someone so...distracting." She waved her hand toward Avisse, whose stern face cracked into a smile.

"You'd hate it in Rontaia. It's sunny and hot most of the year down there."

"I love it in Rontaia, in point of fact." Lila had spent a whirlwind of a winter solstice week there with a group of painted-faced friends what seemed like a lifetime ago. Even in winter, the midday sun had forced them back to the private painted-only hotel in Cliffside, built into the rock so it stayed cool through the heat of the day. She couldn't imagine living down there, but it was a great place to vacation. She didn't remember half of it, but what she remembered was among the most fun she'd ever had in her youth. "Don't you take long daytime naps down there too? I could get into that."

"I was never much of a napper, but we do lie low in the middle of the day. Are you sure you're okay?"

"I'm absolutely splendid, thank you."

"You mind if I go ahead and bring in those crates then?" Avisse asked almost apologetically.

"Please!"

Lila glanced at, but forced herself not to stare at, Avisse's round behind as she marched out the door.

"Looks like everything is in order, as usual." Lila signed the receipts, and Avisse tore her copies off and slid them across the desk. "The way things are going, I'll be placing another order before you know it. We already have over a hundred names on the waitlist."

"Look at you, spreading joy through the city one vibrating olli at a time."

"Give the people what they want, I say."

"And what about what you want, Ms. Lila? Does anyone give you that?" Avisse moved around the side of the desk one slow step at a time. Lila stood, pushing her chair back awkwardly, blood rushing in her throat.

"I—" was all she managed before Avisse's lips were on hers, strong hands gripping Lila's biceps and pushing her back against the bookshelf, her taut thigh pressing between Lila's legs. Lila slumped against the hard wood as Avisse devoured her mouth, hands running over her shoulders and up to cradle the back of her head. Was the door open? Was this happening? What was happening?

Avisse gave her no time to think as she wrapped her other leg around Lila's, molding to her thigh and sliding up and down against the silky fabric of her dress. Lila lost herself in the deft sweeps of Avisse's tongue, the powerful clench of her thighs, the spiraling oh gods don't please not yet—

Avisse pulled away from the kiss, fixing Lila with hot, dark eyes as she eased the pressure between Lila's legs but stayed clenched around her thigh. She kissed Lila's neck, fingers sliding up to untie the top laces of her dress. She licked and sucked her way down as she peeled the dress from Lila's shoulders, massaging her chest, dragging her fingers across Lila's nipples. Lila moaned as lightning shot through her nerves. Avisse's fingers danced and stuttered over and over as her sucking, lapping mouth inched ever closer. Her tongue flicked over Lila's nipple, then she clamped down and sucked, and Lila let out a sharp cry of delight that startled even her.

She glanced over at the door, which was in fact open. She was briefly aware of footsteps approaching. Avisse looked up at her with a mischievous grin, then moved over to suck the other nipple for a long second. Lila bit her hand to stifle another cry, then quickly covered herself as the footsteps grew closer. Avisse stepped back, wiping her mouth, as Aven entered the room with their usual jaunty, carefree step. They opened their mouth to speak, took in the scene, then shut their mouth in a wry smile. They gave a little one-fingered salute, then turned and spun back through the door, shutting it carefully behind them.

"I like them," Avisse said with a grin.

"I consulted on Aven and Tera's marriage, as it happens." Lila smiled as she thought of Tera and Aven's fear and hesitation at the beginning compared to how inseparable they were now. "Seems like it worked out all right."

"Tera's the one with the hazel eyes that could cut you in half from across the room?"

"You noticed."

"I always notice people's eyes. Yours are like the Naeili Bay in the morning sun."

Heat spread from Lila's cheeks down her neck as Avisse held her gaze.

"I'm afraid that sunstroke from before is coming back." Lila picked up her hat and fanned herself, biting her lip to stop her smile from spreading too wide.

"I'm sorry, I know I come on strong sometimes." Avisse looked down, and Lila let out a breath she definitely knew she was holding. "You're just really beautiful, is all. And it gets lonely on the road. So, I thought about you. A lot." When she looked back up, her eyes burned hot and guileless into Lila's, bringing back a touch of the dizziness from before.

"You see, I told Aven we should move my fainting couch into this office because you never know when you're going to need one." Lila leaned back against the bookcase, unsure what she would do if Avisse kissed her again, how she'd stop herself from coming apart at the slightest touch of her hand.

"I wouldn't want you to get overstimulated before dinner." Avisse took a small step toward Lila, rolling her shoulders ever so slightly. "And I need to go board my horses." Her fingers found Lila's, intertwining, her voice lowering as her mouth grew closer. She rose up on tiptoes, using Lila's fingers for leverage, and kissed her gently, leaning in so her small breasts pressed against Lila's chest. Lila's mind went blank as their bodies molded together, lips joining in a languid dance full of patience and promise. Avisse hummed into the kiss, then pulled back, lids half-closed, mouth curved in a sleepy smile.

"I need to take my girls to our stable in the fourth. The walk back will be a good stretch for Theo and me."

"That's...that's good!" Lila's lids fluttered as her senses returned. "And you'll come back for dinner?"

"I wouldn't miss it. What're you cooking?"

"Oh!" Lila shook her head. She couldn't cook worth a damn, so she was planning on getting something to grill, but she wasn't sure what Avisse did or didn't eat. "I'm going to grill, but I wanted to check to see if there was anything..."

"I eat everything, but Theo can be weirdly picky. He doesn't eat much, to be honest, but as long as there's bread, he'll be happy."

"Oh, perfect. My butcher has these amazing fennel sausages, and there's an allvendor in the next stall over. I'll get a few dips and some nice flatbreads to go with them. We should be all wrapped up and ready at, say, seven?"

"Seven it is. I've brought something special to drink, a little taste of Rontaia. I think you're going to love it."

"Sounds perfect. I guess I'll see you and Theo tonight then."

Avisse slitted her eyes, grabbed Lila by the jaw, and pulled her in for one more long, slow kiss, leaving her breathless and slumped against the bookcase.

"See you tonight," she said, wheeling her empty dolly out the door.

5

Lila changed into a no-nonsense gray sleeveless shirt and a pair of lightweight black pants to grill in. It was a good move, because the heat lingered even after the sun went down, and the grill got much hotter much faster than she'd hoped. She stood back, mopping her forehead with a handkerchief, sighing at the makeup stain she left on it. She should just have time to slip back inside and freshen up before—

"Look at you, mistress of fire!" Avisse stood with one hand on her hip, the other holding a bottle of wine with light purple wax around the top. Theo lurked just behind her, several books tucked under his arm, as if afraid of the fire.

"The grill's got the better of me at the moment," Lila admitted, stepping toward Avisse as if drawn by a magnet. Avisse wrapped one arm around her and kissed her cheek, eyes flashing with muted desire.

"Delighted to see you, Theo." Lila pressed her hands together at her chest and bowed in the Endulian style. Theo's eyes lit up, and he repeated her gesture, awkwardly because of the books under his arm.

"What is inside me is open to you," he said solemnly.

"And me to you," Lila indulged him. "Would you like to go look at the river tales book again?"

"I read it once already, but I'm going to consult it again after dinner if that's all right. I brought several other books for comparison, one a collection of Maer legends from the Silver Hills, and the complete *Elder Tales* from the Time Before." He brandished the books, which were hefty and well-worn. "I thought I recognized some common threads in a few of the stories, and I'd like to investigate those further."

"Theo is doing an independent study course in narratology." Avisse put a hand on Theo's shoulder. "And I only know what that is because he's explained it to me a dozen times. I only like to read stories, not study them."

"I would argue that all reading is a form of study." Theo shifted the books to his other arm, tucking his wispy hair behind his ears as he stared at the fire. He opened his mouth again, then closed it, looking up at his mother, then at Lila, with a weak smile. "But I don't want to bore you with my little theories. What's for dinner?"

Lila shook her head as a smile crept over her face.

"Fennel sausage and a spread of spiced veggie dips from the market, with all the flatbread you can eat."

Theo's smile widened, and his eyes grew round.

"Be careful what you promise, Lila." Avisse put a warm hand on Lila's shoulder. "Theo never ceases to surprise you."

Theo eyed the last round of flatbread with longing, but he still had a quarter piece and several dollops of dip on his plate. It was the principle of the thing, Lila surmised; eating with company, he no doubt had freer access to bread than usual, and he didn't want to waste his chance. Avisse had eaten three whole sausages and picked the pieces Lila had been too full to eat off her plate, chewing and laughing with gusto. They drank a lovely bottle of lavender wine Avisse had brought from Rontaia—"Because I noticed you had it on your dress, and your perfume, and even in the lobby"—and every sip warmed Lila's heart.

Theo had stopped pontificating and sat in a food-induced stupor while Lila and Avisse chatted and polished off the bottle. Avisse told of a street brawl she'd narrowly avoided in Guluch, a triple rainbow she'd seen over the river near Endulai, and the boredom of the long, lonely stretches of road.

"Sometimes when I'm driving, I try to replay books I've read in my head but change the ending, imagining what would happen if the characters made different decisions. Other times I watch the houses and villages we pass by and try to picture myself living there, wondering what my life would be like." She downed the last of her glass, lifting the bottle to stare at its meager contents by the light of the candle.

"And occasionally, I try to picture what my life would be like if I lived in my destination." She looked around, staring up at the sky, the carriage house, the stately buildings surrounding them. She turned to Lila, eyes glowing with the wine and the candlelight, and her pinky slid over to brush against Lila's. Lila lifted hers over Avisse's, letting the warmth creep up her hand, along her arm, and through her chest.

"You might like it here."

"I'm starting to see its charms."

Her pinky tightened against Lila's, and their knees touched under the table, sending further waves of warmth up Lila's thighs, which she ignored as best she could. Sandaled footsteps sounded on the gravel, and Lila turned to see Sylvan rounding the edge of the woodpile with a small package under his arm, his face painted bright green with light green lips and yellow accents. *You are like a wise frog on a lily pad awaiting the sun's return,* Lila might have said if she were still painted. She'd always been good at color compliments, and she sometimes missed the little repartee of painted greetings.

"Good evening, Lila, Avisse." He kissed the air around Lila's face and bowed slightly toward Avisse, then turned toward Theo. "And this must be our young scholar, Theo." He studied the boy for a moment, then pressed his hands together at his chest and bowed in Endulian greeting. Theo stood and returned the gesture.

"You didn't tell me he was a practitioner," he chided Lila with a friendly lilt to his voice.

"I didn't know—"

"He's not exactly—"

"Mother—"

"Oh, but he is." Sylvan sat down in the fourth chair, and Theo sat too, his sleepy eyes now wide and bright. "It's in the air all around you." Sylvan's fingers fluttered in a circle in Theo's direction. "Did you learn in Rontaia?"

Theo stared, as if star-struck, then nodded quickly.

"At first, yes. I went to see the quarterstaff fights and stayed for the meditation sessions. Someone gave me a pamphlet with an old poem in it, which I now know to be part of Cloti's *Treatise on the Thousand Worlds*, but I was only six at the time."

"I had to drag him away," Avisse mused.

"And you've been to Endulai as well." Sylvan spoke with certainty, and Theo nodded again.

"We were passing by during the Red Festival, and I persuaded Mother to spend a day there."

"Then you weren't very far from where I learned that some of the legends in this book have their origins in the truth." He slid the package across the table, and Theo's eyes grew wider still. Theo looked to Avisse, who blinked her approval, then carefully peeled open the brown paper. His intake of breath was audible as he unfolded the wrapping to reveal the gold-embossed green cover of the *Tales and Legends of the Agra*, the very same book Lila had in her study.

Theo opened it with care, tracing his fingers over Sylvan's signature on the inside cover.

"*To Theo, May you never stop seeking the truth the world tries to keep from you. —Sylvan Kirin.*"

Theo's eyes grew wet, and he closed the book and clutched it to his chest. He took in a deep breath and let it out as a shaky sigh.

"This is the honor of a lifetime, Dr. Kirin."

"Please, call me Sylvan. I don't believe in honorifics. And I'd be more than happy to chat about the book with you if you're not too tired."

"Oh no, not at all. I mean, that is, if it's okay with..." He turned his big eyes to Avisse, who blinked her acknowledgment once again.

"This fits in perfectly with your curriculum. I think we can count it as lecture hours."

Theo practically bounced off his seat.

"Would you happen to have a lamp we could borrow?" Sylvan asked Lila. "It's too nice of a night to be indoors, but this candle's not quite enough for proper study."

Lila hurried inside to grab a lamp, pausing for long enough to touch up her makeup and freshen up under her arms after a long day of walking in the sun and grilling. Sylvan had arrived right on cue. Everything was unfolding according to plan.

She delivered the lamp to Sylvan, who barely paused his conversation with Theo to wink at her.

"Hey Lila, I'd love to see this spa and bath facility you were talking about. You said the renovations were just finished?" Avisse stood, gesturing subtly with her head. Lila glanced at Theo, who was engrossed in conversation with Sylvan. "Sweetie, we're just going to go have a look around. You'll be okay with Sylvan?"

"Fine, mom," Theo said without looking.

Avisse giggled under her breath as they made their way across the dark courtyard arm in arm.

"You had that all planned out, didn't you?"

"A complete coincidence, I assure you." Lila bumped Avisse with her hip, which hit closer to Avisse's tight waist. She released Avisse's arm for long enough to unlock the heavy door, then turned the deadbolt behind them out of habit once they were inside, though in the second ring, behind a gate, there was really nothing to worry about. Lila gasped when she turned around to find herself trapped against the door, her face bracketed by Avisse's biceps, the smell of cinnamon, wine, and sweat enveloping her in a cloud of heady need. Avisse's mouth curled into a wicked smirk, her eyes half-slitted but hard with want. As the heat of Avisse's body radiated into her, Lila melted against the door for support, heart racing and mind spiraling.

The kiss, when it came, was so soft it made Lila want to turn inside out. Her hands found Avisse's waist, felt the strength of her muscles beneath the linen, her fingers working the fabric free and sliding across the warm curves bulging over the top of her pants. Avisse leaned into her, and Lila kept her touches gentle to match the soft sweeps of Avisse's tongue, the tender nibbles of her lips. Lila swelled against her gaff, longing for pressure, but Avisse gave her only soft touch and slowly building heat. Just when Lila felt ready to explode, Avisse pulled away from the kiss, pushing off the door, and bit her smiling lip. Lila pressed her palms against the door until her mind stopped spinning and her breath returned.

"You have a way of making me forget whatever it was I was going to say or do." Lila pushed away from the door, standing under her own power. Avisse reached out and took her hand, pulling her toward the center of the lobby.

"You were going to show me the baths, and then the spa." The *fuck-me* undertone of her voice was unmistakable, and Lila followed, walking awkwardly due to her swollen state, which the view of Avisse's behind did little to abate. "I gather the renovations are complete?"

"Well, there's always something that still needs work in a place this old."

Lila took the lead once they passed through the doors to the baths. Avisse was wowed by the number of brightstone lights; apparently, they weren't nearly as common in Rontaia, which made sense, given how much farther it was from the newly discovered mines. She was awestruck by the red sandstone, which still impressed Lila every time she saw it, and more than a little curious about what lay beyond Sylvan's big bronze door.

"It's some kind of pre-Endulian shrine. Sylvan's having it restored as a pet project." Lila had prepared the half-truth in advance. She felt bad about it, but it was too much to get into when what she really wanted to get into was Avisse's pants.

Avisse let out a low hum that was almost a purr when she entered the spa, whose low orange lighting gave her skin an ethereal glow, accentuating its reddish tones. She fondled some of the accoutrements, ran her hands over the calfskin massage tables, then popped up to sit on one, her legs swinging over the edge.

"C'mere." She held out a hand toward Lila, eyes soft and inviting. Lila swallowed hard, wishing she had a glass of water to wet her dry mouth, but as their fingers touched and Avisse's boots hooked around her thighs and pulled her in, she forgot all about that. She forgot about everything else as Avisse's arms wrapped around her neck and her mouth crushed against Lila's, hot and wet, her eager tongue rendering Lila breathless and desperate.

Avisse's legs clamped tighter around Lila's waist, and she pulled herself up, forcing Lila's hands to grip her plump buttocks to support her. Avisse ground against her, heat pulsing through thin layers of fabric, clutching Lila's hair as she devoured her lips. She was so light but so strong, clinging to Lila, practically riding her from a standing position. It was almost more than Lila could take without spilling. She had to flip the script, quite literally, or risk an awkward, messy end to their encounter.

Lila stepped toward the table, lifting Avisse bodily and setting her down on her back without breaking the kiss. It was Lila's turn to pin Avisse's biceps this time. She pressed into the kiss for a moment before releasing her suddenly, staring into the hot, dark depths of her eyes. Avisse gasped as Lila grabbed her by the ankles and pulled her to the end of the table, standing between her legs. She roughly wrenched off one boot then the other as Avisse shimmied out of her shirt, revealing perfect small breasts with stiff brown nipples. Lila unbuckled Avisse's belt and wrestled her out of her pants, salivating at the sight of her, the smooth expanse of her skin gilded by the spa lights, the thick mound of hair between her legs, the soft curves and solid lines of her body. Lila licked her lips, running her fingernails up and down Avisse's muscular thighs.

"Gods, I want to taste you so bad."

"Please," Avisse whispered, pulling her legs back and taking her knees in her hands.

Lila fell to her knees, dizzy with lust at the sight of her, pink and glistening amid a cloud of dark brown hair. She nosed in, taking in her rich perfume, and licked a slow, salty trail up the crease of her leg, Avisse's heat searing her cheek only inches away. Avisse gasped as Lila ghosted her lips over her before licking her way up the other side, tangling her fingers in the thick curls of hair above. She returned her attention to Avisse's center, breathing in the very essence of heaven itself. With the first taste, the first, long, slow stripe painted with her tongue, Lila closed her eyes and lost herself in the silken pleasures of Avisse's body and her growing moans echoing off the ancient stone.

It had been so long, and Lila's hunger knew no bounds. She swam in Avisse's pleasure, bathed in it, baptized herself in her cries of delight. Her hands roamed freely over Avisse's tight body, all of which was within reach. She took full advantage, massaging her breasts, toying with her nipples until she found the pressure that made her moan just so. She slipped her fingers into Avisse's mouth to be suckled and licked. In between Avisse's climaxes, Lila climbed atop her, straddling her body as Avisse devoured her lips, then lowering back down when her kisses grew more desperate. Lila kissed her way up and down that sweaty, lithe little body more times than she could count, pouring more of her heart and soul into pleasing her each time even as she grew closer herself.

As Avisse's cries became hoarser and she arched off the table, Lila dug deeper, gripping her flexed buttocks and rising with her. Avisse's legs wrapped around her neck, locking her in tight. The world went dark, dragging her into the relentless undertow of Avisse's climax. As she tumbled in those dusky waters, Lila experienced a moment of euphoria that was almost dissociative in its intensity, a loss of self, a oneness unlike anything she'd experienced with the finest philters available on Alchemist's Row.

As Avisse pulsed against her mouth, sharp cries of almost-pain ringing off the walls, Lila's mind released from its moorings, and her body followed. A wave of pleasure welled up inside her, not just from her loins, but from some deeper place, the one she'd felt hints of during Sylvan's meditation session. She exploded, mind and body, struggling to hold onto Avisse's quivering hips, which slowly lowered onto the table as her legs relaxed their hold around Lila's neck. She stayed with Avisse to the end, breathing into her, laying tiny kisses all around as Avisse's hoarse breaths slowly settled.

When at last Lila dared to look up from the crux of her legs, she saw Avisse with arms splayed out, covered with a fine sheen of sweat, lips puffy and eyes closed. She had never seen a more beautiful sight.

"Skundir's balls and taint, Lila," Avisse mumbled, reaching down to run her fingers through Lila's hair. "You really know how to show a girl a good time."

Lila stood slowly, leaning forward with elbows on the end of the table to hide the dark stain that no doubt covered the front of her pants where she'd spilled copiously through her gaff.

"The pleasure was all mine." She picked up a towel from the rack on the table and gave her face a quick wipe.

Avisse sat up, using Lila's arm as leverage, and pulled in close for a slow, soft kiss.

"So I noticed." She pulled back from the kiss, glancing down at the wet spot on Lila's pants with a smirk. "I love that."

Lila turned away, blushing furiously, unsure how to take it all.

"I *do*," Avisse said softly, tugging Lila back to face her. "That happens to me sometimes too, when I'm really enjoying pleasuring someone." She kissed Lila again, hands creeping up the back of her neck, somehow stirring her anew. "I think it's cute."

Lila tried to pout, but Avisse kissed it away. Avisse took her by the shoulders, and Lila stared deeply into Avisse's eyes, dark and all-consuming in the low light of the spa.

"I need to go see to my kid right now," she said. "But we're in town for another few nights to give the horses a rest." She slipped away from Lila and hopped off the table, grabbing the towel and wiping roughly between her legs. "And I was really hoping that tomorrow night we could find a way to get some more alone time so I could return the favor."

Lila closed her eyes, breathing out through her nose as Avisse's fingers traced up her stomach, zeroing in on her nipples, and began circling them as they stiffened beneath her touch.

"That would be—" Her words ended in a gasp as Avisse gripped both her nipples through the thin fabric of her shirt and twisted gently one way, then the other. Lila swelled against her sticky gaff, unable to form a coherent thought until Avisse let go and stepped back, still naked and somehow even more beautiful than before in the orange glow of the spa.

"Wouldn't it?" She pulled on her underthings and pants, then hopped up onto the table to put on her boots. "Ready when you are." She hopped down, still naked from the waist up; her breasts had a slight sag, with upward-pointing nipples, and Lila's mouth watered at the sight of them.

"Aren't you going to…" Lila gestured vaguely toward her chest. Avisse grabbed her hand and pressed it against her, rubbing Lila's fingers over one breast, then the other, over her shoulder, and up her soft neck.

"If you insist." She turned, showing off her well-muscled back, which soon disappeared beneath her shirt, leaving only her tight shoulders, biceps, and forearms bare to tempt Lila.

"Of course, I've got a little cleanup to do." Lila dabbed the towel against her pants, for what little good it would do.

"You could spill some massage oil on yourself." Avisse picked up a pitcher of oil from the little stand beside the table, and Lila took it with a shrug.

"It's not going to fool Sylvan, but I guess it's plausible enough." She poured a bit of the oil over the stain, where it spread into an even bigger stain, surely ruining the pants. Such was the price of ecstasy, she supposed.

"You're wearing Lila's lipstick again."

Avisse touched her lips, covering a smile in the process, and Lila covered her smile as well.

"I wanted to try it on, you know, just for a laugh."

"You should try using the stick instead of kissing. It wouldn't smear so much." Theo kept a remarkably straight face, but Sylvan burst out laughing, leaning on the table for support.

"I'm just going to go freshen up." Lila excused herself with a little wave at Theo and a meaningful glance at Sylvan, who regarded her with amused curiosity. She hurried up the stairs and out of her pants and gaff, tossing the soiled mess into her hamper. She washed herself quickly in the basin and put on fresh gaff, pants, and lipstick, then hurried back downstairs.

"I think your son might be onto something," Sylvan was saying. "I don't know much about these Maer stories, but they sound an awful lot like the ones from the *Elder Tales*, and not a few of them have obvious connections to the Agra stories as well. We're thinking of co-writing a paper."

"A wha—you're—" Avisse couldn't seem to finish her thought, standing with one hand on her chest and the other half-covering her mouth.

"He's perfectly capable of writing it himself, but I can help him with the academic language. And as a full professor, I have access to publishing outlets that he as a mere student does not. It will be his first scholarly paper." He put a gentle hand on Theo's arm, and Theo's sleepy eyes beamed with pride. "But certainly not his last."

"I assume you don't mind, Mother?" Theo asked hopefully.

"Of *course*, I don't mind. Theo..." She took his hands and lifted him to standing, then pulled him into a bear hug, which he accepted limply. She pushed him back to arm's length, eyes agleam in the lamplight. "I'm so proud of you." She turned to Sylvan, still holding Theo's shoulders. "Thank you," she said.

"The thanks goes to your son, for bringing this fascinating bit of scholarship to my attention. I have been neglecting this side of my career of late, and he's given me just the push I need. But I have other scholarly matters to attend to at the moment."

He winked at Lila as he stood. "I'll have those books sent by first thing tomorrow morning," he said to Theo. "I assume you'll be in town for at least a few days?" He glanced at Avisse, who nodded, her hand grazing Lila's thigh.

"Yes, and we need to get back to our stable. The third ring gate closes at midnight, doesn't it?"

Lila nodded. There was no way in or out between midnight and quarter dawn without a gold pass.

"I'll leave them at the desk, and you can pick them up whenever you like. I'll also leave my address, where you can send your outline and your opening argument, along with your return address in Rontaia. I'll send my response via the Inkwell, and you can bring your draft next time you're in town."

"Sounds great, Dr. Kirin."

"Just Sylvan, please."

Theo shook his head. "If we're working on an academic paper together, I'm afraid I must insist, for the duration of our collaboration at least. Good night, Doctor."

"Good night, Theo." Sylvan gave Theo a deep Endulian bow, then shared air kisses with Lila and Avisse. "I'll be by tomorrow night, in case you might be around."

"You never know." Avisse pulled Lila's arm in close and snuggled against her as Sylvan strode across the courtyard. Her head fell against Lila's shoulder, and she hummed into Lila's hair.

"You don't have to schlep all the way out to the fourth ring, you know." Lila turned and tucked Avisse into her chest, wrapping her arms around her back. "My bed is plenty big, and Theo could sleep on the couch in the study."

Avisse groaned into Lila's neck, her breath warm on Lila's skin. "I'm afraid I can't accept." Her voice was tinged with whine.

"And why in the Thousand Worlds not?" Lila glanced over at Theo, whose eyes were closed, his mouth slack in sleep. She slid her hands down, slipped them inside Avisse's waistband, and found the warm, soft curves of her behind. Avisse let out a gentle groan that vibrated through Lila's chest.

"I don't like being beholden to people."

Lila's hands slid further down, cupping each buttock and lifting, pulling them apart just a little. Avisse huffed into her neck, then her lips wrapped around Lila's windpipe, soft and wet, her tongue flickering up and down. Her hands found Lila's behind and gripped her tight, crushing their bodies together. Lila's blood pumped hot and wild, her hands kneading and massaging, every part of her leaning in but trying not to move too much for fear of waking the child. They stayed in this torrid fugue state for some time before they finally pulled apart slowly, fingers sliding around to hips, then tangling together as they stood facing each other in the now cool night air.

"Stay with me," Lila pleaded. "Wake up next to me in the morning."

Avisse glanced over at Theo, who had one eye half-open but quickly shut it.

"Okay," she said with a wry grin.

Theo's mouth quirked into a smile, and he clenched his fist, eyes still closed.

They lay in bed, Avisse pressed tight against Lila's back, one arm clamped around her chest. With Theo in the next room, they seemed to have decided anything more was off the table, so they snuggled, neither of them sleeping, pressed into each other's warmth.

"This might be the biggest bed I've ever slept in," Avisse murmured.

"It was hell getting it up the steps, I can tell you that. It's built for four if the need should arise."

"And how often is that?"

"I have my moments." Lila blushed, thankful for the dark to hide it. "Or used to, anyway. It hasn't seen more than one since I moved from the fourth ring."

"Maybe you were saving it for me, and you didn't even know it." Avisse's voice had a sleepy, self-satisfied glow that made Lila's heart flutter. She gripped Avisse's hand and wiggled in against her.

"Too bad we can't take full advantage."

"We could take partial advantage." Avisse's lips breathed hot in her ear as her teeth clamped down gently and her fingers crawled inexorably toward Lila's nipple. Lila hissed in a breath as Avisse gave her a soft pinch and held on, twisting gently. She released, sliding her hand along the curve of Lila's waist, inching ever closer. Lila never wore her gaff to bed, since it was too restrictive, and she was tenting her bloomers, straining toward Avisse's touch but terrified at the same time. She knew Avisse wasn't like that—surely, she knew, wouldn't care, didn't mind—but as her fingers slid along the fabric and teased Lila's tip, Lila's heart raced in panic. Avisse's tongue slid into her ear as her fingers fondled Lila gently, like she was handling a delicate flower.

"Is this okay?" Avisse asked, licking behind her ear as her fingers circled so softly Lila feared she might faint.

"Y-yes," she managed. "I just—"

Words failed her as Avisse milked her earlobe and slid her hand down, still holding on gently through the fabric, then back up. She wrapped one leg around Lila's hip and rolled her onto her back, straddling her thigh and pressing kisses along her cheek, then her lips. Avisse's mouth was hot and ready, and Lila gave in to her kisses as Avisse ground into her thigh and continued her gentle stroking. Lila's breath came in ragged bursts between kisses, and something else was going to come in ragged bursts if Avisse kept this up much longer. Avisse's other hand pressed into her chest, and she began moving her hips, sliding along Lila's thigh with slow, powerful strokes. She gripped Lila tight as she sped up, and Lila gave an inadvertent squeak.

Avisse's eyes darkened, and she clamped a hand over Lila's mouth as she ground against her thigh, holding her with an iron grip. A wave of ecstasy welled up inside Lila as Avisse rode her leg with furious, controlled strength, gritting her teeth and clamping her hand tight to Lila's mouth, shoving her head deep into the pillow. Lila moaned into her hand as Avisse stifled a groan, the trembling of her powerful thighs sending Lila over the moon, spilling and bucking. Avisse collapsed onto her, still holding her firm, covering her face with warm, wet kisses. They lay, sticky and soaked with sweat, unwilling to peel their bodies apart, as the night air slowly cooled them.

Avisse finally rolled off to the side, letting her arm flop over Lila's stomach. Lila locked fingers with her, wondering how she had lived the past thirty-two years of her life without this woman by her side.

6

Lila slipped out of Avisse's embrace and tiptoed to the washroom. The door to the study where Theo was sleeping was closed, so she did her business and washed up as quietly as possible. She ran her fingers over her jaw, feeling the subtle bumps that would become the beginnings of stubble by day's end but were too short to shave now. The transcendent alchemist's creams could only do so much, but she rubbed some in anyway, adding a bit of orange-ish tan around her cheeks and finishing it with a subtle blush of lipstick. Being around Avisse made her want to look more natural, but she had to put a little color on her skin or risk looking like a ghost. She would have to tell Avisse about being an Unpainted one of these days, but there was so much to unpack. Why did she still feel guilty after all these years, when it was *they* who'd expelled her from their cult for being who she was? No sense ruining the little time she had with Avisse with her tragic backstory. She tapped a dab of lavender oil on her throat, tousling her hair in the mirror and smiling. For it being this early, she looked pretty damned good.

Lila heard movement from behind Theo's door as she passed back to the bedroom, pressing her backside against Avisse's sleep-warmed body. A strong arm curled around her, and a gentle hum breathed in her ear.

"Good morning, Lavender Girl." Avisse sniffed as she snuggled into her neck. "I love that smell on you." Her fingers stroked Lila's chest, sending tingles all across her skin.

"Did you sleep all right?"

"Like a bear. You're nice to hold onto."

"You're nice to be held by."

"Mmm…" Avisse's lips brushed against Lila's ear as her hand slid down and took hold of her, unsurprisingly hard already. "I could hold you all day," she whispered, squeezing gently.

A faint thud sounded somewhere in the apartment, followed by another, then padding footsteps. Avisse let go, and Lila pulled a sheet over herself, suddenly mortified. Avisse's giggle did nothing to assuage her guilt, nor did the sound of the washroom door opening and closing.

"Don't worry. He's not going to barge in on us. I didn't raise him in a barn."

"A stable, I imagine?"

"It's a much more civilized environment, better suited for the development of the whole child."

"Speaking of the development of the whole child, don't they require sustenance? In the form of pastries, I was thinking?"

"I don't usually spoil him like that, but since he's your guest, I suppose if you offered, he'd be wrong to refuse."

"The same might be said of you."

"I would be especially wrong to refuse woodberry pastries. We don't get those down in Rontaia."

"I should think it would also be wrong of you to refuse a kiss if your host demanded it?"

Lila turned to face Avisse, propping herself on one elbow. Avisse rolled back on the bed, spreading her arms above her head.

"It would be wrong of me to refuse you anything you wish."

Lila's skin flushed with desire. She put a hand on Avisse's chest and closed in, eyes locking before lips, hearts melting together through the soft languor of their kiss. They pulled apart as they heard the washroom door open and Theo padding down the hallway.

"I'll run and get some pastries. Tea's in the kitchen if you want some. I won't be long."

"You better not be."

Avisse touched her cheek, eyes soft with sleep and their kiss, then blinked toward the door.

"Good morning, Theo," Lila said before remembering and offering an Endulian bow.

"Good morning, Ms.—Good morning, Lila." Theo bowed back. "The couch was quite comfortable. Better than the bed at the inn above the stable. Plus, library." He gestured toward the bookshelf.

"Well, help yourself, of course! I'm off to get pastries. Anything special you'd like?"

Theo's eyes flew wide.

"Ooh, do they have sugar flowers?"

"Sometimes? If not, I'll get a little variety. Your mother wanted—"

"Woodberry. She always talks about it. I don't get it. It's too sour for dessert. Which, I guess pastries for breakfast aren't exactly dessert, but it's too sour for breakfast too. It's too sour for anything if you ask me. Which I suppose you didn't. I don't talk to people much if you hadn't noticed."

"You're fine. No woodberry for you, then. Your mother's awake and will be out to make tea in a few, I suspect. I'll be back shortly."

She turned to grab her keys, but stopped when Theo said in a small voice,

"You make her happy."

Lila turned around, her mouth half-open.

"I—what?"

"My mother." He glanced at the door, ducking his head a little and lowering his voice. "She's had a rough time of things ever since Mama Jillia died when I was little. She doesn't show it, but I think it's hard for her. But since she met you? She smiles more." He sat back, staring at the bedroom door, then turned an almost blank face toward Lila.

"Um, thank you," she said, trying to hold back unexpected tears. "I didn't—"

The door opened, and Lila blinked rapidly and jangled the keys.

"Sugar flowers for you then, and definitely no woodberry."

"Ugh, did he give you the woodberry speech? I let him try mine once when he was like three and he's never forgotten." Avisse looked better right out of bed than most women did in their evening finery, her hair falling in stiff waves down to her strong shoulders, left bare by her skimpy top. She leaned in and kissed Theo on the forehead. He only squirmed a little.

"Good morning, sunshine."

"Good morning, Mother. I trust you slept well?"

"Best night of sleep I've had in years." She put an arm around Lila's back, pressing into her side. Apparently, they weren't pretending to keep secrets. "I'll get some tea started while you get the pastries." Her kiss was brief, but it stirred Lila more than felt appropriate, given the presence of Avisse's son in the room, watching them intently. She whirled down the stairs and out into the courtyard, hurrying as she heard the bakery cart's bell receding in the distance.

She ran into Sylvan in the courtyard on her way back, his eyes drawn with fatigue but bright with hope.

"Long night?" She offered the bag of pastries, and he sighed in relief, pulling out one of the sugar flowers and crunching into it.

"Mmm, I haven't had a sugar flower in years. Takes me back to my childhood."

"That was for Theo. I hope you enjoy it." Lila smirked at the look of horror on Sylvan's green-painted face.

"Oh, gods, I'm so, *so* sorry, I—"

"I'm messing with you, Sylvan. I got two." He sighed into another bite, closing his eyes and humming with satisfaction. "So, how's progress down there? Is the Well, you know, All?"

"It's more of a Well of Not Much at the moment," he said, covering his mouth as he spoke, still chewing. "One of the pieces needs to be remanufactured, I'm afraid, and I'm still working on the mineral balance in the water. I'm almost finished interpreting the schematics for the crystal ball, and you'll never believe who I'm commissioning it from."

"It couldn't be the Silver Dock workshop, could it?"

"It could *only* be the Silver Dock workshop. From everyone I've talked to, they're the absolute best there is in delicate glassware such as this. Which means, in all likelihood, your...special friend Avisse will be making an extra special delivery."

Lila wrapped Sylvan in a big hug, forcing him to hold the remains of his sugar flower to the side. She let him go, brushing a few flakes of pastry from her dress.

"That's wonderful news, Sylvan! Well, I won't keep you. I've got company." She lifted the bag, and Sylvan nodded, a weary smile on his face.

"Tell Theo I'll have the books sent over just as soon as I'm home. Wish me luck catching a carriage at this hour."

After tea and pastries, Avisse stood, stretching her magnificent, tight little frame.

"I've got to go look after my girls. They need a good stretch, and I expect you have business to attend to as well."

Lila's heart sank. She'd been putting off thoughts of the countless tasks that awaited her as soon as she walked through the doors of The World Within.

"Sadly, you're right. Who would have thought opening multiple businesses at once would be so much work?" She stood, standing awkwardly across the table from Avisse. "You're welcome to stay here, for as long as you're in town, unless you'd rather be close to your horses. Of course, you'd need to look after them, I didn't mean, I just—" Lila shook her head, blood pounding in her temples as Avisse rounded the table and took her hand.

"We'll be back in time for dinner." She tiptoed up and pressed a soft kiss on Lila's mouth. "But this time, I'm cooking."

Lila let out a nervous laugh, her heart fluttering as she glanced down into Avisse's smiling brown eyes.

"I'll be looking forward to it all day."

Avisse bit her lip, brushing her fingers on Lila's hip, then turned to Theo.

"Get your satchel ready and fill your water bottle. We've got some walking to do."

"Can't I just stay here and read? I'll get behind on my lessons, and I really want to get started on the outline for that paper with Sylvan."

Avisse crossed her arms over her chest, and though Lila couldn't see her eyes, the way Theo reacted told her the look had been withering. He stood grumpily and marched into the study to collect his things.

"An hour of exercise a day minimum on the road, and three when stationary," he recited in a bored drone. "The mind is an extension of the body, and ill health of one contributes to poor function of the other."

"Plus, you know you like seeing the architecture in Anari!" she called after him.

He sat down on the sofa, putting a few things into his satchel.

"But I can't read while I'm walking, Mother." He stood, returning to the kitchen, his pout somewhat diminished. "It feels like such a waste."

"And you can't talk to your dear old Mother when you're reading." She put an arm around his shoulder. "Maybe you can tell me about this Endulian practice of yours I've been ignoring for the past few years."

His eyes brightened, but there was a wariness to his tone. "Will you really listen, or are you just trying to cajole me?"

"You can give me a test at the end."

"And if you fail the test, you get us a carriage back."

Avisse turned to Lila, calculating in her head.

"How much is a carriage back from the fourth ring?"

"At peak hour? Probably about twelve lep."

"I guess I better not fail then." She held out her hand, which Theo shook solemnly.

"See you tonight." Avisse blew Lila a kiss, which she captured in her palm and drank like sweet lavender wine.

The day passed in a blur of deliveries, interviews, minor emergencies, and of course heaps of paperwork. Tera kept all the invoices and bills neatly filed, labeled, and ready to sign, but sometimes the mere act of picking up the pen was more than Lila could handle. She glanced at the Silver Dock order sheet, whose numbers hadn't increased in several days. She wasn't sure it was enough for free shipping, and she wasn't about to pay fifty poul just to see Avisse again. Well, of course, she would, but she'd rather see her and have money in her pocket to take her out to a nice restaurant. She leafed through their catalog, eyeing the glass sculptures of nudes, which were quite fetching. Some were solo figures, while others were intertwined in delicious poses. The fine print listed the various sizes available, along with the prices, with discounts for bulk orders. If the painted faces' appetite for vibrating ollis was drying up, maybe she could tempt them with some art. It might be risky, but she didn't think money was the issue. Painted faces always had plenty of that while the rest of the city struggled to get by. She just needed to find the right product to get it from them.

After closing, she sat with Tera going over the books, assisted by a delicate white tea with a floral aroma she couldn't quite place.

"Things have slowed a bit, but we're still going at a more than sustainable pace." Tera closed the ledger, eyebrows arched in what looked like pleased surprise.

"You had your doubts?"

"Even with the sweet deal Aven got us, the mortgage is hefty, and combined with a not-inconsiderable maintenance budget, I had my reservations, yes. But I wouldn't have gone into it if I didn't believe in you." She slid her hand across the desk, and Lila accepted it, her heart warming with Tera's unaccustomed touch. Tera wasn't exactly standoffish, but she wasn't one for sudden gestures of affection.

"I damned sure couldn't have done it without your keen eye and Aven's clever hands."

"You have no idea." Tera's mouth hitched into a smirk, and Lila found herself blushing along with her. "Speaking of which, I gather things are going well with the delivery woman?"

Lila's blush deepened, and she could not hide behind her teacup forever.

"I haven't been this crazy about anyone in a long time."

"Is she staying again tonight?"

Lila nodded, checking the water clock and wondering when Avisse and Theo would arrive. "She's cooking dinner for me."

"And her boy?"

"Theo, yes, he's staying too. He's quite the little scholar."

"Sylvan seems quite taken with him. I gather they're…writing a paper together?" Tera's voice rose in incredulity.

"If you'd met Theo, you'd understand. I swear, he's smarter than me by a long shot. Sounds like a little mini-Sylvan, all into the Endulian stuff. He even bows in greeting." Lila put her hands to her chest and demonstrated. Tera smiled beatifically and repeated the gesture quite naturally.

"I shall have to meet this Theo."

"You'd love him. And Avisse too. They'll be here before too long, I should think." Lila touched her chin, feeling the slightest beginnings of stubble. "Listen, I've got to run and freshen up. Do you mind locking up? And if you're still around, we'll have a drink?"

"Mmm…not tonight. I've got a date with my spouse. I even bought them a little something special." She patted her bag with a mischievous grin that made Lila a trifle jealous. She'd always had a bit of a thing for Aven, and she wondered just what Tera had bought, what she was going to do to them. But thoughts of Avisse swept that from her mind, and panic began to set in. She needed to wash up, shave, and put on her evening gaff if there was going to be any action.

"You two kids have fun." Lila shouldered her bag, winked, and left Tera holding her tea in both hands. She waved to the bath and spa attendants filtering out, then swept out the door, pleased to see the courtyard empty and the door to her carriage house closed. She hurried upstairs and gave herself a quick but thorough wash and dry, adding a drop or two of lavender oil here and there, since Avisse clearly liked it. She shaved, forcing herself not to hurry, since a shaving cut was among the most embarrassing things that could happen to her. She put on her evening gaff, which separated her bits to one side and the other, forming a soft cleft in the middle that made her feel sexier and more like herself. She changed out of her day dress, which was an elegant blue number, into a more casual soft pink and purple floral dress with thin shoulder straps. She was sometimes self-conscious about her wide shoulders, but Avisse's hands seemed to like them, and she'd always thought they were nicely sculpted.

The knock sounded as she was checking her makeup in the mirror. She swished a sip of water and spat it out. Whatever. She looked fine. It was fine. She hurried down the stairs, her heart racing faster with each clack of her heels on the wood.

Avisse was dusty and sun-kissed and smelled like leather and fresh hay. Her hands gripped Lila's waist, pulling herself up for a hard, wet kiss, lingering just a moment before letting herself down gently, her dark eyes sparkling in the evening sun.

"Miss me?"

"An inordinate amount, in fact." Lila looked over Avisse's shoulder at Theo, who watched unabashedly. "Did she pass the test?"

Theo sighed, staring down at his dust-covered shoes.

"She only missed one question, and it was a trick question. I have to give her credit. She's a better listener than she lets on."

"You must be thirsty if you walked all the way from the fourth ring!" She gestured toward the stairs, and Avisse trooped up, her satchel bulging. She brushed against Lila's crotch with her hip as she passed, a sly smirk on her face.

"Let's not forget about the five or so miles we walked the horses," Theo grumbled as he climbed. "Was I allowed to sit and read while Mother walked them? Of course not!" His voice grew fainter as he neared the top of the stairs. Lila shut the door, smiling to herself as she followed them up.

Lila sipped her wine, watching Avisse chop root vegetables, her triceps flexing with each quick movement of the knife. Lila shifted in her seat, fanning herself despite the nice breeze flowing through the open windows. Avisse's strong hand held the ends firmly as her knife flashed with a flurry of precise cuts, slowing as it approached her curled fingers. She'd brought her own knife and sharpener, which was a good thing. Lila's knife was dull, and she'd lost her sharpener in the move and hadn't bothered to replace it, since she didn't cook all that much to begin with.

Avisse scraped the perfectly even cubes into a bowl with the back side of the knife, then set to work on the onions, which she reduced to a neat pile almost before the tears formed in Lila's eyes. When she spread out the thin steak on the cutting board and started pounding it thinner with her fists, Lila's gaff grew uncomfortably tight, and she had to loosen her grip on her wineglass for fear she might break off the stem.

"Theo, how are your studies coming?" Avisse called in between pounding.

"They'd be coming a lot better if you'd stop beating that meat," he called back.

Lila choked on a mouthful of wine, and Avisse half-turned, hands greasy and covered in little bits of meat and onion, and flashed her a wicked grin.

"It's not going to beat itself," she called back, a smile in her voice. "But I'm just about done." She pummeled the steak a few more times, her round ass jiggling with each blow, then poured the diced vegetables on top of it. She rolled it into a neat cylinder in a matter of seconds, tucking the ends with practiced gestures. She pulled a pre-cut length of string from her apron and looped it around and around, cinching it with a few deft twists of her fingers. She tied it off so it looked like something you'd buy at the butcher's shop, ready to put in the oven. As she watched Avisse do the same to the other two roulades, Lila couldn't help imagining Avisse using those same skills to tie her up like a piece of meat. The kitchen grew unbearably warm, though the oven had just been lit.

"Pour me a glass of wine while I get these in the oven and wash up?"

Lila nearly poured the glass to overflowing, as her attention was distracted by Avisse's backside and her shoulders, which moved rhythmically as she scrubbed her hands vigorously in the basin.

"Well, all right!" Avisse said, leaning in to sip the top half-inch of wine, showing a hint of cleavage as she did so. She stood up straight and lifted her glass to clink with Lila, her eyes warm and bright.

"Here's to the most beautiful woman in the seven rings."

Lila blushed furiously as tears threatened to form in the corners of her eyes.

"Hush, you," she said quietly, staring down at her wine, then back up into Avisse's smiling face.

"Make me." Avisse stepped closer, setting down her glass, her lips wet with the wine.

Lila glanced at Theo, who was deep in his studies, half obscured by the door frame. She put down her glass, slipped her hands around Avisse's waist, and pushed her back against the counter so they'd be out of sight. Lila licked her lips, sliding her hands up under Avisse's armpits, and lifted her onto the counter as their lips crushed together. The world disappeared as Avisse wrapped her limbs around Lila, enveloping her, devouring her. Lila's hands roamed, finding all the perfect soft and hard parts of Avisse's body. It was all she could do not to tear her clothes off piece by piece and have her way with her right there on the kitchen counter.

Avisse slowed the kiss after a moment, pressing against Lila's chest and leaning her forehead in to touch hers.

"Gods, the things I want to do to you," Avisse whispered.

"You can do anything you want to me," Lila breathed.

"I know," Avisse said in a low voice. "And I will." Her arms and legs released their grip, and Lila took a half step back, throbbing between her trembling legs at Avisse's tone, the hint of dark menace in her gaze. She leaned on the table for support and took a long drink of her wine for further support.

Avisse slid her fingers around the stem of her wineglass, cupping the bowl in her palm. Gods, why did her every little gesture have to be so arousing? Lila felt her face flush as she watched Avisse's lips meet the glass, the light purple liquid slide through her unpainted lips.

"I'm going to go bother Theo for a bit while they cook." Avisse's eyes asked Lila to join her. Lila's heart melted at the invitation; as much as she liked Theo, the fact that Avisse wanted to share this family moment with her meant a lot. Was it possible they'd only known each other for…how long was it now?

Theo looked up at them suspiciously as they sat, Avisse next to him on the couch and Lila at the desk, the only other place to sit.

"Shouldn't you be cooking dinner or smooching in the kitchen or something?"

Avisse pushed his shoulder gently.

"Dinner's in the oven, and that's not *all* we think about, you know."

"It's nothing to be ashamed of, Mother," he said earnestly, putting a hand on her knee. "And I hope it isn't awkward for you, Lila. Having me around. I know about kissing and adult privacy, and I respect it absolutely." He put a hand over his heart, eyes somber and earnest.

"Nothing to worry about, I'm sure." Lila waved it away, hoping that he wouldn't notice her blush, or if he did, that he would understand. "But tell me what you're reading there."

"It's the Endulian history book Sylvan lent me. Remember, Mother, what we talked about, regarding the continental origins of the Naeili practice?"

Avisse rolled her eyes.

"Yes, the one question I supposedly 'got wrong' in your test, and I filed a formal protest. I'm still waiting for adjudication."

"Well, the jury's still out, I'm afraid, but this book does make a convincing case for a simultaneous development, or possibly an interconnected development of similar systems on the continent and in the Gulf in the pre-Endulian period. According to this author, it is impossible to determine the precise origins of the discipline because no written records exist from that time, and archaeological data is inconclusive." He flipped through the book, brow furrowed, until he found the passage with his index finger, which he then raised in the air as he spoke.

"The epistemological foundations of the continental origin theory are built on data that does not exist and cannot be known. The entire theory is unprovable and therefore invalid except as a tool for furthering systems of colonial oppression on an ideological level."

He snapped the book shut, twisting his mouth as if trying to chew on the words he'd just spoken.

"I'm not sure I quite understand what all that means," Lila admitted.

"It means the Fatlanders are trying to claim everything we invented, as usual."

"It's not saying Endulian practice was a Naeili invention, Mother; it's saying—"

"It's saying the Fatlanders' claim isn't true."

Theo blinked several times, then nodded.

"It's saying that the claims of a continental origin aren't substantiated by the available evidence. But it's also saying there's no conclusive proof of a Naeili origin. We simply don't have the data."

Avisse opened her mouth, then apparently thought better of it and poured lavender wine into it instead.

"You're going to make your mother very proud someday, Theo."

"Are...are you not proud of me now, Mother?" Theo's voice quavered a bit, his big eyes fixing Avisse with a doleful stare. Lila's heart clenched.

Avisse stared back at him for a long moment, then a snort escaped, followed by a cackle. Theo's face broke a moment later, and before long they were leaning against each other, heaving with laughter. Lila found herself laughing with them; though she was still confused as to what had happened, she was glad to be part of their little joke.

Theo told them more than they ever wanted to know about the pre-Endulian period, which wasn't much at all, though as Lila thought about Sylvan's Well of All, she began to pay more attention.

"And their belief in the oneness of time and space, of the individual and the universe, remains at the core of the Endulian movement of today, though it takes different forms." Theo stared up at the ceiling, then turned to his mother. "The roulades smell ready."

7

"Mmm, gods, Avisse, that was divine." Lila ran her finger around the edges of her plate, then licked the juice off her finger, blushing as she noticed Theo and Avisse watching her. "Sorry, I'm used to eating alone. I forgot my manners." She removed her finger and wiped it daintily on her napkin.

"In some cultures, it's considered a compliment to the chef to use your fingers," Theo said reassuringly, then furrowed his brow. "Not in Anari, though, as far as I've read."

Avisse tapped Theo lightly on the back of the head, and he glared at her as if deeply offended. Lila stifled a giggle.

"I'm no expert in Anari culture, but I'm pretty sure it's rude to correct one's host on matters of local etiquette." Avisse smiled, reaching a hand across the table to intertwine it with Lila's. "Especially when they're saying such nice things about your mother's cooking."

Lila squeezed her fingers. "How long did you say you were staying?"

Avisse's face fell for a fraction of a second before her smile widened and her fingers tightened around Lila's.

"The horses should be ready in three or four days." Her middle finger caressed Lila's palm, sending little shivers through her arm straight to her heart. "I hope we won't be overstaying our welcome?"

"Understaying, by far."

"Can I go to the library with Sylvan instead of walking the horses one of those days?" Theo put on his big eyes, which Lila could see now was a trick Avisse was well used to, but she acquiesced with a nod.

"How could I say no to a chance to visit the greatest library on the continent? You'll have to plan out your visit ahead of time to make the most of it."

"Oh, I already have." He scooted his chair back and dashed to the study, returning with a notebook. He flipped to a page filled with neat bullet points from top to bottom. Avisse released Lila's hand to take the notebook, holding it close to the candle to study it.

"What are all these marked 'Cloti 2-12, Cloti 1-17' and so on?"

"The Great Library has prints, under flameglass, of dozens of Cloti's manuscripts from the original cylinder scrolls."

"What in the Thousand Worlds is a cylinder scroll?"

Theo sighed deeply, and Lila and Avisse exchanged confused glances. She knew of Cloti from her Endulian studies; her poems and meditations were said to be the origin of the discipline in the Time Before, but Lila had never heard of a cylinder scroll. Theo opened his mouth to speak when a gentle rap sounded on the door.

"It must be Sylvan." Lila stood and hurried down the stairs.

Sylvan stood in dark gray paint and a trim shirt and pants, unlike the loose robes he usually wore.

"I hope I'm not intruding?"

"Not at all! Theo was just telling us about cylinder scrolls."

"Ooh, yes, the Great Library has the best collection in human lands. I believe Theo wanted to see some of Cloti's in the original Ormaer. I can't imagine he can read it, though apparently, he can read modern Maer, which as I understand it is less different from Ormaer than Southish is from our ancient tongues. It's a field wide open for scholarship, which I'm sure—"

"Which I'm sure you'd have more luck talking about with Theo than with me. I can barely speak Southish." Lila kissed the air around his cheeks, and he followed her up the stairs.

Theo bounced up from his chair, bowing deeply to Sylvan, who repeated his gesture, hands at his chest. Avisse did the same, awkwardly, and Sylvan unshouldered his satchel and unpacked several hefty tomes, which he handed to Theo one at a time.

"I found a few more books I thought might be of interest, which you're welcome to take with you when you travel to Rontaia, provided you promise to return them."

"I solemnly swear." Theo put his hand on his heart, balancing the heavy books on his knees.

"Those could be germane to our paper, as they concern the evolution of languages, which may mirror the passing on of knowledge and traditions. This one focuses on the island languages, and it was written by a Naeili scholar, I'll have you know. The big one is about the continental languages, including Islish, Southish, and a few lesser-known tongues spoken in the East. And the third one, the one bound in real hide and printed on fiber paper, is quite special. It's a history of the Maer language, written by a Maer scholar of some repute named Dunil. Sadly, I haven't read it, as it's written in Maer, and he refuses to give translation rights. Which I respect in a way, though it's a shame that such knowledge cannot be shared by those who don't have the privilege of knowing such an obscure tongue. Though I suppose they don't see it that way, which is the whole point, isn't it? Anyway, I thought you might have a crack at it, see if your Maer is up to snuff."

"I've never read anything of this complexity, but I'm eager to give it a try." Theo set the other two books to the side and opened it reverently, running his fingers over the words, his lips moving slowly. "A history of the language...no, languages of the Maer from the...Before Time? Time Before. From the Time Before to the present day." He looked up at Sylvan for approval, his smile widening at Sylvan's enthusiastic head bobbing.

"Yes, it sounds fascinating, doesn't it? I bought it from an exclusive bookseller sight unseen, not realizing it was in Maer."

"I hope you won't let this get in the way of your regular studies, Theo," Avisse said with a warning tone.

"My regular studies take up no more than half of my time, Mother. I'm desperate for real research like this. It's a long trip from Anari to Rontaia and back."

Lila's heart fluttered at the words. *And back.* They were coming back, weren't they? Three or four days wasn't long enough to spend with this woman she suddenly needed more than the breath in her lungs, or with this child who'd wormed his way into her heart as well.

"Speaking of ancient languages and cultures, if I may, I'd like to show you something that might give you food for thought on your journey. With your mother's and Lila's permission, of course."

Avisse's eyes sharpened as she fixed them on Sylvan. "Is this about what's behind that big bronze door in the baths?"

"Lila told me you were clever. You're welcome to join, of course."

"I think I will," she said, caution in her voice.

"Why don't we all go down together, and you can show us your big secret," Lila said.

Sylvan smiled, then his gray-painted face went serious as stone.

"It is, you know." He eyed each of them in turn, his expression never cracking. "A secret. I trust you as a scholar," he said with a nod to Theo, "and you as my friend," he added, gesturing to Lila. He turned back to Avisse, his face softening to a half-smile. "And you I trust because you make Lila happy."

Avisse's eyes glowed at Lila, who did not look away, even though her cheeks and neck were surely flushed, and a lot farther down as well.

Theo stood, rescuing them all from the awkward moment.

"I will take your secret to the grave," he said earnestly.

"Let's hope it doesn't come to that," Sylvan replied with a wink.

Lila drew in a sharp breath when she saw the gleaming bronze arch rising over the well, which had been rimmed with bronze as well. The water was clean and clear, shimmering golden with the reflection of the arch. A wooden pedestal stood next to the arch, with an elaborate set of tubes and wires in disarray atop it, with more laid out on the floor all around. Scrolls, books, and blueprints littered a desk that had been added to the cramped space. The walls had been further patched, and the room was lit with even more brightstone than before, now affixed in neat discs at regular intervals all around the sphere.

"My gods," Avisse breathed.

Theo descended the stairs one careful step at a time, examining the well, the arch, and the pedestal. He knelt to study a large blueprint laid out next to the pedestal. Sylvan followed, gesturing for Lila and Avisse to join them.

"Is this like an Endulian cradle?" Theo asked, glancing up briefly from the blueprint.

Sylvan nodded, turning to beam at Avisse.

"The direct predecessor, I believe, though the design may be a thousand or more years older."

"Are those even real?" Avisse asked, incredulous, glancing at Lila, who shrugged. She'd used the Inkwell, so she knew the technology to communicate across distance was real, but there were so many rumors about the cradles. Most people didn't actually believe you could sit in a chair, put on a magic circlet, and visit other worlds.

"Very much so," Sylvan said brightly. "I've seen one in use, at Endulai. I don't have the training for it myself, not yet, but this..." He stepped forward, gesturing toward the arch and the well. "This channels the earth's energy in a much more efficient way, so it requires less training, in theory anyway. If these blueprints are accurate—and I have every reason to believe that they are, given their source—almost anyone could use the well, assuming they know how to operate it. Which is no easy task, I should add, and requires a great deal of highly specialized and very expensive equipment, even by my standards."

"You would use it to access the Thousand Worlds?" Theo asked, his voice soft and earnest.

"That's a way of putting it, yes. Once this device is complete, assuming it works, which it should, you can visit, though not interact with, any time, any place, throughout history. Even…other worlds, other realities, versions of this one…" His voice trailed off as his eyes grew distant. He turned to them, hands clutched together at his waist. "Any knowledge you might seek, be it ancient history or something buried deep in your own past, or even hypotheticals or alternate scenarios, can be discovered through the Well of All."

"Wouldn't that take the fun out of scholarship?" Avisse stared at the scrolls and books laid out on the floor.

Sylvan shook his head vigorously. "Scholarship is the study of truth based on the available evidence. This would just open up the field of evidence available to scholars. And it's not like there would be Wells of All on every street corner. There are only a handful of places where the earth's energy is suited to the endeavor. It's why the temple was built on this site, above the Well."

"Won't that create problems of inequality of access?" Theo asked.

"Not if I don't get the damned thing finished." Sylvan sighed, gesturing toward the mess of wires and tubes on the platform. "The cradle for the crystal ball needs to be perfectly channeled or none of this will matter. And that is what I'm working on right now. It's not my strongest suit, I'm afraid."

"I don't know if I'll be much help," Theo admitted, staring at the complex diagrams. "I'm really only good with words."

"Ah, but you'll be so much help because your fingers are smaller and nimbler than mine." Sylvan held up his gloved hands, which were neither particularly thick nor thin. "And four hands are better than two."

"Can I stay and help?" Theo turned toward Avisse, his eyes widening, and she let out a single cackle.

"No need for the big eyes. You can stay. I'll come and get you in a little while."

"No need to hurry. I'm not tired in the slightest." Theo stood, his eyes already fixed on the wires and tubes.

"And you," Avisse said, pointing to Sylvan. "Will not let Theo touch anything dangerous."

"I would sooner cut off my own leg than let any harm befall your son."

"If it does, I'll cut it off for you."

8

Lila felt Avisse's eyes on her as she walked up the stairs. When they got to the top, Avisse roughly gripped her ass, pushing her against the doorframe, hot lips sucking on Lila's shoulder, which was sure to bruise if she kept it up. Lila closed her eyes as Avisse's hands shifted, sliding up to grip her hips as she pressed in from behind. Lila's mind and body were on fire with need as Avisse ground against her, kissing and licking her way up Lila's neck. Avisse pressed into her once more, then released, spinning her around, staring her up and down with a predatory gleam in her eye.

"You said I could do anything I want to you." She closed the negligible distance between them, breathing into Lila's neck, the soft tips of her breasts just touching Lila's chest "But I'd never do anything you didn't want." Her lips found Lila's neck, kissing softly, leaving wet spots as she moved up toward her lips. Her hands settled gently on Lila's hips, holding her with restrained strength.

Lila's body thrummed, but she held still, letting Avisse's touch and her own building desire send shivers through every nerve. Avisse leaned in as she tiptoed up to capture Lila's lips, fingers tightening around her waist like she wanted to pick her up and throw her down and do unspeakable things to her. Lila's lips opened, her tongue drawing Avisse in, hoping to show her how badly she wanted her to do those things.

Avisse slowed the kiss after a moment, sliding her hands up to rest on Lila's chest, then pulled back, their lips sticking together as they separated.

"Tell me what you want me to do to you." Avisse's eyes were dark and deep, her voice still thick with the kiss.

Lila's heart leapt with panic even as she swelled against her gaff. This was exactly what was supposed to happen, exactly what she wanted. Why was she still so scared?

She took a deep breath in through her nose and let it out, then slowly lifted her dress to reveal her lavender silk gaff, which covered her from mid-thigh to her waist. She'd designed it herself since most of the tucking gaffs were uncomfortable and got in the way during intimate moments. Sometimes she liked to be completely naked with people, but other times she liked the feel of the silk securing her, the way her cock fit snugly against her thigh, how it formed a soft cleft between her legs that felt good when rubbed just right. She'd had a dozen made in a variety of colors, but she'd picked lavender for Avisse. And, she supposed, for herself.

Avisse took a step back, her eyes wide with wonder.

"It's beautiful," she whispered, staring between Lila's legs, then back up at her face, which must have been deep scarlet by now.

"I want you to touch me here," Lila managed, almost short of breath. She held up her dress with one hand and moved her other hand to the cleft between her legs, rubbing a little, feeling the swell and the tingle through the silk even from this little bit of contact. "As you would any woman. I want you to finger me and make me come."

Lila's heartbeat echoed in her chest like a great drum as Avisse's eyes softened, still fixed on Lila's center. She stepped closer, her fingers trailing up Lila's thighs, eyes running hungrily up her body, which tingled in response. Lila whimpered as Avisse's fingertips glided up her length, feathering across her cleft, then down the other side, fondling her balls with the gentlest touch that stirred an ache deep within.

"Higher," Lila breathed.

Avisse stared into her eyes with a desire so raw and frank it made Lila's stomach drop. Lila sank against the doorframe as Avisse's fingers crept up, tightening in the soft flesh of Lila's cleft, the silk blunting the calluses on her fingers but not erasing them. Avisse massaged her with slow, deliberate strokes as her other hand made quick work of Lila's dress and tossed it aside. Her lips and tongue wandered over Lila's neck and chest, never lingering long enough on her sensitive nipples to push her over the edge. Her fingers continued their insidious game, homing in on her weak spots and dancing all around them, keeping her in a constant state of near explosion, a dull ache that kept building without limit. A numbness crept through her limbs, a tingling in her chest and head, and something stronger, more primal, coiling deep within.

"Please," she whined deep in her throat. "Avisse, please."

Lila gasped as Avisse gripped her cleft tight and plastered her mouth to Lila's left nipple, the more sensitive one, and sucked so hard it almost hurt. Avisse pumped and flicked with her tongue as her fingers gripped Lila tighter and tighter, bracing her thigh against her hand and pounding Lila against the doorframe over and over. Lila clutched her tight shoulders, moaning like a moonstruck wolf as she spilled a river through her gaff, down her leg, and onto the floor.

Avisse stopped pounding and stayed pressed against her, grip loosening, mouth releasing, covering Lila's chest with little wet kisses leading up her neck to her mouth. Lila put a hand on her cheek and kept her in the kiss, taking time to breathe together, to be together in a way she too seldom was with anyone.

Leaning against the doorframe with Avisse in a soiled gaff with her pleasure puddled on the floor beneath her felt more romantic than anything she'd experienced in a long time. The warmth of Avisse's hands on her chest, the softness of her lips, the thick line of muscle on the back of her neck—Lila kissed back harder now, suddenly hungry for more, hungry for everything, all of it, right now.

"Babe," Avisse said in between kisses, a smirk in her voice.

"I want to taste you." Lila's hands slid down Avisse's tight hips, her fingers creeping between her legs. "I want to make love to you with my mouth."

"Babe!"

Lila shut her mouth with another kiss, levering against the doorframe to stand up straight, one hand sliding back to grip Avisse's round ass while the other traced a gentle line up and down the seam of her crotch, fingernails stuttering over the fabric. Avisse's mouth opened to her, hungry lips and tongue pulling her in. Lila took full advantage, plundering her mouth as her fingers continued their delicate work.

Avisse furiously unbuckled and pulled her pants halfway down, and Lila's fingers found her wet and ready, a garden of pleasure waiting to be harvested. She removed her fingers and pulled back from the kiss, staring into Avisse's hot, dark eyes as she slipped her fingers into her mouth one by one. She closed her eyes as the taste ran through her like sweet, musky wine, filling her with an elation stronger than any drug.

When she opened them again, the raw want in Avisse's eyes tugged something deep in her gut. She crouched, wrapped her arms around Avisse's thighs, and lifted, shifting her body so Avisse's torso flopped over her left shoulder with surprising ease. Avisse let out a squeal of surprise, which turned into a yelp of delight as Lila trundled through the bedroom doorway, Avisse clinging to her back.

Lila stopped at the edge of the bed and half-flung Avisse onto it, cushioning her landing a little with an arm behind her head. She crouched over Avisse on all fours, gazing down into those brown eyes, now sparkling with desire. Lila pulled Avisse's shirt up with one hand, revealing two perfect little mounds tipped with stiff brown nubs hungry for Lila's mouth.

She wasted no time, worshiping Avisse's breasts with her lips and tongue as she yanked her pants the rest of the way down. Avisse let out a series of muted whines, pulling her shirt over her head and arching into Lila's touch, hands curling in her hair, legs wrapping around her waist. Lila was drawn inexorably down the soft curve of her stomach, along the trail of fine hairs leading from her navel to the perfumed thicket between her legs. Avisse spread her legs wider than Lila would have thought possible, revealing her perfect pink flower nestled amid the soft hair.

Lila made love to her as if in a dream, peeling her petals back one by one, lavishing each part of her with every caress her heart and tongue could devise. Avisse guided her with gentle hands in her hair and subtle variations in her breathy song. Her body pulsed and squirmed, legs clamping tight around Lila's neck, heels digging into her shoulder blades as her hips raised up off the bed.

Lila pushed deeper, lost in the flood of Avisse's pleasure, her stuttering cries, her fingernails digging into Lila's scalp. Lila's tongue ran wild, pushing past fatigue and need for breath, her hands gripping the taut lines of Avisse's shaking hips as her own pleasure surged, coiling in her gut and sparking through her loins. Avisse let out a hoarse cry, shaking and flooding Lila's face and the bed beneath.

Lila froze against her, spilling once more, a jagged, spine-deep bolt of ecstasy, and collapsed with Avisse onto the soaked sheets. Lila stayed pressed tight as Avisse's body pulsed again and again, more slowly each time, until her fingers released their grip on Lila's hair and her legs unwrapped themselves and flopped awkwardly to the sides.

"Giiiiiirl," Avisse moaned. Lila grinned from between her legs, still giddy with pleasure. She kissed Avisse's thigh up to the point of her hip and laid her head on Avisse's belly, soft with a hard layer of muscle beneath. Avisse's fingers ran gently through her hair, her calluses tickling behind Lila's ears, sending little shivers down her back, but she remained where she was.

"I feel like I've known you forever," Lila said, hearing her voice vibrating through Avisse's body.

"I want to know you forever." Avisse's words filled her heart with a sloshy wet feeling, and Lila wrapped her arms tight around her. "Gods, I sound like such a sap."

"You don't," Lila said softly, pushing up onto her elbows. "I think we meant the same thing."

"Kiss me."

Lila crawled to her side, careful to keep her sticky, soaked gaff away from Avisse's body, and Avisse rolled over toward her. Their lips met in a moment of softness prolonged by fatigue. When they separated, they lay breathing together, side by side, for a while until Avisse's eyes closed and her breathing steadied.

Lila crept off the bed, stripping off her wet gaff and tossing it into the corner, where it landed with a sickly splat. She quickly toweled off and pulled on a dry pair of the loose bloomers she wore for sleeping, then slid back onto the bed. Avisse stirred, her arm sliding over Lila's hip, and Lila pulled her close, away from the wet spot, clutching her to her chest. Avisse snuggled in, a ball of warm skin and firm curves, interlocking with Lila's, a perfect fit.

Lila did not sleep, too distracted by the heat of Avisse's body and the memories of the things they'd done, which had her stiff and straining once again. She breathed through it, holding her partner tight, savoring the smooth expanse of her back, the downy soft hair on her nape, the heat of her breath on Lila's chest.

They would need to go retrieve Theo soon, though she was sure the boy would be happy to stay up all night working on Sylvan's fantastical project. She wondered if it would really work, if Sylvan really believed it, or if it was just another one of his fancies.

It must be nice to have that kind of money; he'd spent thousands of poul, tens of thousands, at least, on the project, enough to feed Anari's poor for a month or more. And for what? For a chance to visit the past, or some other world, if such a place really existed, to gain knowledge to write down in some book or debate with other scholars while real people were struggling to earn enough to feed their families.

Not that Lila was entirely blameless. Her shop catered to the painted faces, and while not all of her clientele were rich, they were all comfortable. She was in the second ring. No one bought luxury sex toys or pleasure creams or got spa treatments or spent hours in a mineral bath, then went home to a squalid apartment they shared with two other people working three jobs to make ends meet. Here she was, in her spacious apartment in her very own building in her private courtyard cuddled up next to the strongest, most beautiful, most independent woman she'd ever met.

Lila chided herself for feeling guilty. She deserved happiness. Everyone did. Her hand slid down to cup Avisse's behind, stirring her desire further. Avisse snuggled in closer, humming into Lila's collarbone, vibrating her entire chest.

"You're insatiable," Avisse murmured, kissing Lila's collarbone and sucking on it a little as she pressed into Lila's stiffness with her stomach.

"I can never get enough of you." Lila hiked Avisse's thigh up, letting her fingers slip between her legs, finding her wet again, though her fingertips could barely reach because of the angle. Avisse moaned as she sucked on Lila's collarbone, then flung her leg over Lila, toppling her onto her back and landing astride her, pinning her biceps above her head.

"I have to get my kid, but I'm in town for two more nights." Her body settled atop Lila, grinding slowly back and forth. "And there are quite a few things I'd like to do to you in that time to give you something to remember me by while you wait for my return."

"Promise?"

"On both counts."

Avisse squeezed her biceps hard, still grinding against Lila as she lowered down for a kiss that was so slow and soft it almost made Lila spill again.

9

Lila's time with Avisse caught up with her hard the next day. After a leisurely breakfast and a far-too-brief goodbye kiss, she pushed open the already-unlocked doors and walked into the maelstrom of unfinished business that had piled up since she'd spent two days working only *most* of her waking hours instead of all of them. Tera followed her around with a stack of papers to sign as she dealt with a problem with the bath pump that needed to be fixed right away and contractors who had to be paid up front. She was almost late for her consulting client, a delightful older woman who was marrying another woman for love after her arranged-marriage husband finally passed and wanted to spice up her sex life with her new wife.

She drifted into the shop afterward and was immediately drawn into a conversation about binders with the mother of a transcendent youth who couldn't come in himself. Lila sent her away with several to try and offered a free morning consultation the next day, which the mother gladly accepted. Lila wondered how many of the undergarments the shop sold had been purchased for youths who couldn't come in themselves. She was more than happy to consult, but she'd need to let people know such a service was available when the shop was not open, since minors weren't allowed in during business hours. She could start by having Tera make a sign. She had the most beautiful handwriting, and she'd be doing the booking in any case.

Lila cast a longing glance at the spa door as she returned to the office to meet with a representative for High Waist, one of her more popular lingerie suppliers. She badly needed a massage in the lavender-scented quiet of the spa, but with sales of the glassware tapering off, she needed to make a splash some other way. The new lingerie line was almost as hot as the model who accompanied the representative, a muscled, androgynous person with close-cropped hair and a face painted in swirls of blue and gold. They weren't a painted face, she didn't think—some non-painted performers wore paint in the course of their trade—but their makeup was as exquisite as their physique, and they moved with a calm grace that showed the pieces to excellent effect.

"Would you consider joining us for a demo day?" she asked the model, who quirked a smile as they glanced at the representative, a squat woman in her forties with high, painted-on eyebrows.

"If you put in an order of a thousand poul or more, we'll do a demo day. Fifteen hundred and we'll do two." She punctuated the last remark by jabbing two fingers in the air as if she were poking Lila's eyes out.

Lila pursed her lips. A thousand poul was a big commitment, but with this model, she could probably move the stuff.

"I think we can make this work. Let's dig into your catalog and get down to specifics."

An hour later, Lila had signed an order for fifteen hundred sixty poul and gotten three demo days out of the deal. Both she and the representative were mopping their brows in the warm air; the model sat reading in a chair by this point, a heartstory if the picture on the cover was any indication, balancing the book on one toned thigh crossed over the other.

"I've got to say, I am impressed," the rep said, standing and shaking Lila's hand. "To go from your little shop in the fourth, which was nice, don't get me wrong—" She blinked apologetically. "Not everyone was sure you were going to make this work. But you've made a believer out of me. I've never seen anything like this, not even in Rontaia."

Lila's weary heart warmed with the compliment.

"Thank you. I look forward to surprising people for a long time to come."

Lila collapsed in her chair when the rep had left, tilting the almost-empty water pitcher into her glass and draining it in one gulp. Gods, she wished she had a glass of hotstone, but the day wasn't over yet. Or was it? She glanced at the water clock, which shocked her by telling her it was half dusk. The metallic clank of the main door locking echoed in, and a tap sounded on her office door.

"Come in!"

Aven peered through the door, then entered quietly, as if afraid they were disturbing her.

"Everything all right?" she asked.

"Fine. Fine!" They sat on the chair opposite her, crossing their legs, then uncrossing them and crossing them in the opposite direction. "How are you?"

"I'm exhausted, honestly. But I just signed a deal with High Waist for fifteen hundred poul that got us three demo days with that stunning model—gods, did you see them?"

Aven bit their lip, nodding and raising their eyebrows.

"You know I only have eyes for Tera, of course, but I can appreciate a talented model."

Lila smirked.

"You have eyes for everyone who breathes, Aven."

Aven let out a nervous laugh that turned into a real one.

"Be that as it may, I actually did come here for a specific purpose." They re-crossed their legs, fingers clutching together. Lila blinked them on. "What I'm here to say is, what Tera and I are saying is—"

"Wait, are you here on behalf of both of you?"

"Well, we thought it would be awkward if we were both here. We didn't want it to feel like an ambush—"

"Mission definitely not accomplished." Lila crossed her arms over her chest, unsure how to take Aven's words and their tone, which didn't have the admonishing edge she'd expect if they were telling her something bad.

"It's nothing like that, it's just…"

"Spit it out."

"We think you should take tomorrow off and just…enjoy your time with her. Let us take care of the place. We can handle anything that comes up."

Lila's mouth hung open, words refusing to form. Taking a day off wasn't something that had ever occurred to her as a possibility, except for holidays. She'd sent Tera and Aven home early a couple of times when there wasn't much to do and she had plenty of help in the shop, but could the place really run without *her*? And what would she do, go walk the horses with Avisse in the summery heat that was taking its sweet time to dissipate?

"I'll take your silence as a yes." Aven stood, moving closer and taking her gently by the elbow. "Tera says I am to escort you out of the office under strict orders to leave any unfinished paperwork for her to deal with in the morning."

"Strict orders from Tera, huh?" Lila smirked, letting Aven lead her away from the desk.

"She's a very gentle person, but you don't want to get on her bad side, I can assure you."

"Don't threaten me with a good time."

Aven released her elbow to hold open the door for her. She breathed in deeply as she entered the lobby, which was peaceful, quiet except for the tinkling of the fountain echoing in subtle harmonics off the domed ceiling. The light streaming in through the round windows was that of sunset, casting orange, pink, and purple shadows across the cracked stone. Avisse would be back soon, and Lila hadn't washed up or changed, but she drifted toward the fountain, staring up at the dome, letting the scents of jasmine and lavender wash away the day's troubles. The door creaked open and clicked shut; Aven had left, and she was alone in this space for the first time in as long as she could remember.

Avisse made dinner again, raw fish marinated in greenorange juice, vinegar, and chilis, served with garlic noodles and a crunchy salad made of goldeneye roots and roasted pumpkin seeds with a creamy dressing.

"Gods, Avisse," Lila said as the spicy-sour aftertaste of the fish lingered in her mouth. "This is phenomenal!"

"Full credit to the fishmonger in the Cypress Market, who had fresh speckles on ice."

"You went all the way out to the Cypress Market?" It was in the fourth ring, and pretty far out at that.

"It's not that far from the stable, and Theo needed the extra exercise if he's going to spend all day in the Great Library tomorrow."

"Sylvan won't forget, will he?" Theo sounded hopeful, but his eyebrows furrowed with concern.

"If he made you a promise, he'll keep it," Lila reassured him. "And as it happens, I'm free tomorrow. I might join you walking the horses if you don't mind the company."

Avisse's head swiveled toward Lila's, her face lighting up with an infectious smile.

"How do you mean, free?"

"Tera and Aven said they'd look after the shop so I could take the day off and spend it…" Lila let her hand creep over Avisse's. "If you're not too busy, of course."

Avisse clutched her fingers, using them as leverage to climb halfway onto the table and kiss her full on the lips, the spicy, garlicky tang of the food mixing with the wine to make a heady bouquet.

"We can take a carriage if it's too sunny," Avisse said, stuffing a forkful of noodles into her mouth. "We don't want you getting too worn out by the day's endeavors."

"And you'll pick me up in the carriage to bring me back here?" Theo asked excitedly. If he caught the subtext of Avisse's words, he hid it well.

"I don't see why not. You walked almost double today."

Theo smiled into his noodles, which were the only thing he seemed to be eating much of, though Lila noted that he did take at least three bites of the fish and the salad, as if it was a family rule. Her heart warmed, in a twisting, aching sort of way. He was such a good kid; she wondered about his other mother, how often he thought of her. How often Avisse did. What it must have been like. How he must see Lila, dating his mother.

What it would be like if she and Avisse became more serious, if she became part of this family somehow. But surely she was getting ahead of herself; this was a long weekend fling, and while it felt like so much more, there was no sense fantasizing about—

"He *said* I could help out again tonight, Mother!"

Lila shook her head as the conversation jarred her back into the moment.

"*If* he comes by and *if* he *specifically* invites you. Otherwise, you stay in and study."

Theo dropped his fork on his plate, making a loud clattering noise. Avisse tensed, and Lila with her.

"Sorry, Mother. And Lila. That was rude." He picked up the fork, carefully speared a piece of fish, and slid it into his mouth, then set the fork down gently. "I really think I was helping him. He gets all wrapped up in his own thoughts sometimes and he needs someone else to help him untangle them."

"Sounds like someone I know," Avisse said, warmth creeping back into her voice. "Now, how do you like the fish? Really."

"I like it better than saltwater fish, to be honest, but it's still fish." He scooped up a bit of the goldeneye salad and crunched it thoughtfully. "This stuff's not bad though, for vegetables. A little starchy, but still." He glanced up at Lila, then took another bite.

"Well, I think you're lucky to have a mother who's such a fantastic cook."

"It does get a little old eating road food for weeks at a time," Theo admitted.

"There are limits to what you can do while traveling across country, but I happen to pack an excellent picnic lunch," Avisse said proudly.

"Maybe tomorrow you can show off that prowess. There's a nice little market just a few streets down, a bit on the expensive side, but they have the best cheese stall in the city."

A tap sounded at the door. Theo pushed back his chair and went running down the stairs, heedless of his mother's exasperated huff.

"Sylvan!" Theo's delighted voice rang out, and the brief conversation that filtered up the stairs left no doubt as to Theo's success worming his way into Sylvan's plans.

"How about we go say hi to Sylvan and take a little stroll? There's a lovely sculpture garden just down the block that's lit up with brightstone at night, unless you're—"

"Sounds perfect." Avisse stood, kissing Lila briefly, then hollered down the stairs. "We'll be right down!"

Avisse's skin glowed golden red in the light from the brightstone lamps, which were artfully hidden amid succulents and lava rocks between the sculptures. Most of the pieces were ancient, busts or statues from the Time Before missing arms or the tops of their heads. Some were in excellent shape, considering their age, with only a little pocking of the surface—and brass plaques on the ground—revealing how old they really were.

They stopped in front of a sculpture of two female figures intertwined in an embrace such that it was impossible to tell where one body ended and the other began.

"Goals," Avisse murmured, slipping her arm around Lila's waist and pulling her tight.

"Princess lovers," Lila read on the plaque. "It's over two thousand years old."

"I bet their families were pissed."

"I don't know. Maybe they were more enlightened back then. Sylvan says civilization re-forms itself over and over but becomes more primitive each time, while thinking itself more advanced."

Avisse let out a chuckle. "That sounds like the sort of thing Theo would say."

"They've probably read some of the same books."

"I guess. I try to keep up when I can, but I was never much of a reader. And with my job, it's hard."

"Ugh, I haven't even finished a single heartstory since I opened the new place. I used to read several a week."

"I should have known." Avisse turned Lila by the hips, so they were facing each other. "You're such a romantic." Her eyes shone in the dim light of the garden, where they were nearly alone, save a few other couples drifting by, doing much the same thing.

"Only with you," Lila murmured, putting a hand on the small of Avisse's back and pulling her close as their lips met. Avisse hummed into the kiss, hands kneading Lila's hips, tongue caressing her, melting her resolve, not that Lila had any when it came to Avisse. Soon they were making out like teenagers, groping each other to within an inch of their lives, until the crunch of feet on gravel signaled the approach of other visitors. They pulled apart with a giggle, turning away from the smiling elderly couple, who gave them a patronizing wave as they wandered past.

"I think I've seen about enough statues," Avisse said, sliding a hand down to cup Lila's ass. "This garden is lovely, but everything is a bit too…neat. Let's get back to your apartment and make a mess of each other."

Back in the carriage house, Avisse stripped Lila with her eyes, then her hands, then her mouth, tearing away layer after layer of inhibitions and insecurities, replacing them with blissful affirmations. Lila lay spread on the bed with Avisse writhing over her, seemingly everywhere at once, fingers and lips streaking pleasure across her body like shooting stars. She had not the strength to wrap her limbs around this velvety strong beast ravishing her; she lay captive, her back arched toward Avisse's caresses, fingers and toes stretched to their utmost as she struggled to draw breath. She gasped as Avisse's weight lifted, her body sinking at the sudden loss of touch. Her vision went dark, and warmth cradled her face as Avisse's strong thighs framed her, breasts draped and flattening against her stomach, hot breath flowing across her throbbing length, fingers kneading Lila's thighs.

Avisse sank down onto her ready mouth, and Lila devoured her with lips and tongue, gripping her tight hips, which began moving with slow, powerful strokes. Lila quickly found a rhythm with her, lavishing attention on every part within reach, gripping Avisse tighter to get closer. *She had to get closer.*

The touch of Avisse's fingers froze Lila's mouth for a moment as she let out a high-pitched gasp. Avisse fondled and cradled her like she was a crepe-paper doll, soft fingers running delicate lines through her folds and along her length. Lila redoubled her efforts, even as Avisse spread her folds and began massaging them, wet fingers probing every crevice, bringing each hidden nerve to the surface. Lila gasped as Avisse's fat tongue licked a long, slow stripe down her length, fingers stretching her foreskin up to pin her cock to her belly. Avisse hunched her back as she kissed and licked her way back up, swirling around Lila's tip, tongue lapping her belly and only occasionally brushing against her sensitive head, then licked her way back down.

Lila gripped Avisse's hips and poured her heart out through her tongue as Avisse lapped her up and down, giving a little more play to her head on each pass, bringing her closer and closer to the precipice. After a glorious eternity, Avisse homed in, first with a set of fluttering flicks that had Lila mewling like a kitten, then a thorough battering with her tongue that sent stars shooting through her vision and her back arching off the bed. Avisse pressed onto Lila's face and rode her harder, lips locked in tight, bathing her in a whirlpool of ecstasy. Lila's unearthly moans were muffled by Avisse's last quivering clench around her face as Lila came, a seemingly endless river of bliss prolonged by Avisse's heroic mouth.

A dull ache spread through her lower back, and she sank down onto the bed, hands still gripping Avisse, tongue still lapping slowly as the twitching subsided. Bathed in Avisse's taste, cradled in the comfort of her thighs, she could think of nothing else in the world she wanted. Through Avisse's touch, she had forgotten, for a moment, what parts she had. She was simply a woman being made love to by another woman.

They cuddled for a while afterward, not speaking, kissing each other's wrists and jawlines and collarbones until they had to make love again. The cycle continued until they were spent, boneless and sweaty, arms flopped over each other, two fallen soldiers half-dead on the field of battle.

Sylvan's knock woke them, and Avisse threw on Lila's robe, which was much too long and dragged on the floor a bit behind her. She hurried down to meet her son while Lila lay in the heady perfume of their lovemaking. She smiled at Theo's excited babbling and Avisse's good-humored responses, which kept up for quite some time. She briefly awoke as Avisse snuggled in beside her, scooching away from the wet spots and grappling her tightly back to sleep.

10

Morning came like a dream, tea and pastries and smiles all around. Theo scribbled away, making notes for his big library adventure, referencing this book and that from the increasingly large pile Sylvan had loaned him. Lila gazed out the window at the heavy doors and sun-gilded dome of The World Within. For today, she would spend her time in the world without.

Sylvan's knock came right at ten, as he'd said. His face showed surprisingly little sign of fatigue, though it might have been the bright yellow paint he wore, an old trick Lila remembered all too well from her time as a painted face.

"Who's ready for some good old-fashioned scholarship?" he asked after a hurried exchange of bows with Theo.

Theo stood up straight, looking several inches taller than usual, satchel over his shoulder and notebook under his arm.

"Lila says it's a two-mile walk, but I'm used to that. I walk at least six miles a day."

"I guess I'll just send the carriage away, then?" Sylvan cocked his head toward the window, where a luxurious covered darkwood carriage with matching dark brown horses stood waiting.

Avisse glanced out the window, then took a step closer, nearly pressing her nose against the glass.

"That's a Seliver," she said in an impressed tone. "Not the fastest, but you could eat soup while riding in one of those."

"We get to ride in a Seliver?" Theo pressed both hands against the window.

"It's the only carriage my father had free. Come on! Those cylinder scrolls aren't getting any less ancient!"

They clambered into the velvety confines of the cabin, which felt more like a parlor than a carriage. While Lila wasn't sure she would have eaten soup in there, the ride was smooth enough that she was able to apply a fresh coat of lipstick. Theo gripped his mother's hand tightly, grinning like a fool. Sylvan didn't seem inclined to prattle on as he usually did, and they rode in quiet comfort, each of them no doubt absorbed in their own little world.

Lila watched Avisse taking stock of the carriage, testing its materials with her fingers, studying its appointments. She surely thought it frivolous, but she was a woman who appreciated quality, and Lila had never seen anything like it. She'd never seen anything like Avisse, either; the way her eyes flashed from hard to soft in an instant, how she held herself, upright but at ease, the forked veins running up each of her forearms. Lila tugged at her collar. All this velvet in the carriage did have the disadvantage of making it warmer than it needed to be, especially with the continued autumn heat.

They stepped out of the carriage at the valet circle in front of the library's great bronze doors, which would open with the pull of a single finger on the handle. Lila hadn't been inside the Great Library in more than a decade, and part of her longed to join them, to wander its arched galleries and spiral staircases to balconies lined with more books than the imagination could conceive. Avisse's hand on her hip dissipated these images like mist before sun. Lila turned, adjusting her hat against the bright sky, and slipped a hand around Avisse's waist.

"Would it be too forward of me to insist on lending you my carriage for the day?" Sylvan asked. "It's awfully hot, and I know you'll be doing plenty of walking with the horses. The least I can do is get you there and back without you melting into a puddle."

Lila glanced down at Avisse for approval; she didn't want to seem weak, but she knew her limits. In this heat, it was going to be a struggle to walk all the way to the fourth ring and then walk further from there.

"We accept, with great thanks." Avisse bowed to Sylvan in the Endulian way, and he bowed back, a sly smile on his face.

"The library closes at quarter dusk, and I expect we'll want to stay until the very end, so why don't you plan on meeting us here then?"

Avisse slid into the carriage next to Lila, interlocking fingers, eyes gazing out the windows. Lila took off her hat and ran a hand through her hair. Avisse giggled, turning sideways and plunging her fingers into Lila's hair, no doubt making a mess of it, but it felt nice to be cared for like this. Avisse clambered onto her lap, strong fingers running across her scalp, massaging the back of her neck. The gentle sway of the carriage pressed Avisse against Lila, stirring her desire. Soon Avisse's hot lips were on hers, kissing her slowly as her fingers worked their way around to fondle her ears. It was positively stifling in the carriage; Lila wished she had worn a lighter dress, or none at all, wished she could tear Avisse's shirt off and lick and suck her, wished her fingers could find their way through the stiff fabric of her pants to her perfectly luscious core, wished Avisse could ride her fingers, grinding against the knuckle of her thumb, panting into her mouth, sweat dripping onto her forehead—

A double tap sounded on the roof of the carriage. They had arrived. Avisse's lips unstuck themselves from Lila's, her face flushed and limned with sweat. Lila glanced at the carriage's convenient mirror, then quickly pulled out her handkerchief to mop her face and touch up her lipstick, leaving a cherry red smear that would never wash out.

"It seems we leave a mess wherever we go." Avisse smirked, climbing off Lila's lap, running a hand between Lila's legs and lingering for a moment. "Come on. Let's go get some fresh air and take my girls for a walk."

The air outside was a little fresher than that in the cabin. A faint breeze redolent with hay and manure tamped the late morning's heat down a bit, but the sun was at full strength, almost summery in its intensity. Lila followed Avisse into the busy stable complex, where scores of riders, drivers, overseers, and stablehands bustled about with horses of every size and color. Lila's family had a carriage and two horses, and she'd never thought much about them other than as a way to get from place to place, but the size and strength of the animals was intoxicating. Avisse walked differently here, with a confidence and ease in her stride that made her, impossibly, even more alluring.

"Let's go see my girls," Avisse said, her step quickening as she entered the shade of a huge stable. Lila followed, dodging piles of horse manure and the stablehands scurrying around after them with shovels and buckets. She'd worn her most comfortable boots that still looked good with a dress, but she rather hoped not to have to scrape that from her soles. Avisse was pulled in for a hug by a tall woman in a leather vest, who held her close for long enough that Lila's heart curled in on itself in jealousy. As they released, Avisse gestured toward Lila, her radiant smile burning away any doubt. The woman ambled over and put out a long, callused hand.

"Calla. And you must be the famous Lila we keep hearing about." Her grip was firm but not crushing. She pulled Lila in close and spoke low in her ear. "You treat her right, now. She's a keeper." She released Lila, giving her an approving head-to-toe glance, then motioned Avisse with her chin down the long row of stalls.

"Your girls are ready to run. I got you a slot booked in the park path. You'll be glad for the shade, I expect."

Lila mopped her brow and neck with her spare handkerchief, though at this rate she was going to have to re-use her lipstick-stained one as well. She was feeling light-headed already, and they hadn't even begun walking. She took a long sip from her full water bottle, which she had been saving for the walk itself, but she realized that had been a mistake.

Avisse drained half her bottle in one gulp, then gestured toward Lila.

"Drink up and we'll fill these before we go. The water from the pump here is as cold as I've ever had." She held an arm halfway toward Lila, as if ready to catch her if she fell. Lila felt foolish, but it wasn't so far-fetched. She supposed she hadn't done a very good job of hiding her condition.

She removed her hat, smiled, and drank some more, though when she got like this, her stomach felt bloated, and it was hard to drink very much at one time. Once Avisse had filled their bottles, she took Lila's arm and led her down the row of stalls, where all manner of horses stood munching or snuffling or staring at her with their huge, shining eyes. The air was humid with hay, manure, and horse breath. While Lila normally enjoyed the smell of a stable, combined with the heat it was starting to get a bit overwhelming. She took Avisse's arm, more for moral than physical support. Avisse's fingers clenched around hers, loosening, then releasing as she slowed and came to a stop.

"Just look at you two majestic creatures," Avisse cooed, pressing against the post between two stalls, one arm wrapped around the neck of a horse in either stall. One was shiny and black, the other tawny dappled with brown spots. Both were long, lean, and powerful. Avisse leaned her head toward the black horse, which huffed into her ear as its huge lips mouthed the side of her face in what must have been a kiss.

"I love you too, Senna." Avisse laid a loud smack on the horse's nose, then turned to the other horse, which snorted in her face several times before bumping her with its nose.

"I know, I know, I miss you too, Duvie." She rubbed her nose against the horse's, then clapped the sides of its head with both hands.

"Who's ready to go for a little walk?"

Lila stepped back as Avisse maneuvered the two animals out of their stalls, holding onto their reins with one hand and cajoling them with a velvety soft voice Lila had never heard her use. Lila tugged at her collar; the air in the stable had grown unbearably hot.

"I want you to meet a very special friend, and I want you to be extra gentle because I don't think she's used to horses, okay?" The dappled horse nickered gently and stepped forward, head lowered toward Lila's outstretched hand. She wasn't unused to horses, having grown up with a stable on the grounds, but it was true that she hadn't so much as touched one in a number of years.

"Lila, this is Duvelle, but I call her Duvie. She's a softie, but if anyone messes with me or Senna, she's got a mean streak." The horse's hair was not as smooth as some, almost a little wiry.

There was a gentleness in her eye that made Lila take an instant liking to her.

"She's a sweetheart."

"Yes, you are." Avisse scritched the horse's ear, pulling gently on the reins and leading the other one forward. "And this sleek drink of dark water is Senna. She's a little shy."

Senna moved forward timidly, sniffing Lila's hand before moving her nose into it. Her hair was smooth and glossy, and her ears flickered as Lila's hand ran the length of her muzzle, then underneath, where it was softer. The horse lifted her head, snorting soft, warm breath on Lila's face as her wet nose brushed her cheek.

"She likes you," Avisse said, a hint of surprise in her voice. "Sometimes it takes her a little while, but she knows a good heart when she sees one, don't you, girl."

Lila's heart warmed at the compliment, though she wasn't sure if the horses truly did like her. She wanted them to; they were part of Avisse's everyday life, and she wanted to be part of that, too. Gods, how could she be like this after so short a time? It must be the heat getting to her. She uncapped her bottle and took a drink of the water, which was indeed some of the coolest, most refreshing she had ever tasted.

They made their way out of the stable and into a long open area that ended in a set of eight gates with a high stand occupied by a pair of women holding clipboards. Avisse checked in with one, who directed them to a gate marked number 3, which funneled them down a fenced-in bridleway. It diverged from the others, and soon they were alone, walking with the horses in tow along a beaten path with tall grass on both sides. It was hard to believe they were still in Anari; she turned around and could see the three towers twisting in the distance, and a couple of other buildings as well, but nothing more. With the looming mass of the Imperial Park ahead and the line of trees to the right, it felt like they were somewhere on the road between cities.

"It's nice out here," Lila said, though in truth the breeze had started to wane, and the sun had just reached its midday peak. She uncapped her bottle and took another sip; it was about two-thirds full now, not enough to last long in this heat.

"To be honest, I hardly ever come into town when I'm here, except for deliveries." Avisse switched both reins to one hand and offered an elbow to Lila, who took it gratefully, as the heat was getting to her. They were approaching the forest's edge, the dark shadows cool and inviting.

"And I literally never knew this part of the city existed. I've been to the Imperial Park once or twice, but my family was never one for the outdoors." *For obvious reasons,* she almost said. Gods, she was going to have to tell Avisse about having been a painted face, but she didn't know if she could bear to say the words out loud.

"Well, we'll be in the forest soon, so we'll get some shade then. I noticed you're not a big fan of the heat."

Lila's danger sense tingled at Avisse's words. Had she somehow guessed? Was she fishing?

"I guess I'm just out of practice, being cooped up in the shop all the time of late."

"And I get nothing but practice. Not too much shade between here and Rontaia, except for a couple of stretches near Endulai where there are trees planted along the road. The northern segments are all farmland, and it's pretty rough in summer. But I'm used to it, I guess."

"You're made of heartier stuff than I am, that's for sure." Lila breathed a sigh of relief as they reached the first shade of the forest, though it wasn't a whole lot cooler. She leaned against a tree and took a swig from her bottle, which was half empty by now.

"Take a break, girls," Avisse said, and the horses stopped, snuffling around the roots of a nearby tree. "And you, girlfriend, are talking nonsense." She leaned an arm against the tree, lifting a callused finger to Lila's cheek, sending a chill along her jaw and down the back of her neck.

Lila shook her head, unsure if the flush in her cheeks was a sign of impending heatstroke or just the effects of Avisse's touch, or her words.

"Girlfriend?" She angled into Avisse's hand, which cupped her cheek lightly.

"I'll be yours if you'll be mine." Avisse placed a hand on her chest and tiptoed up to kiss her lightly, then lowered back down, biting her lip, eyes dancing in the forest's shadows.

Lila felt dizzy from the kiss, and from the heat, and maybe the sight of Avisse's teeth biting into her plump lip had something to do with it, but she wasn't sure she could move from the tree's support just yet.

"I do. I will! I mean..." She closed her eyes, managing a shallow breath, then a deeper one. When she opened her eyes again, Avisse was studying her with concern.

"Are you sure you're all right? I really think the heat is getting to you. Here, why don't you take off your hat and sit down for a little while." Avisse helped her down, taking her hat and crouching next to her. Lila's heart beat unreasonably fast, and her breath came shallow. Avisse unscrewed the cap of her water bottle and poured a little onto her handkerchief, then dabbed it on Lila's temples and the back of her neck. "Close your eyes and just breathe for a minute."

Lila complied, the air suddenly feeling cool where the handkerchief had been. Avisse's hands pressed it gently against her forehead, bringing sweet relief and a gradual clearing of her mind. Her heart's panicked beating slowed, and she opened her eyes, forcing a smile at Avisse's serious demeanor.

"Drink," Avisse commanded gently, and again, Lila complied, taking the offered bottle and letting a few cool sips flood her mouth and make their way down her parched throat.

"I'm feeling much better already," Lila said in a small voice. It wasn't a lie, but she wasn't sure if she could stand, either. Though Avisse had brought her back from the brink, she was still ill from the heat, with the long sleeves and gloves she had no choice but to wear in the sun. She should probably take them off, she thought; her hands were sweating, even though she'd worn her lightest, most breathable pair, but it seemed like an awful lot of effort.

"Skundir's balls, let me get those gloves off you." Avisse peeled the gloves from her hands and laid them carefully atop her satchel. "And those boots aren't doing you any favors, either." She unlaced them and pulled them off, much to Lila's mortification; they surely stank, as much as she'd been sweating, but Avisse made no sign of having noticed or cared. She wet her handkerchief again and dabbed the inside of Lila's wrists and the soles of her feet, which were ticklish, but the cool water felt so good, it almost didn't matter.

"I'd love to get that dress off you too, but the next driver'll probably be through here before long, and we wouldn't want to cause a scene." She smirked, glancing at Lila's neck, which flushed beneath her gaze.

"Maybe when we get back home, we can order a tray of ice from the alchemist." Lila's mother had occasionally had to be treated with ice baths on hot summer days, as she was especially prone to heat exhaustion and stubborn about doing her own market shopping, no matter the weather.

"That sounds like a lot of fun." Avisse winked at her, bringing another flush of heat to her cheeks.

"You absolutely must stop flirting with me so shamelessly. You're only making matters worse."

"Oh, gods, sorry!" Avisse half-stood, covering her mouth. Lila giggled, and Avisse's expression melted into a rueful smile. "Gorgeous *and* funny. How did I get so lucky?"

Lila shrugged, shifting to see if she was ready to stand. Avisse lowered to a crouch, holding out a hand for support, but Lila sank back down.

"I need a few more minutes."

"Take all the time you need."

The black horse nudged Avisse's behind. Avisse swatted her on the muzzle without turning around.

"Be patient, Senna! You know we'd do the same for you."

"You can run them ahead if you want. I'll be fine—"

"Zero percent chance of that happening. In fact, I was thinking maybe she could carry you back."

Lila shook her head, forcing a smile, but as she glanced out at the sun-drenched field just outside the forest's shelter, the idea didn't sound half bad.

"How far did we walk?"

"About half a mile."

"Gods, is that all?" Lila covered her face with her hand. She'd always been a strong walker, and she kept fit. It was just the damned sun and the heat. Not for the first or thousandth time, she cursed her foolish ancestors who'd decided that inbreeding for pale, fragile skin in a climate like this was in any way not a terrible idea. If Avisse hadn't guessed by now, Lila needed to come clean. She felt a little better now that she'd rested. She reached for Avisse's hand and pulled to standing with her help, though she leaned against the tree for support.

"Easy does it." Avisse's hand hovered near her bicep, as if afraid she might topple over.

"I'm fine, really. Well, not entirely fine, obviously, but the dizziness is gone for now. You really knew what to do."

"Living in Rontaia, we get hot spells that last for months at a time. I've seen my share of people pass out from the heat."

"And yet there are painted faces there, aren't there?" Lila asked in as innocent a voice as she could muster.

Avisse nodded, squinting at Lila, though there was no sun.

"Not as many as up here, but there are. Mostly on Brachys Hill and the Bluffs. Their houses are built deep into the rock where it's cooler. But you see them in the market now and then." She was hedging her words, Lila could tell. She didn't much like the painted faces; no one did. Hell, even when she'd been one, Lila had hated them, but it was still hard to say the words.

"I'm—" Lila took Avisse's hand, swallowing hard and daring to look her in the eyes, which had grown serious, thoughtful. "That is, I was born and raised as a painted face here in Anari. Until just short of my second majority at twenty-two." Avisse nodded, fingers holding Lila's tenderly as Lila fought the treacherous tears that threatened to surge forth. Did Avisse really need to know her family saga right here and now?

"What happened?" Avisse asked quietly. "It's fine if you don't want to talk about it," she added quickly. "I just...I don't really understand the whole thing, to be honest, but I wondered before, with how you reacted to the heat, if you might be..."

"Unpainted is the word we use. I still wear sun cream to protect my skin, and hats and gloves and long sleeves obviously, and of course just enough makeup to highlight my natural beauty." She tilted her chin, showing off her profile, hoping her makeup hadn't run too much from all the sweating and mopping.

"As to what happened..." She gripped Avisse's fingers tight and breathed in deeply through her nose. She pictured her family as a set of pencil sketches, fading behind dusty glass on a mantelpiece. Faded sketches couldn't hurt anyone, and they certainly couldn't make anyone cry, no matter what the figures they depicted had done. No matter their betrayal.

"Listen, you don't have to—"

"My family disinherited me a month before my second majority," Lila said in a leaden voice, reciting a script she'd long practiced but never spoken aloud. "They used the morality clause, which hadn't been enforced in over a century, claiming that my transcendent status disqualified me from claiming right of inheritance."

Avisse's eyes darkened, her hands sliding up to grip Lila's forearms.

"Those evil fucking bastards," she growled. "Those sick, twisted, hateful fuckers." Lila got the distinct impression that if she asked Avisse to murder her parents, she'd do it without hesitation. By now, Lila's own hate had faded to the point that even she didn't want them dead, just forgotten.

"I kind of robbed them blind on my way out, if that helps."

"Fuck, Lila, I'm *so* sorry. What they did was unconscionable. Talk about morality!"

"The only morality they know is money." Lila wiped away a few tears that had slipped out. "They don't even care that I'm transcendent. At least not my mother. Not really. She even threw me a party when I came out, though I suppose that was more for her than for me, a queer badge of honor for the house when it was convenient." Lila thought of the lavender dress her mother had had made for her in secret, using measurements from the tailor who made her suits. It hadn't been the best fit, but she'd kept it, even after she left her family and their shitty, cloistered world behind.

"Well, I'm glad you're rid of those assholes. I sometimes forget that sort of thing still exists."

"And I sometimes forget there's a good reason they paint their faces and stay indoors during the heat of the day." Lila eyed Senna, who took a half-step forward and brushed her soft nose against Lila's cheek, almost as if she understood what was happening.

"So, what do you think, do you want me to help you up onto her? You could hold onto her mane, and I'll ride behind you to keep you steady."

Lila ran her hand along the horse's head and down her neck, which rippled with muscle beneath a coat of sleek black hair. Lila hadn't ridden since she was a kid, and certainly not bareback, but there was no way she would make it back through that sun. She ran her fingers through Senna's mane, which was rougher than her hair, thick and strong, perfect for gripping.

She nodded to Avisse, who smiled and began collecting her things.

"Show me what to do."

Lila leaned into the horse's neck, clutching the mane, as her legs were too weak to hold her upright. Avisse's thighs clamped tightly around hers, keeping her from sliding to one side or the other. One arm wrapped tightly around Lila's chest, while the other held the reins. The heat of Avisse's body pressed against her combined with the sun lulled Lila into a sleepy haze. With her boots and gloves still off and her body not doing the work of walking, she made it back to the stable feeling only a little bit dizzy.

Calla set her up with a bucket of cool water for her feet and another with a towel for her neck and forehead. By the time Avisse had finished dealing with her horses, Lila was feeling more or less herself again. She dried her feet, put her boots back on, and made it to the waiting carriage with minimal help from Avisse.

Avisse opened the little windows as they rolled through the streets, letting in just enough air to keep Lila from overheating. She dozed, leaning against Avisse's shoulder, until the carriage stopped. She opened her eyes to see the familiar surroundings of her courtyard and Avisse's indulgent smile.

"Let's get you upstairs and peel these clothes off you."

"You always know the right things to say," Lila murmured, though there was no way she'd be up for anything other than a long nap after what she'd been through.

Avisse helped her up the long stairs and unlaced her dress as Lila stood, barely able to hold herself upright. The warm breeze flowing through the open windows was a blessing on her bare skin. Avisse held onto her back with strong hands and lowered her onto the bed wearing only a lacy pink gaff that was damp and stained with sweat. She lay spread-eagled, motionless, as Avisse brought a bowl of water and a washcloth and wet her body all over, cooling her skin and raising goose bumps across her arms and legs.

"Thank you," Lila whispered, eyes half closed.

"You get some rest now. I've filled your water bottle and left it here on the nightstand. I'm going to go get something to make a nice summery dinner and then go pick up Theo. I'll be back in a little while, okay?"

"K," was all Lila managed before sleep pulled her under.

11

Lila heard the carriage roll up as she lay half-awake, tangled in her sheet, her body unable to decide if it wanted to be naked or covered. Theo's voice, too loud at first, then shushed. Lila smiled as quiet footsteps crept up the stairs. She took a drink of water and sat up, pulling the sheet around her torso. The floor outside her door creaked.

"I'm awake," she called.

Avisse slipped in, opening the door just enough to let her slim frame through, then closing it daintily behind her. The dim light of dusk reflecting off the dome softened the worry lines on her face, and when Lila stood and let the sheet drop to the floor, Avisse's smile wiped them the rest of the way off.

"Someone's feeling better."

"I've felt worse." A sudden chill swept over Lila's body which, combined with her awareness of how disheveled and dirty she must look, had her reaching for her robe. Avisse pushed out her bottom lip in a little pout as Lila slipped it on. "Once I've had a bath, I'm sure I'll feel like my old self again."

Avisse moved closer, one slow step at a time, stopping to take Lila's hand and kiss it gently.

"I know you're still pretty worn out, and I was hoping..." She kissed the inside of Lila's wrist, pulling her closer as her lips worked up toward her elbow, sending sparks of desire racing through Lila's body. "I was hoping I'd get to take care of you tonight."

The dizziness returned as Avisse's lips continued their journey upward, reaching Lila's shoulder, then her neck, palms pressed gently against her chest.

"I think I'd like that very much," Lila breathed as Avisse kissed her chin and all around her lips. Her hands slipped inside Lila's robe, fingers gently kneading her chest. Her lips finally found their mark, pressing with soft, sweet heat, turning Lila into a statue with blood rushing hot beneath her immobile exterior.

"Mother!" Theo's voice called out from beyond the door. "Sylvan said I could go help him again tonight!"

Avisse pulled back, eyes deep and liquid, mouth quirked into a soft smile.

"After dinner, love," she called, half-turning toward the door. She turned back to Lila, brushing her chin with her knuckles.

"We stopped at the market and got some things for a cold summer soup and some lovely brown bread. I thought it might be just the thing."

"Gods, what am I going to do when you're gone?"

"Miss me terribly and count the days until my return?" Avisse's eyebrows raised hopefully, then lowered as Lila gripped her cheeks and pulled her in for a soft kiss.

"I miss you already." Lila's heart felt ready to burst at the thought of almost two months without Avisse by her side, in her bed, in her life.

"I'm not gone yet, and I aim to give you more reasons to miss me before the night is over. Why don't you go get cleaned up while I make dinner."

The soup was as delicious as it was refreshing, a mix of summer squash, flat onions, and chilis, with dried shrimp and plenty of sweet cream. Theo inhaled his soup and half a loaf of bread, all the while waxing poetic about the cylinder scrolls, about the languages of the Time Before, about his theory that the famous Cloti had actually been a Maer, not a human. Lila wasn't sure exactly who or what a Maer was; no one she knew had met one. Some said they were just a mountain tribe of exceptionally hairy people, but others claimed they were an entirely different race, like the Timon, fabled dwarves of the mountains.

"Or perhaps the human language of the Time Before evolved into the Maer language somehow, or vice versa." Theo shook his head, puzzlement etched on his face.

"Maybe once Sylvan gets his wishing well operational, you'll have the answer." Avisse pointed at him with a slice of buttered bread.

Theo stopped mid-chew, mouth twisted at an odd angle.

"I don't know if it works that way. I'm not even sure if I'd want it to work that way. I mean, is it really fair to go back in time and find the answers to questions like these if only a few people are able to do it? Who gets to decide which truths are worth seeking? It's an impossible question."

Lila's head spun with the possibilities, and with the idea that a child of Theo's age could even begin to consider such things.

"Perhaps you and Sylvan could co-write a paper on the ethics of the Thousand Worlds," she suggested.

Theo smiled, eyebrows raised as if he was impressed.

"There are tomes devoted to the subject, but this new, or should I say newly rediscovered, piece of technology might open new areas for study. I shall bring up this question tonight. Speaking of which, Mother, as you can see, I've finished my soup, which was delicious, by the way, best you've ever made—the dried shrimp was an excellent addition, and I'm more than happy to help clean up—"

"Go." Avisse waved him off good-naturedly. "Have your fun, but *no* time travel or running off to any other worlds, you hear?"

"On my honor as a scholar." Theo put his hand over his chest.

"And you'll be back by midnight at the absolute latest."

"On Sylvan's honor as someone who doesn't want to get on your bad side." Theo giggled at his own joke, and Lila and Avisse joined in. Avisse motioned him on with her chin, and he raced to pick up his satchel and flew off down the stairs.

"Gods, you've raised such an amazing kid." Lila took a sip of her water, which she'd flavored with a few drops of greenorange. She half wished for a glass of the lavender wine Avisse had brought but knew it would do her no favors in her condition.

"Honestly, this is all Theo. I've set a few boundaries and given him space, but he's always been like that. He takes after Jillia." Avisse pursed her lips, blinking and smiling.

"She was your wife?"

Avisse nodded. "Took ill with Ulver's cough when Theo was little. We all got it—you remember the wave that went through eight years ago?"

Lila nodded. The painted faces had been largely spared, due to the luxury of their cloistered lifestyle. But in households that had been infected, it had been especially deadly, given their susceptibility to lung infections.

"Theo and I got the usual two weeks of hell, but Jillia..." She took a sip of her wine, looking out the window to her left, blinking rapidly as one does when fighting off tears. "She never got better."

"I am *so*, so sorry." Lila reached her hand toward Avisse, though not close enough to touch her; it didn't feel right somehow.

Avisse shook her head. "It's fine. It's been a long time now, and I go days and even weeks without thinking about her. But until I met you, there hadn't been anyone..." She looked up, her eyes wet with tears now, and stretched her hand to take Lila's, her fingers warm and strong.

"You mean you haven't..."

Avisse barked a laugh. "Oh, I have, don't get me wrong. A woman's got needs. But nothing...nothing like this."

Lila's eyes began leaking, and she made no move to stop them, makeup be damned.

"Me neither. Not for a long time. Not since..." Lila searched her memory for someone she'd felt like this about. Felix, maybe, who'd shown her what it meant to be transcendent, how to open her heart to another. But she'd been so young then, a roiling mass of unexpressed feminine joy; she might have felt that way about anyone who'd given her a chance to just be. She sighed, rubbing the back of Avisse's hand with her thumb.

"It's been a long time for me too," she said. "And now you're leaving tomorrow, and I had such big plans for tonight, but I'm still not one hundred percent. I feel like I've ruined everything."

"Hey," Avisse snapped softly, standing and moving closer, still holding onto Lila's hand. "You haven't ruined anything." She placed Lila's hand on her hip, moving her own hands to Lila's hair, pulling Lila's face to her chest. Lila inhaled Avisse's scent through her shirt, salt and horse and forest breeze, as she pressed between her soft breasts.

"You smell amazing," she murmured, nuzzling to the side, mouthing a breast through the thin fabric, feeling the nipple pebble between her lips. Her hands crept down around Avisse's behind, cupping her as she nibbled her gently through her shirt. Avisse's fingers clutched deep in her hair, pulling her in, and Lila sucked in earnest now, having wet the fabric enough that she could feel every bump and ridge. Her hands gripped Avisse more tightly, pulling her closer, feeling her heat bleed across the few inches that separated them.

"Fuck," Avisse moaned, pulling Lila's head back, eyes dark and shiny. "You make me want to do such things to you…" She took Lila by the shoulders, surprising her with the gentleness of her grip. She leaned over and planted a long, soft kiss on her lips that left Lila short of breath. Avisse pulled back, staring down at her, eyes softening a bit.

"What kind of things?" Lila whispered, her chest tingling with the wings of a thousand butterflies.

"For starters, I'm going to peel the clothes from your body and lay you down in that big bed of yours."

Lila nodded, heat spreading across her cheeks, down her neck and so much further. Avisse put a finger under her chin, and Lila rose like a puppet on strings, awaiting the commands of its master. Avisse kissed her again, so briefly Lila's heart lurched when she pulled away, eyes pointed toward the bedroom. Lila pushed her chair back, eyes locked on Avisse's, and backed toward the door, feeling her way along the wall with her hands as Avisse stalked after her, unbuckling her belt and kicking her boots off in the hallway. Avisse shed her pants and pulled her shirt over her head, small breasts jutting out, framed by bushy armpits. She stood in the doorway in nothing but a pair of thigh-length underwear, bulging with curves and muscles.

"Turn around," Avisse said in a low voice as she stalked into the room. Lila complied, her skin buzzing as Avisse quickly undid the laces on her dress and stripped her to her shift in a matter of seconds. Strong hands moved up her thighs, sliding the silky shift up, fingers grazing her already stiff nipples. The shift tangled in her hair for a moment, and then she was free, wearing only her gaff, Avisse's firm hands warming every inch of her body she touched. Soft lips worked their way across her shoulder as Avisse pulled Lila's hair back, wrapping it around her hand to tilt Lila's head just a little and expose her neck. Lila's stomach dropped out as Avisse's breasts pressed into her back and she began gently mouthing her neck, lapping and flicking with her tongue. Her other hand slid around, massaging Lila's chest, fingers feathering over her nipples, sending tiny shockwaves through her body.

Lila groaned as Avisse's fingers pinched gently and held on, her lips and tongue working their way up to her ear. Her groan rose to a plaintive note as Avisse's lips clamped down on her earlobe and began milking it in time with the subtle twists of her fingers on Lila's nipple.

"Mmm, I love the noises you make," Avisse whispered into her ear, letting go with her fingers, which roamed with the lightest touch, goosebumps rising in their wake. "I want to learn every note of your songs."

She released Lila's hair, turning her gently around with one hand on her shoulder and the other on her hip. Lila felt small and delicate in Avisse's arms, despite their difference in size; the way she touched, the grip of her hands, so full of calm control. Lila was desperate to give in to her. Avisse moved in slowly for a kiss, her eyes soft and oddly serious, her kiss doubly so. Lila melted against her mouth, into her arms, heart wide open and ready to be plundered.

"Why don't we lie you down now." Avisse walked Lila toward the bed and lowered her down, keeping one arm under her back, as if she needed help. She didn't, not exactly, but she was weak, and it felt nice to have the support of Avisse's strong arms. She scooted toward the center of the bed, and Avisse helped move her legs, smirking at the bulge in Lila's gaff.

Avisse looked into Lila's eyes with such beautiful hunger. Her gaze drifted downward, lingering on Lila's lips, traveling down her neck and to her chest. Lila's nipples budded from her gaze alone, and the thought of what Avisse might do to her. Avisse's eyes traveled down to Lila's stomach, which still showed the lines of her muscles, despite how lax she'd been about hitting the bars.

The way Avisse's eyes softened when they fell between Lila's legs turned her insides to jelly. It wasn't the look of someone who saw that part of her as a tool to get fucked with or an annoyance to work around. Avisse saw her as she was, wanted her for who she was, and was about to do unspeakable things to her that would have her moaning in ecstasy.

Avisse smirked, eyes devouring Lila from head to toe, then glanced around the room, her mouth twisted in a mysterious smile. She seemed to focus on the chest of drawers and the two wardrobes.

"What?" Lila leaned up on her elbows, her mind racing with curiosity and desire.

"I've been thinking, a cosmopolitan woman such as yourself who runs a fine establishment like the Pleasure Palace must have a few...tools of the trade around, for personal entertainment purposes?"

Lila's already-flushed face must have darkened three shades as Avisse's gaze returned to her, eyebrows raised in question. Lila nodded, glancing toward the wardrobe where she kept her supplies. *Oh shit,* she thought as Avisse crossed the room, rolling her hips, rounded ass jiggling tantalizingly with each step. Lila covered her mouth as Avisse threw open the wardrobe to reveal dozens of dresses in every color. Lila giggled hysterically, then pointed to the other wardrobe when Avisse turned a quizzical eyebrow toward her.

"Now *that's* more like it!" Avisse stood before the treasure trove, as Lila called it, her personal collection of sex toys, outfits, and accoutrements, arranged on orderly shelves, drawers, and hooks. She had hardly touched the contents since she'd moved, other than the sensitivity cream and a few toys she used for masturbation; she hadn't had a single partner sleep over since she'd left the fourth ring. Not even Cyntia, who she'd sworn to all seven rings she would not lose touch with.

Avisse ran her fingers over the chains and restraints, examined the collection of ollis and straps, and picked up a few of the jars to read the labels. She pulled open one of the drawers, where Lila kept some of her racier underthings. When she turned around, she was holding the pink satin egg, which she held up to her chest as if she thought it might be a bra.

Lila covered her giggle, which became a full-fledged cackle as Avisse examined it from all angles, trying to figure out what it was or how it would be used. It would look strange to the uninitiated, a pair of oval pink satin cups with a washable liner, connected on one side, with various silk ribbons to attach it. Lila cupped her hands between her legs, and Avisse closed the egg and placed it between hers, mouth opening wide and eyebrows nearly reaching her hairline.

"Show me how to put it on you." Avisse knelt between Lila's legs and tucked her fingers into the hem of her gaff, her eyes seeking approval, which Lila gave. Avisse pulled down her gaff in one long, slow movement, leaving Lila feeling oddly exposed. She didn't mind so much once she was in the act, but seeing everything so plainly was sometimes more than she could bear. Which was the whole point of the egg in the first place. Her cock lolled about, half-aroused, half-confused, as she was, which was an advantage, as it would be impossible to fit the thing on if she were fully erect. She took a deep breath to steel her nerves and sat halfway up, taking the egg and spreading out the laces. Avisse watched, her eyes sparkling with fascination.

"First, you scooch the bottom half of the egg underneath, like so." Lila spread her legs wider to make room for the contraption. "Then you make sure everything's tucked downward, like this." She tucked herself down and closed the egg quickly, as the awkwardness was giving way to awkward arousal with Avisse's eyes following her every move. "Then you lace it up through these loops here—"

"Let me do that part." Avisse's voice was soft as she leaned in, breasts dangling, eyes focused, and threaded the lace through each loop. Lila swelled within the egg, giving it shape, but it held her in check, as it was intended to do.

"Now you have to tighten it. Just pull here, like you're tying a shoe."

Avisse bit her lip as she slowly pulled the laces taut and the egg tightened, securing Lila in soft, restraining comfort, but it was still too loose. Avisse glanced up at Lila, eyes questioning.

"I'll say when," Lila assured her.

Avisse pulled the laces tighter. Lila took a deep breath as the egg closed around her and a tingle stirred deep within.

"Right there," she whispered.

Avisse tied the laces with precise gestures, then ran her fingers softly over the smooth exterior. Lila couldn't feel her touch through the padding, but the sight sent a tingle into the pit of her stomach. She lay back, blowing out a long, slow breath.

"It's beautiful." Avisse continued touching the egg, cupping it from beneath, her fingers squeezing a little now, testing it, sending waves of hot need streaking through Lila's body. "You're beautiful."

Her lips found Lila's stomach, her hands sliding to the sides to frame Lila's hips. She kissed her way up Lila's body like she was planting a garden, sucking with her lips, then swirling with her tongue on each spot, covering her stomach and chest with whorls of pleasure. Her hands followed, holding Lila's ribcage, fingers stretching upward, gripping her more tightly as her lips and tongue worked their way inexorably toward Lila's nipples.

She straddled Lila, hovering with her breasts just touching Lila's skin, her stomach resting atop the egg, adding a touch of pressure. She licked slow circles around each nipple, grazing the pebbled areolas, sending Lila into a dizzying state of near-ecstasy. When Avisse's tongue started flicking against one of them, Lila gasped, gripping Avisse's hair and pulling her close.

"Suck," she whined.

Avisse raised her head, a devilish gleam in her eye, and threw Lila's arms above her head, pinning her biceps with strong, callused hands. She hovered above her, lips glossy and thick, pressing the egg between her thighs.

"Patience," she whispered, then fell on Lila's mouth, devouring her, pressing into her with her entire body until Lila was ready to burst. But the egg kept her secure, kept her on the edge but not over it. Not yet. Avisse pulled back from the kiss, lightening the pressure of her body, and returned her attention to Lila's chest, which she studied with hungry eyes.

"Now, where was I?"

Lila wished she had restraints to keep her arms secure as Avisse worked her over with her mouth and fingers, teasing one nipple, then the other, then both at the same time. She stopped suddenly, a mischievous gleam in her eye, and scurried off the bed. She opened the treasure trove and retrieved a jar, which Lila recognized immediately as the sensitivity cream, and sniffed it.

"Strawberry?"

Lila nodded, her face burning as the smell hit her, knowing what it felt like, wondering how much more intense it would be with Avisse doing the touching. The cream went on cold, then quickly warmed her nipples with an icy heat, which flared as Avisse's fingers circled, teased, and gently twisted. Lila's breath grew short, her voice escaping in unexpected moans and squeaks, which she stifled by pressing her forearm over her mouth as Avisse applied her lips to the endeavor.

Lila closed her eyes, channeling the deep well she'd found in Sylvan's meditation, the cracks in her core that Avisse was tearing open with her ravishing lips and tongue. The entire universe was inside her, revealed now by Avisse's tender ministrations. She was lovable. She was loved. *This* was real, and nothing could ever take it away from her.

Avisse's mouth grew less gentle. She pulled Lila's nipples in one at a time and held them, laving each with her tongue before moving on to the next, back and forth, with relentless determination. Lila's body began to shake, and Avisse increased the pressure on the egg, riding it gently but steadily. Avisse breathed heavily through her nose, and she sucked so long and hard that Lila let out a sharp cry. Avisse released, her eyes hot and wild, gripping Lila's ribs and grinding against the egg now.

"Gods, I fucking love you so much," Avisse whispered. Stars swam in Lila's vision, surrounding Avisse like a celestial being come down to earth to fuck her into the Time to Come. Avisse increased her speed and pressure, gripping Lila's ribcage so hard that Lila was sure to bruise, but she didn't care. Avisse rode her to a velvety earthquake that had Lila biting her arm to avoid crying out so loud Theo and Sylvan would hear them all the way down in the Well. When at last Avisse collapsed atop her, sweaty and heaving for breath, Lila wrapped her arms around Avisse's strong back and held her tight. Avisse's body slowly relaxed, her breath settling, her legs slumping to the sides, but Lila kept her arms exactly where they were.

"I'm never going to let you go," she murmured.

"I'm never going to let you," Avisse whispered in her ear.

12

Lila woke to an empty bed and a leaden void in her stomach. She slid into her bathrobe, relieved to hear the sound of water in the washroom; at least Avisse hadn't slipped out without a warning.

"Good morning, Miss Lila." Theo bowed Endulian-style, and Lila forced a smile and repeated his gesture. He sat with one of Lila's books on his lap, his bulging satchel strapped tight on the couch next to him.

"Looks like you're all ready for your trip."

Theo closed the book gently, as if with regret. "I suppose. I spend half of my life in the carriage, so it's not exactly difficult, but I always get a little restless the first day."

"I guess you have plenty of books to keep you company." She gestured toward the satchel, her mind sharpening as the sound of water in the washroom stopped. Avisse must have finished washing up and would be getting dressed now.

"Oh yes, I'm never bored, and especially not this trip. Sylvan has loaned me quite a few books from his personal collection, some of them in languages I don't read perfectly, which is always a good way to while away the days." He glanced at his satchel, then out the window. "I'm going to miss him." He turned back toward Lila, his face contorting with embarrassment. "I'm going to miss you too, Lila! You've been so good to me, and to my mother. I've never seen her this happy."

Lila waved off his words, too choked up to respond right away. She sneaked a rumpled handkerchief out of the pocket of her robe and dabbed her eyes.

"I'll miss you too, Theo. I've learned a lot having you around. I expect Sylvan has, too."

"You should see the Well of All. It's just about finished, save the crystal ball, which I expect we'll be delivering when we return in a month and a half."

Lila's heart leapt at his words, but she merely raised her eyebrows gently. "Do you think so?"

"Sylvan said as much. He said he had requested that my mother deliver it when he'd commissioned it from Silver Dock. I get the impression he tends to get what he wants."

"That he does," Lila said with a chuckle. Her heart leapt as the washroom door opened, and she turned to see Avisse stroll out, pulling her wet hair back into a ponytail and tying it.

"Good morning, beautiful." Avisse took Lila by the hips and kissed her, making her immediately forget how disheveled she was, how she hadn't put on her makeup, how she no doubt had morning breath.

"I might say the same thing about you." Lila rubbed noses with her, then kissed her again.

"Who's stopping you?"

Lila saw Theo raise his hand out of the corner of her eye, and she laughed and said it anyway.

"Good morning, beautiful."

They kissed again, then Avisse settled back down on flat feet, biting her lip.

"Do you have time for breakfast?" Lila asked hopefully.

"I went out early and got some things for the road, and a few pastries because there's nothing like this between here and Rontaia." She gestured toward the kitchen table, where plates and cups were laid out. "Let me get the tea going while you wash up."

They ate with awkward false cheer, pretending it was just another morning together, that they weren't about to be separated for six long weeks. The sugar flowers were like paste in Lila's mouth, the tea faded and bitter. As she picked at the crumbs on her plate, she saw Avisse drain the last of her tea and set her cup down with what felt like finality.

Tears welled up, spilling down Lila's cheeks and falling in fat drops onto her plate. The kitchen was silent except for her quiet sobs, which she stifled as best she could, burying her face in her handkerchief. She heard the scoot of a chair, a few soft footsteps, felt the warmth of Avisse's body behind her. Strong arms wrapped around her shoulders and chest.

"It's okay, baby." Avisse's voice faltered as if she was on the verge of crying, too. "I'll be back before you know it, and next time we'll stay a little longer."

Lila nodded, dabbing her tears and sniffling, embarrassed that this scene had to happen in front of Theo.

"I know you will." She sat up straight, and Avisse released her a little, sliding her hands up to Lila's shoulders. She dabbed her eyes again, looking down at her makeup-stained handkerchief, just another of the day's many indignities. She blinked apologetically at Theo, who studied her with serious, concerned eyes.

"I won't tell you not to cry, Lila," he said as if he were an adult trying to comfort a child by pretending they're grown up. In any case, it only made her tears flow more freely. "But don't forget your Endulian teachings: wherever my mother goes, there's a part of her that's inside you, and you in her." Lila sobbed, an ugly, moaning sound, and covered her face with her handkerchief to hide the tears and snot running down her face.

"Skundir's balls, Theo, I'm not dying. I'm just going to Rontaia." Avisse's strong hands slid up and down Lila's biceps. Lila felt her breath in her ear as Avisse lowered down to kiss it. "I love you," she murmured, "and I swear I'll come back for you."

Lila reached over her shoulder to pat Avisse's head, then turned awkwardly sideways to blow her nose, then dab her eyes and ruined makeup with the few remaining clean, dry spots of her handkerchief.

"Thank you for your words of wisdom, Theo. You honor the Endulian practice."

He nodded with a faint smile.

Lila stood, turning toward Avisse, whose eyes were a little red and wet, but she didn't look like the mess Lila felt.

"We really need to…" Avisse fingered the hem of Lila's sleeve, and Lila nodded, looking down, trying not to cry anymore.

"Can I call you a carriage?" Lila said brightly, eager for a distraction.

Avisse shook her head, pulling her close and kissing her on the chin. "We're going to be sitting for the better part of the next two weeks. We could use the walk."

"Right, of course." Lila held Avisse's firm biceps, which even in Lila's tear-sodden state gave her a tingle of desire. "Well, then, I suppose—"

Avisse shut her mouth with a kiss that was much less chaste than expected, given the presence of a child. It was also much briefer than she would have liked. Avisse pursed her lips, shouldered her bag, and motioned Theo forward with her chin.

"Come on, kiddo."

Theo picked up his own heavy satchel off the back of his chair and approached Lila awkwardly. She swept him up into a strong hug, which he returned with unexpected enthusiasm, his warm hands clutching around her neck.

"I'll miss you, Lila, and I look forward to seeing you again when we return."

"You can send a message via Sylvan's account at the Inkwell, if you like." Lila said it to Theo, but she glanced at Avisse out of the corner of her eye.

"I've never used that before, but—" Avisse glanced at Theo.

"We will." Theo clapped Lila on the shoulder, once again acting like the adult in the situation. He glanced at Avisse, who nodded, and he joined her at the top of the stairs.

"Drive safely," Lila said, blowing a kiss, sickened that these would be the last words she'd say to Avisse before she was gone from her life for such a long time.

"I'll think of you every day and every night," Avisse said over her shoulder, eyes staying locked with Lila's until she disappeared down the stairs.

Lila spent the day in a fog. Numbers made no sense, and letters weren't much better. People spoke to her, she responded, they went away. She holed up in her office, shuffling through papers, staring into space. Tera and Aven left her alone for the most part, occasionally delivering her something to sign, a sandwich, a cup of tea. She smiled and thanked them, and they drifted away on soft feet. Tera lingered in the doorway after one such delivery, and Lila pushed her smile wider and raised her eyebrows.

"We're closing up, and I just wondered if there was anything..."

"No, I'm just going to stay here for a little while, thank you."

"Sylvan's in the basement, just so you know."

"Of course, he is." Lila's thoughts drifted to his strange contraption, and she wondered what he was doing down there. Theo had said they'd almost finished it.

"Might be a good distraction." Tera turned, standing in the open doorway, her eyes softer and less piercing than usual. "And he could probably use the company too."

Lila cracked a half smile, picturing Sylvan all alone in that strange round room with its golden arch and mysterious podium.

"Might as well." She stood with a sigh. "It's not like I have anyone to go home to tonight."

Tera turned her face down, no doubt to hide her blush. Of all the pairings Lila had helped put together, Tera and Aven were the couple she was most proud of. Tera's attitude toward sex had been one of almost scientific fascination, and as far as Lila could tell, Tera was the first *woman* Aven had been with, but the bond that had developed between them showed no signs of weakening.

"Give Aven a kiss for me."

"If you want to kiss Aven, you'll have to do it yourself." Tera blinked, the gold in her hazel eyes shining like tiny blades. "See you in the morning."

The pool room was eerily silent, the water still as glass now that the pumps were turned off for the night. Two brightstone lights had been left on for safety, casting the walkway between the pools in a warm orange light. Lila paused, inhaling the sulfur scent of the baths, and considered having a soak, but she hadn't bathed since the morning, and it seemed like a lot of bother to shower and remove her makeup. As she stood pondering, the thought of Sylvan's machine drew her like a lodestone.

She pulled out the big brass key as she passed along the pools reflecting the arched ceilings glowing red and orange from the sandstone walls. Other than the sound of the lock clunking open, the bronze door opened silently, and Lila made her way down the narrow passageway, lit with brightstones fixed in the ceiling along its length. The door to the chamber was closed. She slid the key into the lock and turned it slowly, hoping to avoid a loud *clunk*, but the sound of the mechanism echoed down the hallway. She sighed and opened the door.

Sylvan stood at the podium, his hands in a pair of bronze gloves held over a glass globe the size of a pomegranate. A shimmer stretched between the shining golden arch and the water beneath it, featureless and smooth like smoked glass. Sylvan stared into the shimmering surface, eyes unblinking, mouth half-open as if with wonder.

Lila gave a start as she noticed that his face was unpainted, shocking in its paleness, though some paint remained on his neck as if he'd hastily removed it. She cast her eyes down for a moment out of instinct, then looked back up again. She was an Unpainted, and Sylvan had done the meditation session unpainted, so he clearly didn't hold to the same standards as other painted faces. What did that make him, then? His eyes fluttered a few times, and the shimmering flickered and went out. He pulled his hands out of the gloves and turned to Lila, blinking rapidly.

"Lila!" he said as if pleasantly surprised, pushing a lever on the side of the podium down.

"Sorry to interrupt you." She made her way slowly down the stairs, studying the machine more carefully now that Sylvan's hands were no longer in it. The gloves were made of bronze mesh, with solid bronze fingertips with little tubes running from each of them and connecting to the elegant bowl holding the glass orb. Beneath the bowl, the tubes entered a wider bronze tube that disappeared into the podium, reappearing near the base and snaking into the water of the pool, which was cloudy with little bubbles.

"Oh, not at all. I was just experimenting with the Sooth Mirror."

"I thought it was called the Well of All." Lila approached the podium, studying the pieces, all of which appeared to be made of bronze, like the arch.

"Yes, that is—technically it's only called that when it's fully functional, which requires a crystal ball of over ninety-nine percent clarity. Like the one I've commissioned from the Silver Dock workshop, and which your beloved Avisse will be delivering in I believe six weeks?" Lila's heart wrenched, thinking of going that long without seeing her, touching her, kissing her. She dabbed at her eyes in case a sneaky tear might be slipping out. "But even with a lesser crystal such as this one, which is about ninety-five percent clarity, the best I could get in Anari, the device can still provide...limited access to the knowledge of the Thousand Worlds."

He peered into the water, twisting his mouth sideways.

"I might need to adjust the levels a bit. Just give me a moment." He dipped a glass vial held on a metal clamp into the well and poured a drop of blue liquid into it. The water immediately turned light pink, and Sylvan held it up next to a sheet of paper with a color scale on it. "It should be good for one more session before I have to adjust the mineral content. Do you want to give it a try?"

Lila's hackles rose as she pictured Sylvan's slack-jawed face staring into the shimmering surface of the arch. She knew this kind of magic existed; she'd used the Inkwell more than once, but the idea of putting her hands in those gloves and staring into it directly went against everything she'd been raised to believe. Then again, most of what she'd been raised to believe had turned out to be false, much of it deeply hurtful.

"Me? Why?"

Sylvan raised his hands as if in defense. "It's fine if you don't want to. I just thought you might find it...interesting."

Lila stared at the arch, then at the water, which had calmed and was now nearly clear, and at the convoluted set of tubes leading from the strange gloves to the bowl holding the glass globe.

"Interesting how?" Her initial shock had worn off a little, and something in his voice made her curious. "And excuse me for being rude, but why are you unpainted?"

"Oh!" Sylvan touched his face, letting out a nervous laugh. "You don't mind, do you? I just...I find it helps me focus when I'm meditating. This," he said, pointing toward the machine, "is a lot like meditation."

"Of course, I don't mind. I think it's great that you're comfortable without your paint. You really blew some minds doing the erotic meditation session unpainted. I wish more people could take off the mask."

Sylvan sighed, smiling. "So do I. But change happens slowly, doesn't it? And I find it helpful to operate from within the system. Particularly when it allows me the financial freedom to pursue endeavors like this."

"Which is...what exactly?"

"Okay, well, as I said, without a truly pure crystal, we can't create a portal. We can't travel physically, or even mentally, as they do with the cradles in the Endulian temples. The connection simply isn't direct enough. But if you're able to focus sufficiently, you can tap into the part of the Thousand Worlds that's inside you and make a connection through the Well to the Worlds themselves."

"So that's what you were doing when I came in? Connecting to the Thousand Worlds in search of some kind of truth or whatever?"

"Yes. No. Sort of. What you get, what you see in the Sooth Mirror, is not the actual truth, as you would experience if you traveled through the portal I believe will be created once we have the higher purity crystal. It's an approximation of the truth, made up of what's in your mind, augmented by what's in the Worlds."

"So, you might just be seeing what you imagine to be true."

Sylvan shook his head impatiently. "No, it's much more than that. I can *feel* the difference, when I look into it—some of it comes from me, yes, but there are things I couldn't possibly know, unlocked by the knowledge I already have. It's hard to explain, but it *is* the truth—just not quite exactly the whole truth."

Lila studied the gloves, wondering what they would feel like, if they would be cold. "What did you see?"

Sylvan's smile widened, showing all of his perfect teeth. "It's so exciting! And I *knew* it, I absolutely knew it, but now I *know* it with much greater certainty. Those who made this device were certainly not human."

Lila's hackles rose again, along with her eyebrows. "Not human? And you want me to put my hands in there?"

Sylvan waved her doubts away. "Not human, no, but no different than us, and quite possibly sharing a common ancestor. Or maybe they *were* the common ancestor. They were Maer, or something like the Maer. You know, the hairy mountain folk we get the brightstone from?"

"So, they're really...not human?" Lila had heard of these mountain tribes, covered in hair from head to toe, but she'd always assumed those tales were exaggerations.

Sylvan stroked his chin, staring into the center of the arch. "I expect there are scholarly works being written as we speak on this very topic. If you saw a woman whose skin was covered in hair like a beard extending over her entire body, would you call her human?"

Lila had seen drawings of such beings in books of legends, but they were always depicted with monstrous or animalistic features like wolf ears, fangs, and claws. She tried to imagine a woman normal in every way but covered in hair. She pictured Avisse's naked body, svelte hips and round ass and perky breasts, covered in a coat of downy fur, and she began to giggle.

"It's hard to imagine, but...I see where you're going with this."

"I have spoken with at least one Maer in the Thousand Worlds, when I was at Endulai, and I can assure you that their minds are no different than ours. And everything in my studies leads me to believe that this technology, and that of the Endulian cradles and the circlets—all of it is most likely of Maer origin. I'll have a hell of a time convincing anyone of this, but hopefully once I get the crystal from Rontaia, I'll be able to *prove* it." He clenched his fist, eyes burning bright. "In the meantime, I'm just testing some little hypotheses of mine, and seeing what some old friends are up to."

"How do you do that?" Lila thought of Avisse, who was no doubt stopped for the night. Was she at an inn, or asleep in the carriage? Was she curled up next to Theo? Lila's heart ached, knowing she would sleep alone tonight.

"You just put your hands in the gloves, think of whatever it is you want to know, and stare into the arch. Oh, and you have to flip this lever first to turn it on." He pointed toward a lever sticking out of the podium with a black leathered knob on the end.

Lila took a step closer, her heart drawing her toward the device as her stomach told her to stay put.

"Listen, you don't have to or anything. I was going to change out the water and pack it in for the night, so if you don't—"

"I want to." Lila stepped up to the podium, willing her stomach to settle. "I want to see Avisse."

"Good, yes, an excellent choice for your first attempt. The stronger your connection to the thing you seek, the easier it should be. Would you like a half dram of soma to ease you in?"

Lila shook her head, her fingers already sliding into the mesh of the gloves, down into the cold pads of the fingers. Sweat beaded on her forehead as she stared into the emptiness in the middle of the arch, thinking of Avisse: her tight ponytail, the hard line of her jaw, the way it softened when she laughed. How her eyes slitted when she closed in for a kiss. Lila's heart filled with longing, but the arch remained empty.

"If you're ready, I'll flip the switch now," Sylvan said quietly.

Lila sighed, smiling, and nodded. "Sorry, I forgot. Go ahead."

The lever moved with a muffled clank, and a faint vibration tingled up through Lila's fingers. Nothing more happened at first, then a mist-like sheen formed in the air, spreading out from the well around the inside edges of the arch, filling in slowly until it was an even screen of dim gray. She narrowed her mind, as she did in Endulian meditation, and pictured Avisse sitting on the carriage, speeding down the road, wind whipping her ponytail behind her. Theo sat inside, reading by the light from an open window. The clatter of the horses' hooves on gravel combined with the grinding of the wheels to form a wall of noise that drew her further in as the vision sped up. Trees and houses flew by, the sky shifting from light to dark blue, then a rainbow of colors as the sun set.

It was dark in the carriage, slivers of moonlight painting pale stripes across the blanket where two shapes lay snuggled together. A muscled shoulder and arm poked out of the top of the blanket, wrapping around the smaller figure, whose long hair flopped loosely across the pillow. Avisse's face, bathed in shadow, nestled into Theo's head. Her gentle snore joined the chorus of crickets outside the carriage. It was warm and cozy, and Lila had never wanted to be someplace so badly in her life.

The vision flickered; at first, she thought it was her tears, or perhaps that her fingers weren't making contact, or that she wasn't concentrating enough. Soon Avisse and Theo's image vanished into the gray, which dissipated like mist. She pulled her hands out of the gloves, turning to Sylvan, eyes wet with tears.

"I think the well's out of kilter," Sylvan said apologetically. "I'll have to drain it and adjust the levels tomorrow. Did you…" He took a tentative step toward her, reaching out his hand as if he wanted to comfort her, but holding back.

Lila nodded.

"And everything was…good?"

She nodded again, smiling through her tears. "She and Theo were sleeping in the carriage. Which seems weird, since…isn't it a little early?"

"Well, using the Sooth Mirror is more of an art than a science. I'm only just now figuring it out myself."

"But was it really them?"

Sylvan nodded, touching her forearm gently. "I think it was, Lila. With the connection you have to her…I think it absolutely was."

She wiped her eyes and face, laughing at the makeup stains on her handkerchief. "I must look a right mess."

"Well, let's go up to the restroom and put on our makeup together then, shall we?"

It felt surreal, after what she'd just witnessed, watching Sylvan put on his paint, but it was a welcome distraction. He applied his base, then layered on his blue-green paint, a little clumsily to Lila's eye. When she was painted, she'd always taken pride in her technique, even though she hated the tradition. She'd choose colors favored by women or undermine traditional male colors with whimsical accents and flourishes she knew would piss her mother off, long before she transcended.

Lila took her time with her makeup, studying Sylvan out of the corner of her judgmental eye. When he began applying the black lipstick he favored, she couldn't stay silent any longer.

"I'm sorry, but your paint is too dark for black. Go with...maybe this sea foam, or even a lavender."

Sylvan flashed a crooked smile, paintbrush hovering in the air, then set it down and indicated his paint box with a flourish. Lila's chest warmed with pride as she dabbed off the black he'd begun to apply and tested the sea foam. It was a nice contrast with the paint, and it caught the color in his eyes a bit as well.

"This will do nicely."

She leaned in close to get a better angle, and it could have felt awkward, but with Sylvan, nothing ever did. She thought back to the kiss he'd given her on opening night, how gentle he'd been, like he was kissing her forehead. Lila had kissed a lot of people, and she'd gotten a variety of reactions— desire, surprise, confusion, even disgust from a few, who'd realized in that moment she was transcendent and been put off by it—but never anything like Sylvan's friendly indifference. It was nice being around someone who just...didn't care about that kind of thing. She smiled as she smoothed out the lines on the top and added a tiny tail on either end.

"See?" She turned him to face the mirror, and his eyes brightened.

"Lila, it looks amazing! Let me do around my eyes too." He reached for the brush, which she held away from him.

"I'd hate to waste *my* lip job on *your* eye job. Come here."

Sylvan smiled, closed his eyes, and leaned in.

Lila lay in bed late into the night thinking of Avisse. Touching herself. Gently, but still, it was almost too much. She turned to the side, tucking her hands beneath her head, but Avisse would not leave her alone, sliding up behind her, arm draped over her hip, fingers roaming. Lila's mind was heavy with fatigue, but just as sleep approached, Avisse's lips would whisper into her ear, sending her into another spiral of half-conscious desire. When she could take it no longer, she tucked herself into a gaff, pinched her nipple, and rubbed herself to a very wet and deeply unsatisfying orgasm.

Once she'd cleaned up and settled back into bed, she pulled two pillows in to her chest, hugging them with all her might. This wasn't forever. Avisse would come back to her. She would hold her in her arms, feel her breath on her cheek, smell the wind on her skin. She just had to sleep and wake up. Sleep and wake up.

Forty times.

Lila pressed her eyes against the pillow so hard she couldn't tell for sure if she was crying.

13

The second day was harder.

She was exhausted from lack of sleep, and no amount of makeup could cover the bags under her eyes. She'd worn a brighter-than-usual shade of red lipstick to distract from them, and she felt like a clown when she looked in the mirror. She decided it would have to do as she realized she had a morning appointment with Ms. Hentry and her son Gaven, the transcendent boy she'd sent binders home for. She downed a glass of water, did a quick touch-up on her eyeliner, and hurried across the courtyard, where she found them standing before the locked door. Ms. Hentry wore a muted tan cloak of fine materials and a burnt-orange-painted face, and her son was dressed all in gray with dark blue paint and a shy smile in rosy silver.

"So sorry to keep you waiting!" She touched Ms. Hentry on the arm, smiling gently at the boy. "Good to see you again, Ms. Hentry. And you must be Gaven."

Gaven's smile widened as she said his name.

"Is everything fitting all right? I'm happy to exchange if you need a different size, or—"

"It fits great." Gaven stretched out his chest, which was nearly flat, the seams of the binder invisible beneath his slightly frilly shirt. "I'm going to need a couple more."

"Of course, right this way."

She opened the door and led them down the old service hallway to the left, which Aven had refinished in reclaimed wood and decorated with some old paintings they'd gotten for a song at an estate sale. They'd done wonders with the old cloakroom as well, adding a changing stall and several wardrobes to display the undergarments most popular with her transcendent clientele.

"You're wearing a medium, so that's this row here. We have several more styles and colors to choose from. Take your time." Lila gave him space, and his mother stood near Lila as he handled the binders, studying them closely.

"You can try them on in the changing room there." Lila pointed to the booth, and Gaven slipped inside, grinning from ear to ear.

"It wasn't easy getting him to come out here," Ms. Hentry said quietly to Lila, with a hint of pride in her voice. "We've been thinking about finding a good alchemist who specializes in transcendent care. I was wondering if you might know of anyone?"

Lila's heart warmed with the question. "I might just, as a matter of fact." She thought of some of the alchemists who supplied the creams she sold in the shop, including the ones she used to slow the growth of hair on her face and body. There were plenty of transcendent folks who took daily philters or monthly infusions for more substantial bodily changes, which Lila had never gotten up the nerve to try. There were stories of bad experiences, since there were no licenses or standards, as there were with doctors. It was mostly word of mouth, and not everyone's experience was the same, but there were a few whose reputations were good enough that she might be willing to recommend them.

"I'll ask around and get back to you if that's okay?"

"Of course. Let me give you my card." The woman produced a gilded card of the sort Lila's mother always carried, with the family name and address—first ring, unsurprisingly.

"I think I found what I need." Gaven emerged from the stall, two binders held low in his hands, both simple beige affairs with padded silk straps.

"I was just talking with Ms. Thelkis about finding you an alchemist."

Gaven smiled awkwardly; Lila was sure he was blushing beneath his paint.

"That would be amazing!"

"I'm going to make sure we find you just the right one." Lila touched him gently on the shoulder, wanting to show support without getting too personal. It was always a fine line. Gaven's smile loosened. She must have done it right.

Once she'd settled their bill and bid them both goodbye, she buried herself in a sea of paperwork and minor annoyances, which got her to lunch. She had little appetite, but she managed to put away several of the pastries Aven always seemed to bring when she needed them most. She sighed at the pile of papers on her desk, which didn't seem to have diminished since this morning, and pushed up out of her chair. She had stewed in her office long enough.

She went into the shop and began straightening things, though the displays all looked good and almost everything was well stocked. Perhaps too well stocked, she worried, glancing around the store, which only held a handful of customers. Maybe this was all a big mistake. She'd overestimated the market for this kind of merchandise. The painted faces and other inner-ring rich who were inclined to purchase sex toys, lingerie, and pleasure creams had already had their fun, and no one was coming from the outer rings to pay her prices. She was ruined, and she'd be taking poor Tera and Aven with her.

She retreated to her office and combed through her files for all the alchemical suppliers of transcendent care products she sold in the store. She didn't sell any of the philters or infusions Gaven would need; she sold mostly simple compounds, creams and lotions to make hair grow or go away, some thought to soften skin or make it thicker, and the like. Some of the alchemists she knew personally, others by reputation, and a few she knew only by the labels on their tins. Surely some of them made more complex body-altering products as well. She made a short list of potential candidates and drafted a note, which she rewrote several times, then made five copies, one for each of them. Aven's head appeared in the doorway as she was folding them up for delivery.

"Everything okay?" they asked in a timid yet chipper voice.

"I've found a suitable distraction." She folded the last note and bound them all together with a piece of twine. "Have you seen Ferdie around?"

"She's off to the glazier, I believe. One of the windows on the side is cracked."

Lila rolled her eyes, picturing the goods she'd have to sell to make up for the price of the repair. The sheer size of the place was a liability in itself.

"Of course, it is. Well, when she gets back, if you see her before I do, I need her to deliver these. The addresses are all there." She crossed the room, and Aven took the notes, studying them briefly before sticking them in the delivery box outside Lila's office door.

"Right, of course." They stood there in the awkward way people have when they need to broach an uncomfortable topic.

"What is it, Aven?"

"Nothing! Or rather, I was wondering, *we* were wondering, if you didn't have anything planned, if you'd like to join Tera and me for dinner this evening. I'm going to grill some eels and greenstalks."

Lila paused, considering the offer. She certainly didn't have anything planned, except perhaps going down to the basement with Sylvan and spying on Avisse through the Sooth Mirror. She'd felt a little guilty for having done it before and already felt guilty for doing it again tonight, though she hadn't done it yet. What better way to distract herself than a pleasant evening with her dearest friends, who she never got a chance to see anymore except at work? But the thought of making conversation, pretending not to be missing Avisse, watching the two of them mooning over each other—it was all too much to bear.

"I think I might need to sulk for a few days more if you don't mind. I'm afraid I wouldn't be the best company."

Aven nodded, hands held behind their back. "Are you absolutely certain? The fishmonger has assured me—"

"Ask me again in a couple of days, okay?" She lifted a hand to cup their cheek, smiling at their blush, wishing it gave her the tingle it used to.

"I will hold you to that."

Lila drifted to the spa, which was fully booked but still felt serene, and to the baths, where several dozen beatific faces floated amid the steam. She eyed the bronze door, knowing that behind it, in the Sooth Mirror amid the golden arch, she'd see Avisse sitting upright atop her carriage, holding the reins, ponytail flapping in the breeze, while Theo sat inside reading or staring out the little window, thinking about the languages of the Time Before.

Lila returned to the lobby, almost dragging her feet, and sank against the wall on one of the stone benches surrounded by vines. She felt empty, useless. A ghost haunting her own creation. If she vanished entirely, The World Within would keep going, and only a few would even notice her absence.

Bathers, spa-goers, employees, and shoppers came and went, and it wasn't until she heard Sylvan's voice that she realized it had grown dark outside and the place had closed.

"Having a little sit and think?"

"More like a sit and mope." She scooted over to make room. Sylvan eased onto the bench beside her, setting his heavy satchel on the floor.

"Probably not one of those things that wants talking about."

"Not much to say, really."

"Just as well. I'm not very good at cheering up the lovelorn. Not something I have much experience with."

"Consider yourself lucky."

Sylvan stared up at the ceiling, which was lit with a few well-placed brightstones tucked away among the vines to give it a greenish, shadowy glow. She noticed his paint now, lime green with black lipstick, which worked with this color.

"I don't know that either of us is particularly luckier than the other. We all live with the hearts we're given."

Lila had no answer for that, so she joined him in contemplating the ceiling's shadows.

"Want to take a peek in the mirror? I changed and balanced the water last night, so it should be good and fresh."

Lila stood before she realized what she was doing.

"Yes, I'd like that very much."

Lila's hands slid into the gloves with only a faint shiver this time, though the metal was still cold to the touch. Her heart was racing, and she worked to slow it by controlling her breathing, as she did in Endulian practice. In through her nose, out through her mouth. Over and over until her mind and body began to settle. She pictured Avisse's face, focused on chopping vegetables, the muscles in her arm tensing with each stroke, her fingers moving with precise motions. Warmth spread through her chest; something about a woman who could handle a horse and a kitchen knife with equal ease made her go all soft inside.

"Is your mind set?" Sylvan asked quietly. He was standing right next to her, though she hadn't noticed him approaching.

She nodded. He flipped the lever and stood back.

The gray sheen formed almost instantaneously this time. Lila quickly found herself watching Avisse and Theo sitting at a picnic table with bowls of soup under a string of paper lanterns. Theo was talking, and though Lila couldn't hear what he was saying, she could tell it was something scholarly by the light in his eyes, and by the way Avisse's smile humored him, even as she stared off into the darkness. Was she looking in the direction of Anari? Was she thinking about Lila, missing her too? Something Theo said jerked Avisse's attention back to him, and she laughed, then fired off what must have been a witty retort. Lila let go with her mind and watched the vision fade, their imagined conversation no doubt continuing at some wayside tavern near Freburr.

She slipped her hands out of the gloves and pulled the lever up. Her face was dripping with sweat, which she mopped with a handkerchief. Sylvan now stood unpainted, which gave her a shock, though less so than last time, watching her with curious eyes.

"Did you find what you were looking for?"

"I did," Lila said with a happy sigh, though tears were not far off. "I probably shouldn't check on her every day, but it...it helps a little bit."

"You may check on her as often as you like. I'm sure she wouldn't mind."

Lila paused, wondering if that was true. Would she want Avisse spying on her in her private moments, watching her, unaware? She blushed as her mind went to places she didn't want it going with anyone else around.

"I'll probably hold off for a while, but thank you." She stepped away from the podium, glancing down at the water, which showed only a few bubbles as evidence of whatever her session had taken out of it.

"Well, I've got a little research to do. I've decided to see how things are going down in the Living Waters. I spent some of the most meaningful time in my life there, made some friends I don't think I'd even be able to describe. I'd really like to see how things have worked out for them." He turned toward the podium, flipping the lever and staring at the mist growing inside the arch as if she weren't even there.

"I'll just let myself out then."

"Pleasant dreams," he said absently, then narrowed his eyes and slid his hands into the gloves.

Lila did have pleasant dreams more nights than not. The days began to take on a predictable crawl as she slowly returned to something like a routine. She soldiered through her initial ennui, which lessened as time went on, though nights were always hard. She avoided visiting the Sooth Mirror, preferring to spy on Avisse in her imagination from the comfort of her bedroom, sometimes with the help of toys or even the egg. Avisse's note from the Inkwell was maddeningly brief, and necessitated an additional use of the egg:

Leaving tomorrow. Trip is sixteen days but we'll be there in fifteen. Thinking of your mouth.

She finally joined Tera and Aven for dinner after a week or so. It was nice, though it did make her nostalgic for Avisse's company. She just had to make it through each day, each week. Before she knew it, Avisse's strong arms would be wrapped around her, hot lips pressed to hers, bodies coiled together like snakes in the dark.

She got several responses to her inquiries to the transcendent alchemists, though nothing solid. One afternoon, she received an unexpected in-person visit from one of them.

"Good afternoon, Lila." Sera, a transcendent woman known for making the high-end depilatory face cream Lila used, stood with a short, blue-haired person Lila had never met before.

"Sera, what a pleasant surprise!" Lila kissed the air around Sera's face, then reached out a hand to her companion, who took it awkwardly.

"This is Eulio, a colleague of mine who specializes in tinctures for masculinization and feminization. We've come to make you an offer."

Lila's eyebrows raised, and she ushered them into her office.

An hour later, they had hammered out an agreement to open a gender consultation clinic in the center, using the same office she used for marriage counseling, which was only occupied a few times a week. They would offer services to all who needed them on a graded scale, based on their ability to pay.

"There is a bottom limit, of course," Sera said apologetically.

Lila would get a percentage of their consultation fee, and all supplies would be purchased through the store. Sera did most of the talking. Eulio only spoke when asked direct questions. Their answers were brief and to the point, but it was clear they had considerable experience in the field.

"I love the space," Sera said as Lila showed them her consulting room, which had dried lavender bouquets, statuettes, and comfortable furniture. "The whole place, really. What you've done here is amazing."

"Oh, I don't know about all of that." Lila felt a blush coming on. She was terrible at accepting compliments.

"Word gets around," Eulio said. "People are impressed."

Why she was more embarrassed at the compliment from the taciturn blue-haired alchemist, she couldn't have said.

"Thank you," she managed. "I hope word of this clinic gets around equally well."

"There will be a few who will be annoyed at the competition," Sera said with a self-satisfied smirk. "But there is such a need for trust in this field, and there's no one I trust more than Eulio."

Eulio inclined their head.

"Then you have my trust as well." Turning to Sera, she added, "And I have your first client." Lila produced the gilded card Ms. Hentry had given her. Sera took it, studying it with eager eyes.

"First ring!" she exclaimed. "Painted faces?" she asked, eyebrows raised hopefully.

Lila nodded. "Nicest folks you'll ever meet. Gaven is the boy's name. Shall I have Tera set up the appointment?"

Sera handed the card back and stuck out a hand, which Lila shook.

"Let's change some lives."

14

They got a half-dozen appointment requests in the next week for the gender clinic, which Sera called The Lavender Room. Lila expanded the store's offerings to include Eulio's tinctures, kept behind glass and only available with an appointment. It was complicated, as appointments for minors had to be made before or after business hours, when the Pleasure Palace was closed. Alchemists were notoriously not morning people, and Lila didn't like having to keep the doors open late. She took turns with Tera and Aven, but since she lived on site, she was in charge after hours more often than not. Sometimes she took advantage of the empty baths, floating in the warm, soothing waters, staring at their shimmering red and orange reflections on the arched ceilings. It was nice being the only one there, if a little eerie. A thousand years of history were baked into that ceiling, and maybe a thousand more years beyond that in the room where Sylvan stood staring into the mist, looking back even further in search of some arcane truths only he would understand.

One evening as Lila was floating in the hottest corner of the baths, her back against the jet where the pump pushed scalding water into the pool, Sylvan emerged from the bronze door, satchel over his shoulder. His posture was slumped but his eyes dreamy as he walked halfway down the path between the pools, then stopped abruptly and turned toward Lila.

"Do you mind if I join you?"

"Not at all."

"I'll have to wash off my damned paint again, which I just put on, but I could use a good soak."

Lila closed her eyes and relaxed, glad she didn't have to worry about such ridiculous customs anymore. She enjoyed her makeup now that it was no longer a requirement, and it was a hell of a lot easier to get on and off. The tinkle of the shower sounded for a while, then a quiet sploosh announced Sylvan entering the pool. Ripples lapped over her chin as he approached and lay on the curved stone chaise next to her, his unpainted face just sticking out of the water.

"Now this I could get used to."

"I could add a bathing fee to your lease if you like." Lila smirked, opening one eye to see Sylvan's reaction. He smiled beatifically.

"Why not," he said. "It's only money, and at least here I know it's going to a good cause."

"It's just a business, Sylvan."

His eyes opened, and he turned to her, sitting up so his head and shoulders were out of the water.

"I think we both know it's more than that."

The water seemed to grow hotter in that moment. Lila wished she could duck under it and swim away like a seal. "If a business can support its owners and bring a little joy into the world, so much the better."

Sylvan shook his head, smiling gently. "That's not what I meant. Not that you aren't doing a world of good—you are. I'm talking about what this place means to you."

"What it—" Lila's mouth hung open, and she sat up too. "What it means to *me*," she repeated, almost to herself.

Sylvan sank back down into the water, half-closing his eyes.

"Never mind. I'm sorry I disturbed your soak."

"No, you're fine, you didn't..." Lila sank down too, turning the phrase over and over in her head. What did The World Within mean to her? Why had her heart run so wild when the idea had first popped into her mind?

They sat in silence, with only the gentle *sloosh* of the pumps and the trickle of the drains filling the air. The warmth of the bath and Sylvan's calming presence induced a meditative state. She gazed down at her pale body, undulating beneath the surface of the water, still a shade six where the sun never kissed her skin. She saw the tunnel of light where she'd faced her yearly examination when she was still painted, the increasingly pale stone, the little bells rung by the examiner peering in through the oval holes in the walls. The deeper bell always sounded at the sixth stripe, whose creamy tone matched her skin perfectly. For years, she'd dreaded that bell, but once she'd accepted herself as a girl, she'd suddenly seen it all for what it was: just another way for those in power to maintain their control. She'd remained painted until she was twenty-one, but it had become a different sort of mask for her by then.

She wondered what her life would have been like if she'd had parents more like Ms. Hentry. If there had been a Lavender Room for her to visit as a teenager. What her body would look like. What her face would look like. Would she be softer? Rounder? Would she have hips? Breasts? She wasn't sure she wanted those things now; she was proud of her body, with the exception of what was between her legs.

Some things were beyond the ken of even the greatest alchemists.

"If I stay in here any longer, they're going to have to skim me from the surface in the morning." Sylvan sat up, water streaming down his face and neck. "Thank you for letting me sit with you."

"We should do this again sometime."

Once Sylvan left, Lila rinsed off in the shower and put on one of the soft robes they kept in abundance in the dressing room, tossing her keys into the pocket. There was no point in getting dressed just to walk across the courtyard. She collected her things and was about to leave when she saw the gleam of the bronze door reflected in the water. She glanced toward the stairs where Sylvan had left; he was surely long gone by now. She fingered the big brass key in the pocket of her robe, hesitated for a moment, then strode down the walkway between the pools.

The silence in the circular room was eerily absolute. Each sandaled footfall down the stone steps echoed back to her in a thousand not-quite-synchronous iterations. She stood before the podium with its gleaming bronze tubes, the startlingly clear crystal ball, and the mesh gloves, whose texture she could feel on her fingers long before she touched them.

She shouldn't be doing this. She shouldn't even be here by herself late at night without Sylvan to step in if something went wrong. She was out of her depth, chasing a foolish vision.

She pulled the lever down. Mist rose from the water, filling the arch in seconds with an even layer of gray nothingness. She slipped her hands into the gloves, feeling a slight tingle as her fingertips slid in all the way to the solid ends. She closed her eyes, digging deep in her memory for the image she'd kept locked away for all those years: the woman in the paisley dress.

Lila had seen her at the market one day studying linens, non-painted but well off, wiry black hair pulled back by a simple yet elegant scarf. Her dress was a tan and purple paisley pattern, sleeves rolled up neatly past her strong forearms. It cinched tight at the waist, curving over her tight hips and high bosom, a perfect fit to Lila's young eyes.

She'd hardly considered wearing a dress at that point, though she'd studied her mother's and sister's wardrobes with great care. Something about the way this woman carried herself had struck Lila—not just her dress, nor her figure, nor her sharp-eyed expression as she expertly examined the weave of the cloth. It was the ease with which she carried her womanhood, the *strength* of her, that stuck in Lila's mind as she lay awake that night and many nights afterward. As she built up the image of the woman she wanted to become, she'd always look back to the woman in the paisley dress studying linens in the market. She was unpainted, unselfconscious, and unfettered by concern for anyone else's opinion of her. In Lila's mind, anyway, she was truly free.

Lila had often imagined herself living as that woman, choosing the colors and styles she would cover herself with. Sometimes she wondered, if she'd been born into a different body, what it would look like? Would she be slender like her mother or curvy like her sister? Would she be as tall as she was now? What kind of muscles would she have? Would her behind be round and jiggly or hard and muscular? And gods, what a nightmare it would be to have monthly cycles to deal with!

As she grew into her teenage years, sometimes she would strip naked and stare into the mirror, covering her privates and pushing her arms together to create the illusion of breasts. There was no way to tell what she would look like, of course, given how different people in the same family looked. And she didn't hate her body; she had well-defined muscles, her behind was nicely curved, and people of all genders seemed drawn to her. Still, she would have given anything to know what she would have looked like if her parents' seeds had mixed in a slightly different way.

Lila opened her eyes, and the mist faded. What she saw instead was a near-perfect reflection of the room, with brightstone lights, round walls, and a podium just like the one she was standing at, with a crystal ball and bronze tubes and a pair of gloves. The only thing different was the person standing at the podium.

She was half a head shorter than Lila, with copper hair worn in ringlets that dangled impeccably around her forehead and ears. She was painted a muted pink, with mauve on her full lips and around her eyes. She quirked a smile, her green eyes twinkling. Lila gasped as she recognized the look she had practiced in the mirror a thousand times.

This was *her*.

The woman's face was softer than Lila's, her cheeks wider, her chin more rounded perhaps, but the resemblance was no less clear. Below her painted neckline, her purple and black striped dress swelled with a modest bosom, and the curve of her hips was just visible around the edge of the podium. Lila sucked in a loud gasp, having forgotten to breathe for a moment. Tears streamed down her face, but with her hands in the gloves, she was helpless to stop them. The woman's brow furrowed, her kind face softening into an understanding smile. She looked Lila up and down and blinked approvingly, her smile widening.

Lila's tears poured forth, blurring the vision, and she craned her neck to wipe her eyes on her shoulder.

"My gods, you're..." She gasped for air between sobs. "You're so beautiful."

The woman closed her eyes slowly, then opened them again.

"I'm you." Her voice echoed through the chamber, or through Lila's mind—it was impossible to tell. Lila's body rippled with gooseflesh. This wasn't supposed to be possible—Sylvan had said this was a projection only. The image flickered, and the woman looked around the edges of the arch in annoyance.

"Wait!" Lila cried. "Don't go, you can't go, I—"

The image began flickering rapidly. The woman slid her hands out of her gloves, pressed them together at her chest, and vanished.

Steam rose with a hiss from the well, which was bubbling rapidly, its water frothy and pink. Lila slid her trembling hands out of the gloves and slumped against the podium, sliding down until she lay in a ball on the floor. Her brain felt empty, as if she'd just taken a hundred final exams and failed all of them. Her eyes fell on a rolled-up sleeping mat next to the stairs. She summoned the energy to unroll it and flop onto it.

She lay there, staring at the brightstone lights, listening to the fizzing of the well slowly die down. She was supposed to be feeling something. She was sure of it. But the lights were so bright, even when she closed her eyes. If she rolled onto her side, it was better. She could do this.

She could do this.

"I have to say, I'm less used to seeing you come in from that direction." Aven was adjusting something on the fountain in the lobby, tools spread out neatly on a rectangle of black leather.

"I...uh...yeah." Lila hadn't planned to sleep in the Well all night. She hadn't even known what time it was until she'd entered the lobby and seen the morning sun peeking through the round windows in the dome. "I was doing a little research."

Aven's brows raised, but they said nothing.

"Anyway, I'm going to go wash up and...I don't suppose you'd be a dear and roust up some breakfast?"

"They're such a dear they already did." Tera walked up carrying a tray heaped with pastries and fruit. "I'll just put the water on for tea."

Lila plucked a sugar flower from the tray, a habit she'd picked up from Theo, and tore a long strip off with her teeth.

"Mmm, did I ever tell the two of you how much I love you?"

"It's been quite a while, actually." Aven picked up a tri-fry, studying it for a moment before biting off a corner. "But it's never too late for kind words. And I love you too."

Tera blinked softly, her way of saying the same thing. "Remember, we've got that lingerie demo at noon," she said quietly, studying the pastry tray.

"Fuck, right, fuck!" Lila crammed the rest of the sugar flower into her mouth, picked up another one, and swept past them, calling over her shoulder. "Thank you! I'll be back in a flash!"

The lingerie demo drew quite the crowd, mostly painted faces, thanks to Sylvan, who had passed out little flyers at one of his parties. They'd used up all their chairs and benches, and scores of people crowded in behind them in the lobby, where a long red strip of faux velvet had been rolled out. High Waist had sent a musical duo featuring a goat-harpist and a singer, who wove ethereal melodies that enhanced the languid movements of the models.

Lila watched, spellbound, as the three of them took turns showing off the new line, which featured a lot of pastel colors with black trim. The lithe, androgynous model who'd accompanied the representative went first, followed by a full-figured woman who commanded the room with bold steps and jiggling spins. Last was a chiseled, angular man whose face was painted light blue, along with the rest of his body, in contrast to the high-waisted pink briefs he sported. She got the impression from the way he wore his paint that he was a painted face, but she'd never heard of a painted face modeling before. He bore neat scars under his pectorals; Lila knew some transcendent men underwent surgery, but she had never seen one up close. He was magnificent, and the cool fire in his eyes showed he knew it.

The models changed behind a screen between rounds, and when they'd shown off the full line, Lila brought them together by the fountain for a bow. Applause filled the domed room, impossibly loud, accompanied by a few whistles, which even got a smirk out of the stone-faced man in blue.

The scene in the store was chaotic as everyone crowded the displays after the demonstration. It took her, Aven, Tera, and two assistants over an hour to clear them all out. They sold more than half of the stock, and there were two more demos scheduled. This had turned out to be a lucrative deal indeed, not to mention the hundreds of poul worth of other merchandise the customers bought while they were there.

It wasn't until much later, when Lila was slumped in her office chair after closing time over a cup of lavender tea, that the tears welled up. She'd been so busy all day with the demo and the store and everything else that she hadn't had time to process what she'd seen the night before. The other-Lila. The one born in the body she'd always dreamed of.

Her chest felt hollow, light, as if something were missing. She clutched it with her hands, feeling the hard muscles there, perhaps a bit softer than they once were, as she hadn't been hitting the bars as much since she'd opened The World Within. But not soft like other-Lila. Not soft like Avisse. Not soft like a woman.

Lila clutched her pectorals tight, digging with her fingers so hard it hurt, and took in a deep, hitching breath. She knew this tune by heart, could sing it in three-part harmony in a round by herself. She *knew* it was horseshit. Knew it was just the brain-weasels chittering away in their little cage.

The brain-weasels could rot. She was a woman. A beautiful woman. A desirable woman. An eminently fuckable woman.

Other-Lila had looked at her with approving eyes. Plenty of people gave her a second, a third, and often a fourth look every day. And Avisse...Lila's hands relaxed a little, her pinkies brushing over her nipples as she thought of the things Avisse had done to her. The things she had done to Avisse. What they would do together when she returned.

Avisse's delivery was scheduled for just a week away. When she arrived, there would be no doubt. No hesitation. Lila was going to carry her straight up to her room, lock the door, and bury herself in Avisse's pleasure until they were both gasping for breath.

"How much do horses eat?" Lila asked Aven as they were reattaching a hinge in the door the next morning.

They paused, pulling a screw from their lips and setting it in the hole. "Depends on the horse and what they've been doing." They began turning the screw, crouching to get more leverage. "But I'd say maybe four to eight flakes of hay a day, plus grain if they're working horses." They grimaced as they torqued the screwdriver, sweat popping across their brow. "Why?"

Lila wanted to help them, but she didn't want to get dirty or sweaty, and maintenance was their job, not hers, except in emergencies. She crouched down next to them.

"What about water?"

"They drink a lot." Aven turned the screw a few more times, then paused, breathing deeply, resting their elbow on their knee. "Up to ten gallons a day. Which means they..." They made a delicate flicking gesture with their index finger.

"Oh, gods, that's a lot of piss," Lila said with a laugh.

"Which means a lot of wood shavings to soak it up. We used to get it by the cartload at my house. I would always get in trouble for tunneling in the piles whenever they dumped a fresh load at the stable." They turned back to the screw and finished it with a few hard twists, then stood and leaned against the door. "Why this interest in horses all of a sudden?"

Lila looked down, half trying to hide her smile. "I was just thinking how it would be nice if Avisse didn't have to stable her horses so far away when she's in town."

Aven pushed off the door, eyes lighting up. They raised a finger, then opened the door and stalked out into the courtyard, screwdriver still in hand, Lila on their heels. They walked past the carriage house and stood studying the weedy patch of gravel behind it. They marched to the corner of the house, put their back to the wall, then paced forward. They stopped, kicking aside the gravel, and squatted, tapping on something with their screwdriver.

"What is it?"

"Well, you live in the carriage house, right?"

Lila nodded, a smile growing as it dawned on her. "And it's called that because—"

"This was the corner post of the old stable. Which means the other one should be..." They lined up their arm at a right angle, walked a few paces, and kicked around until they found it. "Yep. There's room here for a stable big enough for two carriages and four horses, I'd say. Though I imagine you're picturing one about half that size."

"How did you guess?"

Aven paced around the space, studying the ground, the carriage house, and the sky, for some reason. They marched back up to Lila with the biggest smile she'd seen on their face since the day they'd forced Tera's mother to give up her Pureline inheritance early.

"I can build it for you before she arrives. Nothing super elaborate, but a roof and stalls for sure."

Lila pulled Aven in for a hug so crushing they wheezed. She released them, holding them at arm's length.

"Have I told you lately that I love you?"

"You can never say it enough, love."

15

Lila worked like a fiend the next week getting everything squared away before Avisse's arrival. She ordered extra supplies for the baths and spa, had another delivery of lingerie sent, and went to Alchemist's Row herself to bolster her stock of transcendent creams and tinctures. Ever since the Lavender Room began taking on clients, even folks who didn't use the service had started coming to The World Within for their supplies. Eulio and Sera offered brief consultations for one poul to transcendent folks who already had a regimen in place and just wanted to get their philters and infusions somewhere safer and less chaotic than Alchemist's Row. As they tallied up their take at the end of the day, Tera turned her ledger around and pointed to a chart showing two lines, a red one slowly descending and a blue one spiking.

"The red line is the high-end sex toys, including orders for Rontaian glassware, which as you know have mostly tapered off," Tera said almost apologetically. Lila withheld a sigh. She'd known that particular vein couldn't be tapped forever. "But the blue line is our alchemical department, which is more than making up for the difference. A lot of it is transcendent supplies, but we're selling more of the sensitivity and pleasure oils as well. And the cosmetics rack we opened got cleared out in two days."

Lila frowned, wondering if it was okay to be making money on people transcending. Most of them were painted faces, for whom money wasn't much of a concern, but not all.

"Can we cut the margins on the transcendent supplies and make it up elsewhere?"

Tera twisted her mouth, flipping through her ledger and running her finger down the page. "The margins on those are already the lowest of anything in the store since the cost is so high. Unless you want to give them away, I don't see how…"

Lila snapped her fingers. "Yes, that's exactly what I want to do."

Tera shook her head, eyes opened wide.

"We'll ask our wealthier clients if they'd like to sponsor the supplies for someone who can't afford them. Not everyone will, but I'm sure someone like Ms. Hentry would. I bet it would make her feel a little less guilty for the stacks of Pureline in her vault."

Tera raised her eyebrows, then nodded, making a note in her ledger. She pulled out the receipts box, flipping through the most recent ones.

"I noticed you've been stocking up on quite a few things. Bath supplies, spa oil, lingerie, not to mention the alchemical products." She smiled, thin-lipped. "Which is fine, of course; it will balance out in the end. I just wondered…"

Lila's stomach clenched; she knew the pressure Tera felt to balance the books. She had always hated that side of the business and was glad to have someone else to worry about it.

"I should have talked to you first. It's just, with Avisse coming in less than a week, I wanted to be extra prepared. I was hoping I might be able to take a little time off when she gets here." She glanced up sheepishly and saw Tera's smile bloom with warmth.

"Of course, how silly of me! You must be so excited!" She set the receipts down and folded her hands in front of her, fixing her glowing hazel eyes on Lila. "Aven's having far too much fun with your stable. I think they miss doing construction."

Aven had spent the morning directing lumber deliveries and herding a small army of carpenters as they worked on the frame. They seemed to relish being in charge, and it was cute seeing their sweet disposition take a turn for the firm with the crew.

"It was just a silly notion, but they really took it and ran with it." Lila smiled thinking of Aven's enthusiasm for the project.

"It's not a silly notion. It's the sweetest thing I've ever heard of. Like something in a heartstory."

Lila dabbed her eyes with her handkerchief. Not that she was crying, not yet. It was just a precaution.

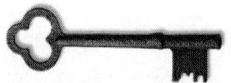

Lila kept her handkerchief at the ready over the coming days. She'd hear a carriage roll by or see a woman in a sleeveless shirt or smell a horse, and her eyes would start leaking for no reason at all. She threw herself into her work as a distraction, spending as much time on the floor of the shop as possible. It was nice, hand-selling lingerie, creams, and toys. She even had the pleasure of selling a full bondage kit to a quiet, yellow-painted woman with fierce gray eyes that absolutely glowed when she handled the straps, chains, and ollis.

"I understand you do...consultations as well?" the woman asked in a low voice, though there was no one else nearby.

"Of course! Check in with Tera at the front desk on your way out. She'll book you as soon as you're ready. You have someone special in mind?"

"My husband and I have...experimented, a little. I think he wants me to..." She paused, looking down at the case in her hands. Lila was sure she was blushing beneath her paint. "I want to surprise him for his birthday next week."

"I'll be sure and squeeze you in before then."

The woman's bright eyes and wide smile warmed Lila's heart and reminded her why she'd opened this shop in the first place. While she did miss the clientele of her shop in the fourth ring, it felt oddly righteous to help bring a little heat to the bedrooms of the painted faces. Maybe if they weren't so repressed, things like the morality clause that had been used to disinherit Lila would finally be stripped from the books. And maybe more families would be willing to help young people like Gaven find themselves before the world decided who they had to be.

The structures of power the painted faces represented wouldn't be torn down overnight. As Tera and Aven's Pureline shenanigans had shown, painted face society was resilient even when the fraud underlying its economic system was laid bare. They still ruled the economy of Anari and most of the South and kept those within their cloistered walls in line with manners and mores like steel spiderwebs. It would take generations to make a difference, and not everyone could be a rebel at open war with the system. Lila hoped the little world she was creating might be a small part of the change that needed to happen in the long run.

As the day of Avisse's predicted arrival approached, Lila grew increasingly unable to concentrate. She took up the bars again, working herself to exhaustion in the morning before the stable crew arrived and again in the evening by lantern light after they left. She knew it wouldn't make much difference, but she had to do something with her excess energy, and she could only pleasure herself so often. She vowed not to on the last two days, though her gaff grew tight and uncomfortable on her freshly waxed body. The slightest breeze or whiff of horse set her off, and she'd have to make excuses to run off to the next room just to move around and calm her loins. It was maddening.

On the last night, she visited Sylvan's round room once more after closing time. He was not there, much to her surprise. Perhaps he was catching up on his sleep to be ready for the big delivery. The ninety-nine percent purity crystal ball from the Silver Dock workshop would supposedly allow him to actually travel through the mirror, or through the Well—she wasn't quite clear how that would work—to see things far away in space or time.

It was beyond Lila's comprehension, and the more she thought about it, the less comfortable she was having it in the basement of The World Within. It seemed like the kind of thing the legends were always warning people about. Then again, looking into magic mirrors wasn't exactly encouraged, but here she was doing it one more time because she couldn't wait another day to see Avisse's face again.

Those deep brown eyes. That reddish-tan skin, rich and golden in candlelight. The knowing smirk as she closed for a kiss. Lila's hands were in the gloves and Avisse reclined in the carriage, laughing at something Theo had said. The door was open, letting in the sun's last rays, which would put them in sync, timewise. Avisse's shirt was untucked, her feet bare, her hair loose around her sun-kissed shoulders. Lila could almost smell the sweat and fresh air lingering around her neck. She inhaled through her nose, and for a moment she was there in the carriage, hearing Theo's scholarly voice, Avisse's amused retort, Theo's protestation. Tears bloomed once again, blurring the vision, but she didn't care. She closed her eyes and could see them still, smell the air, hear the laughter. It was as Theo had said.

Wherever my mother goes, there's a part of her that's inside you, and you in her.

Lila smiled. Annoyingly correct little brat.

It was the longest morning of Lila's life. She bought extra pastries from the cart, all the sugar flowers they had, as well as a heap of woodberry tarts, though the berries were out of season, so they only had the kind made with jam. She spent an eternity on her makeup, trying to keep it subtle but make her eyes pop. She picked her favorite dress, a lavender number with pink and purple flowers that gave definition around her chest and flared nicely at the waist.

She still had moments of that hollow feeling where her breasts would be if she had them; that wasn't going away, and it had been increasing a bit of late. But then she thought of Avisse's fingers on her chest, how her mouth lavished Lila's nipples with such fierce, delicate attentions. No woman was perfectly happy with her body, but when Avisse touched her, Lila felt like the most beautiful woman in the world. If that wasn't enough, she didn't know what was.

Lila was buzzing between the shop and the office, trying to figure out what to do with her hands, when one of the bath attendants came scurrying across the lobby, barely hidden panic written across her face.

"There's been an accident. We need a medical carriage right away."

"Aven!" Lila called out, her voice echoing much too loudly in the dome, catching the attention of everyone in the place. Aven hurried over, and she pointed them toward the attendant and crossed the lobby in as dignified a walk as she could, given the circumstances.

An older bather had slipped getting into the shower and hit her head. There was blood everywhere, including in one of the pools. Bathers milled about in an unruly naked line for the showers, talking in muted voices and casting sidelong glances at the injured woman. She was conscious and smiling, her neck propped up on a towel as the on-duty nurse tended to her wound. The nurse flashed Lila a curt smile.

"I keep telling him I'm fine. It's just a little bump on the noggin." The woman winced as the nurse held a bandage over the wound, wrapping a strip of gauze around her head to keep it in place.

"I'm sure you are, Ms. Kefa," said the nurse in a reassuring tone. "We're just going to secure this and keep you still until the medical carriage gets here."

"Oh, I'll be fine." The woman waved off the idea, pushing with her elbows to sit up, but the nurse put a gentle hand on her shoulder to keep her down. Lila knelt next to her, taking the woman's hand.

"I always prefer to listen to the medical professionals. They get awfully cranky when you don't." She winked at the nurse, then looked down at Ms. Kefa, whose eyes crinkled as she smiled, showing places where she'd failed to wash off her burgundy paint entirely.

"You would be too if you dealt with patients like me all day. My doctor doesn't even want me going to the baths. Says at my age, it's not worth the risk. I'm not going to tell her about this, that's for sure. I'd never hear the end of it."

"Not a word." Lila made a locking gesture at her lips and threw away the imaginary key. She noticed as she glanced down that she was kneeling in a pool of bloody water, which had soaked the bottom several inches of her dress red. She closed her eyes and forced a smile.

"I like your dress," the woman said, glancing over at her. Lila thought she might have stared at her chest for a moment before looking back up into her eyes. "The color really suits you. It's a shame I had to ruin it."

"Oh, nonsense. It'll wash right out."

The woman's eyes crinkled again. They both knew it wouldn't.

By the time the medics arrived, Lila had learned most of Ms. Kefa's life story, and that of her several grandchildren, one of whom was a no-good layabout who squandered his monthly pension without lifting a finger to add to the family coffers. As she was being lifted onto the stretcher, she invited Lila to visit her tailor for a new dress.

"I'd give you my card, but..." She gestured to the blanket covering her still-naked body. "Just tell them I sent you."

"I'll do that. And I'll come check on you later to make sure you're all right."

"I'm sure you have much better things to do with your day, pretty young thing like you." She winked and fluttered her fingers as the stretcher was carried up the stairs and out of the baths.

They had to close the baths for the day to drain, clean, and refill them. Lila stuck around to help smooth out the wrinkles with the clients, which took the better part of the day. It wasn't until she hurried back to her apartment to change that she saw the gleaming black carriage and the two horses, black and dappled, in her newly built stable. Her heart beat double time as she ran across the courtyard, threw open the door, and pounded up the steps.

Avisse stood at the kitchen counter, hands wet from the peppers she'd been chopping. The knife clattered to the cutting board as she turned and opened her arms just in time for Lila to sweep her off her feet and onto the opposite counter. Avisse's legs wrapped around Lila like a vise, and her lips locked onto hers tighter still, drawing Lila's tongue, her breath, her very soul into her. Their chests crushed together, filling the empty place inside Lila. For the duration of that hot, furious kiss, she felt whole again.

A shoe scuffed in the doorway. Lila came up for a breath, which turned into a wheezing laugh as she saw Theo standing with his hands clasped behind his back, the corner of his mouth turned up in a knowing smile.

Avisse wiped her mouth as she disentangled herself from Lila. "Sorry, kiddo. I thought you were studying."

"I was until I heard Lila thundering up the stairs, and then some strange smacking sounds. I thought I'd come to make sure everything was okay."

Lila covered her mouth and nose as a little snort slipped out, but Avisse maintained a remarkably straight face.

"I'm happy to report that everything is more than okay," she said with a tone of bemused condescension.

Theo brought his arms to his chest in an Endulian greeting, which Lila matched for a moment, then surged forward and swept him up in a big but gentle hug.

"It's good to see you, Theo! How's your paper with Sylvan coming along?"

"I submitted my part on time through the Inkwell." His eyes fluttered a little as he said the last word.

"He did it all by himself, he'll have you know." Avisse slid off the counter and touched Theo's shoulder fondly.

"I like to think if I'm grown enough to do research in the Great Library and publish scholarly papers with Doctor Kirin, I should be able to handle walking into a building and handing a packet of papers to a receptionist."

"*So* not a big deal." Avisse's hand slid up the back of his hair, and he shrugged her off.

"Well, I think it's a big deal," Lila said. "I wasn't allowed to use it by myself until I reached my first majority."

"I was thinking of applying for an early majority, actually."

"You were *what?*" Avisse's voice rose sharply, and not entirely in amusement.

"I did a little research when we were in Rontaia. It's a simple matter of passing some tests and having a parent and one other non-related adult certify that you are responsible enough to conduct your own affairs in the public sphere."

"A simple matter, you say? This from the child who has to be reminded to bathe twice a week?"

"Think of the advantages, mother. I could run errands for you when we're in town, conduct business for you. I could be a *partner* rather than a hindrance."

"You're not a—" Avisse closed her eyes and smacked her forehead, then pulled Theo close with the other arm. "I'm not ready to let you go off on your own just yet. There are people out there who might try to take advantage."

"Which is why I've begun my martial arts and knife training."

Avisse rolled her eyes as she pushed Theo to arm's length. "That's not what I mean. There are a lot of things in the world, a lot of situations—I just don't think you're ready."

"I'm not expecting this to happen overnight. I propose a one-year timeline, with certain mutually-agreed-upon goals and metrics. If I met or exceeded the expectations we laid out together, you would certify me."

Avisse glanced at Lila, who was watching, spellbound. "What do you think? Could he be ready in a year?"

Lila's heart fluttered at the question. Not at the thought of Theo gaining his majority early; he was probably close to ready, despite Avisse's unwillingness to let go. It was the fact that Avisse had asked her opinion on how to raise her child. Lila wanted to be part of Avisse's life, and she wanted to be part of Theo's life, too. This kid had lodged himself almost as deeply in her heart as his mother.

"He will be thirteen by then. That's only three years short of first majority. And we know that's bent for apprenticeships and the like all the time. And have you ever met a thirteen-year-old who can read in four languages?"

"Seven," Theo said quietly.

"Don't be a peacock," Avisse quipped. When she turned to Lila, there was worry in her eyes, but hope as well.

"Fair." Theo gave Lila a subtle nod of thanks, then turned his big eyes up to Avisse. "How about you take a few days to think about it and we discuss it on fourthday?"

"You've really thought this through, huh?"

"I do have a lot of time on my hands during the day. I can't read ancient Maer all the time."

"But you can…read ancient Maer?" Lila shook her head. She barely even knew what modern Maer was, let alone ancient. "You're definitely making a strong case for yourself."

"Which we'll discuss on fourthday," Avisse said with some finality. "In the meantime, we have quite a bit of catching up to do." She turned to Lila, glancing down at the hem of her dress, which was stained reddish-brown from the blood. "Starting with, what in Skundir's balls happened to your dress?"

"Oh, this poor old lady fell in the baths and hit her head. They had to take her away in a medical carriage. She'll be fine, but I spent all day dealing with it. When did you get in?"

"Just before noon." Avisse slipped her arms around Lila's waist and pulled her close, sending her heart racing. "Tera checked the cargo in. She told us about the bath fiasco. Sounds like a drag." She leaned in for a kiss, and the world disappeared. It returned with dizzying suddenness as their lips parted.

"I've forgotten it already."

"We need to get you out of that bloody dress and into something fresh." Avisse's voice had a low hum in it, sending vibrations through Lila's core.

"Shall I chop the rest of the peppers while you help Lila change?" Theo's voice was cheerful as he moved for the big knife. Avisse tensed, then relaxed.

"Careful with those fingers, kiddo. You've only got the ten of them."

Theo picked up the knife reverently, squared a halved pepper on the cutting board, knuckles facing the knife, and made a careful slice. He glanced up at Avisse for approval, and she blinked softly at him.

"A little thicker, and then square them. Leave one for me to slice into the salad."

She steered Lila toward the hallway, one gentle hand on her waist.

"What are we having?" Lila asked.

"Duck bone rice. My aunt's recipe."

"Ooh, I've never had that before. Sounds amazing."

Lila opened the bedroom door, and Avisse shut it gently behind her, leaning against it, biting her lip. She must have bathed and changed clothes, but she looked more rugged clean than most people did covered in dust. She pushed off the door, stalking casually across the room. Lila froze in place. She'd imagined being alone with Avisse every night for almost two months, but now that she was here, Lila couldn't move a muscle.

It didn't matter.

Avisse touched her gently, untying her laces and peeling her dress off like she was a porcelain doll. When Lila stood in nothing but her lacy pink evening gaff, which she'd worn all day for the occasion, Avisse ran her callused fingers over her body, sending frissons of delight everywhere she touched. Her lips ghosted over Lila's chest, brushing across her pebbled nipples, eliciting a whimper she could not contain.

"I've wanted you," Avisse whispered as her lips kissed a wet circle around each nipple, "so badly." Her hand slid down between Lila's legs, finding her cleft, rubbing with the most delicate swirls. "Every night." She laved Lila's nipple with her tongue, swirling, lapping, and flicking. Lila bit her lip to keep her moan inside her throat.

Avisse's fingers delved deeper, rubbing Lila harder now, sending her into a rapid spiral she was powerless to control. Her lips clamped down on Lila's nipple, sucking it into her mouth and pumping, pumping, sending fireworks exploding through her chest, her core, her mind. Avisse's fingers moved with furious strokes as the other hand gripped Lila's behind, nearly lifting her off the ground. Lila's mind left her body as she came; she would have slumped to the ground like a jellyfish had Avisse not held her up with her strong arms and slowly softening kisses.

When she finally had control of her legs again, Lila pulled Avisse onto the bed, cradling her face in her hands. They kissed slowly for some time until Lila's wet gaff and the silence from the kitchen told her it was time to get up.

The duck bone rice was delicious, rich and earthy, with enough fresh herbs and greenorange juice on top to keep it from becoming too heavy. Theo ate every bite without stopping to breathe, then sat with his hands crossed, patiently listening to Lila and Avisse chatting without interrupting them.

"You're awful quiet, sweetie," Avisse said after a while.

The corner of Theo's mouth turned up in a smile. "I like listening to you two talk."

Lila's heart fluttered at his words, then beat in her throat as Avisse took her hand and squeezed.

"Get used to it, because—"

Theo leapt up at the sound of the knock and was down the stairs before Lila realized what was happening. Sylvan's voice sounded below, intermixed with Theo's excited babbling.

"Sylvan's here!" Theo called up in a high, cheery voice. "He wants to show us something!"

16

"A simple test." Sylvan stood unpainted with his hands behind his back, a serene but smug smile on his face. The podium seemed to glow with the addition of the new crystal, which drew Lila's eye with its reflections of the brightstones in the ceiling and the bronze tubes around it.

"Lila, would you do the honors?" He held out a cup, which Lila took, peering cautiously inside. A pair of twenty-sided dice sat nestled in the felt lining, the kind used to play Slippery Slope.

"Okaaay," she said, dumping the dice into her hand. They were beautiful, cut glass with rounded edges and neatly carved numbers with perfect silver paint. Nothing but the best for Sylvan Kirin.

"Turn your back to me, and I'll turn away and cover my eyes with this." He held up a black hood, like what prisoners in paintings wore to their hangings. "Roll them on the floor, and everyone have a good look and remember the numbers before you put them back in the cup."

Lila shared a glance with Avisse, who smirked in amusement, and Theo, whose eyes were wide with excitement. Sylvan blinked at them, then turned around and pulled the ghastly hood over his head. Lila turned and crouched, then rolled the dice gently onto the floor.

Seventeen and four. She met everyone's eyes, let the dice sit for a moment longer, then snatched them back up and dropped them into the cup.

"Done," she said, standing and turning back toward Sylvan.

He tore the hood from his head, gasping and running his hands through his hair.

"Gods, that was unpleasant. Remind me to never do that again." He shook his head, then turned to the machine again. His face softened, his hands folding together for a moment, then he snapped back to them.

"As I said, a simple test. Rather than going back thousands of years or traveling across the Silver Hills, I'm going to try to travel in time and space just far enough to see what you rolled on those two dice. It should be much easier to access, and the risk should be lower as well."

"Risk?" Lila's heart clenched at the thought of something happening to Sylvan. He was a bit of a fool, but she'd grown quite fond of him, and it was hard to imagine The World Within without him.

"Well, I don't know of any *specific* risk; there's nothing in the texts that speaks of it. But reading between the lines, theoretically, you could become trapped wherever you go if you lose the thread you traveled on to get there. Reality is all connected, but the connections are not infinite; they're highly specific. Sometimes they get severed, and they can't always be reconnected. It's all very metaphysical, and I don't know if I'm explaining it properly, but...yes, there is some risk."

"So, you could disappear and just...never come back?"

"It's been known to happen, very rarely, with the cradles in the Endulian temples. People put on the circlets, lie back in the chair, and just...never wake up. I assume this would be no different."

"It's not very likely." Theo's small voice cut through the conversation. "According to most theorists, there are infinite ways to get to and from anywhere in the Thousand Worlds. So, if someone doesn't come back, it's because they don't want to."

"It's a short trip, so the risk should be minimal. At any rate, it's a risk I'm willing to take. Are you ready to witness history?"

Lila smiled as bravely as she could, her fingers clenched tightly around Avisse's.

"Technically, you're the one who'll be witnessing history," Theo commented.

Sylvan smiled as he flipped the lever and slid his hands into the gloves. The bronze arch glowed brightly, the space within it immediately forming a perfect silver sheen like a mirror. Sylvan closed his eyes, smile fading, face growing slack. Lila hardly breathed as she stood watching him sink into his meditative state. The water began bubbling, and the mirror seemed to vibrate, then Sylvan sort of flickered as if a shadow had passed across him for an instant. The mirror went dark, then faded. Sylvan slid his hands out of the gloves and leaned against the pedestal, eyes bleary and weak.

Lila rushed forward and slid her shoulder under his arm to support him. He smiled faintly, accepting her help to return to standing. His eyes slowly cleared, and his smile broadened as he pulled away from her support and stood under his own strength. He glanced at the cup she still held in her hand, then back into her eyes.

"Four and seventeen," he said, his smile blooming into an enormous smirk as he saw their reactions. "Four and seventeen!" he shouted, his joy echoing off the curved walls. Theo jumped up and down and began shouting along with him, wrapping Sylvan in a big hug, then running over to hug Avisse and Lila in turn. Their enthusiasm was contagious for a while, but as Lila stared at the still-steaming water and the eerily clear glass globe with its array of bronze tubes, a shard of worry lodged deep in her heart.

"Just so we're clear," Avisse said in a sharp voice, "Theo's hands are not going in those gloves." She eyed Sylvan and Theo in turn, then Lila, who blinked reassurance. Sylvan pointed a stern finger at Theo.

"Absolutely not. You're not of majority, for one, whatever schemes you may be cooking up, and your mother would quite literally kill me, so no."

"I didn't ask," Theo said, feigning offense and hurt, though perhaps it wasn't entirely pretend. Lila was sure he had a million questions he'd like answers to. She stared at the crystal ball, wondering what truths it might hold for her if she were only bold enough to ask.

Lila read on the bed by lamplight while Avisse waxed her boots. She'd offered to do it outside, but Lila had insisted. She loved the smell of wax and the sight of Avisse's muscles as she brushed, wiped, and polished. It was homey, having her perform this mundane task in the bedroom, knowing Theo was reading just down the hall unless he'd fallen asleep already. It was like they lived here. Like they were a family.

Lila turned her eyes back down to her book, but the word swam in her vision.

Family.

Was that where this was headed? If she and Avisse found a way to make this work, would that make Lila part of their family? She pictured Theo's little rhetorical flourishes, his reflective pauses, his smiles of delight. Lila didn't deserve to be part of such a family. She was a peddler of sex toys. A purveyor of filth. A Bad Example to the Youth. And a transcendent woman to boot.

"I'm going to go check on Theo." Avisse leaned over to kiss Lila on the cheek, then stood and placed her freshly shined boots on one of the shelves Lila had cleared out for her. She opened the door quietly and slipped out. Lila leaned sideways to watch her pad down the hall, slowing as she approached the study. She peered around the doorway cautiously, then straightened and spoke. Lila couldn't hear what she was saying, but obviously, Theo was still awake. Avisse disappeared into the room. The murmur of their conversation was too muffled to make out. Lila tried to read, but to no avail, and soon Avisse was padding down the hallway again.

She scooched onto the bed facing Lila, who was propped up against the wall with several pillows. "Theo's still awake, reading one of your books on the Thousand Worlds, actually. He says he hopes to...how did he put it? 'Contribute to the practical application of the philosophical' or some such."

"Sylvan does need someone to keep him grounded, I suppose."

"Yes, but why does it have to be my *son*?" Avisse's forehead fell on Lila's knee, then she pushed up on one elbow, stopping to kiss her knee gently. "I do worry about this, honestly. Not for Theo, not exactly. He won't put his hands in those gloves. But what if something happens to Sylvan? Losing important adults in his life, not exactly what Theo needs right now."

"C'mere." Lila reached out her arms. Avisse moved over and snuggled into her chest, draping her body over Lila's. "I think you're right to worry, and I'm going to have a talk with

Sylvan. I don't think he should be using the Well with Theo around."

They sat in silence, bodies melting together, staring at the static shadows on the ceiling.

"What would you want to see?" Avisse craned her head up to look into Lila's eyes. "If you went into the Well."

Lila felt a blush as she realized she hadn't told Avisse what she'd seen in the mirror. "About that." She shifted sideways, and Avisse sat up against the wall, eyebrows raised, perhaps sensing her tone. "Before you brought the crystal, the real one, Sylvan had another crystal, a something something purity one, not enough to travel through the Worlds, but enough to create what he called a Sooth Mirror."

Avisse crossed her legs, eyes serious, nodding along.

"Anyway, it lets you think about anything you want and see...not exactly the truth maybe, but something between what you imagine and the truth? I'm not quite sure how it works, but...I used it to check in on you while you were traveling, to see if you were okay." Lila looked down, cheeks hot, picking her fingernails, suddenly feeling very guilty for this invasion of privacy. Avisse's hands folded over hers, warm and soft, except for the rough spots from her calluses.

"You mean you could ask to see anything in the entire history of the universe, and you wanted to check in on little old me?" She raised Lila's hand to her lips and kissed it, her eyes dark and soft in the lantern light. "What was I doing?"

"Sleeping, the first time, curled up next to Theo. Is that...do you...?"

Avisse smiled, nodding. "When it's not too hot. He's snuggly in the carriage, but never anywhere else. Kind of strange, now that I think of it." She scooted closer, letting one hand drop to Lila's thigh. "You said the first time. There were other times?"

"I saw you eating at a picnic table, with lights."

"The inn outside Tralum. They make the best mushroom stew."

"And on the way back, arguing with Theo about something."

Avisse chuckled. "That could have been anywhere."

Lila fondled Avisse's fingers, thinking about the times she'd seen her through the mirror. If those visions were true, what did that mean about other-Lila? Was she as real as Avisse and Theo? Was she alive in one of those alternate realities people like Sylvan loved to talk about at parties? She'd been a painted face, so in her reality, she hadn't escaped. Was she married? Lila hadn't noticed a ring, but she'd been distracted. Maybe other-Lila had been a disappointment to her mother too, for entirely different reasons. Maybe that was a constant throughout all realities.

"Something on your mind, love?"

Lila sniffed, blinking away would-be tears. "No, just..." She pulled out a handkerchief and turned away to dry herself off.

When she turned back around, Avisse was watching her with kind but wary eyes. Lila sighed.

"Okay, yes. I wondered...I asked the mirror what I would look like, if I had been born...in a different body." She gestured toward her chest and downward. "You know." She paused, biting her lip as tears surged forth. Avisse took her hand, holding on gently, her soft eyes never wavering. Lila dabbed her eyes again, taking in a deep, shaky breath.

"And obviously I've gone through all of this before, but when I looked into the mirror and I *saw* her, I guess it really hit me differently. She was pretty, really pretty—looked a lot like me, but a little softer around the cheeks and chin. And she had..." Lila gestured toward her chest, staring down at their intertwined hands, unable to meet Avisse's eyes. Her tears had started again, but she let them flow.

"She was painted, which I guess shouldn't have been a surprise, since I probably still would be if it weren't for...me being the way I am. But then I think, if I were still painted, I'd be living that cloistered life right now, bound to a thousand little rituals and traditions, kept in a cage of the finest silk. I'd never have found out who I truly was. I'd never have met *you*."

Avisse scooted closer, releasing Lila's hand and cupping her cheek. "You are," she said, her face closing in slowly, "without a doubt," her eyes glassy in the orange light, "the most amazing woman I have ever met." Her lips were soft and warm, her kiss slow and tender. Her strong hands fell lightly on Lila's shoulders, sliding down her arms, leaving goosebumps in their wake. Soon her tongue was hot and wet in Lila's mouth, her touch less gentle as she wrestled Lila away from the wall and pinned her flat on the bed. Lila wrapped her legs around Avisse, who bore down with her taut body, devouring her lips and gripping her biceps so hard Lila feared they'd bruise. If Avisse kept this up much longer, Lila would spill, and she desperately wanted to get her mouth on Avisse. Lila gripped her behind with both hands, bucked with her hips, and flipped her over.

Avisse gave a little squeak of surprise, then grinned up at Lila, whose hands were already grabbing at her shirt. Avisse yanked it the rest of the way over her head, her pert breasts jutting up as she did so, one of them right into Lila's eager mouth. She devoured Avisse like a famished beast, lavishing each sensitive spot with an excess of attention as her fingers explored the wonderland of Avisse's muscles, curves, and perfect angles. Avisse writhed beneath her touch, biting her own wrist as Lila kissed her way between her legs and lost herself in a labyrinth of ecstasy.

The world outside ceased to exist, stars flying by like Solstice streamers as she chased Avisse's pleasure with fingers and tongue. When Avisse arched off the bed so soon, twisting away from Lila's grip, she rode her down, kissing her way back up her stomach and across her breasts to find her lips again. Avisse held her close as they kissed, fondling Lila gently, filling her with a growing lightness. Her hand pulled away, and Lila heard the sound of a lid being opened. When her hand returned, it spread buttery smooth cream all over Lila's gaff, massaging her cleft with maddening thoroughness.

Avisse sat up, pushing Lila down this time. She shifted so one of her legs was beneath Lila, the other atop her in a feat of flexibility Lila would never have been capable of. Avisse lifted one of Lila's legs into the air, pressed against her cleft, and began moving.

"Does this feel okay?" she whispered.

Lila winced, sliding her fingers down to make sure the gaff was arranged to keep her balls from getting squished against her leg, then nodded. Avisse's face grew serious as she pressed against Lila, grinding slowly. The slick pressure through the silk of the gaff almost sent Lila over the edge. She clenched her teeth, closing her eyes and picturing the slow grind of a millstone, which brought her back from the precipice. Avisse tweaked her angle and sped up her movements, the individual muscles in her shoulder showing as she gripped Lila's leg. Sweat beaded on her forehead, and her breasts swayed with each thrust as she pressed one palm into Lila's thigh for leverage.

Lila came unmoored at the sight of her, the desperate fire in her eyes, the corded muscles in her neck. Avisse's breath came in strained hisses as she slid against Lila with frenzied speed, sending her to an oblivion of euphoria. Lila's entire body trembled along with Avisse's as she came, their bodies fusing as if by lightning, then collapsing, spent and heaving, into an unruly heap.

The sliver of moon outside the window cast the room in a magical glow. Lila lay staring at the ceiling, fingers intertwined with Avisse's. This couldn't be real. None of this could be real. The most amazing woman in the world wasn't lying in Lila's bed, having just made love to her more times than she could count. Her brilliant, talented son surely wasn't asleep down the hall, now seeing this as a home away from home, and Lila as something more than just an acquaintance of his mother's. Her outlandish business idea of a luxury boutique in the second ring, complete with a bathhouse, massage parlor, and meditation center, wasn't successful beyond her wildest dreams. And she certainly hadn't opened up the city's first reputable transcendent consultation service. None of this could be happening. Surely she had entered Sylvan's Well of All and was living in an alternate reality.

17

The morning air blew fresh down Lila's collar as she strode back through the gate, a bag of pastries in her hand. The smell of horses and hay drifted over from the stable, where a gentle nicker sounded as she passed. She wanted to go to the horses and touch them, but without Avisse, she didn't know if the gesture would be welcome. She tiptoed up the stairs, avoiding the ones that creaked, and set the bag down on the kitchen table softly, so the paper wouldn't crinkle. She slowly poured a kettle of water and set it on to boil, then crept to the bedroom door, which she'd left open a crack. Theo's door was still closed. Silence reigned throughout the apartment.

Avisse was sprawled out, somehow managing to take up the entire bed despite her diminutive stature. Lila folded her body around Avisse's, nestling into her warmth. Avisse let out a noise between a purr and a growl as she clutched Lila's hair and pulled her in for a sleepy kiss. Her eyes fluttered open, glassy and soft.

"I missed you." She pulled Lila in for another kiss, lingering this time before pulling back and biting her lip.

"I only went out to get pastries, silly."

"You were gone too long."

Avisse slid one arm down to her waist and pulled Lila on top of her, wrapping her legs around her and kissing her deeply. Lila melted into her, sliding against her, heat and breath building so fast she feared she would lose control. Avisse gripped tight with her thighs, grabbed Lila's ass, and bucked off the bed, flipping Lila off and rolling to straddle her. Lila glanced in panic at the door, giving a sigh of relief as she saw that she'd closed it behind her. Avisse gripped Lila's chest, twisting through her dress as she tightened her thighs and ground against her, eyes hot and hard. She leaned in and seized Lila's lips, her body moving in long, steady strokes. Her fingers wormed their way into Lila's dress and found their targets, pinching and twisting hard, so hard. Lila gasped into the kiss, her arms flopping to the sides as she surrendered. Avisse rode her with steady strength, holding her tight until the very end, clamping a hand over her mouth when she moaned in unbridled pleasure.

They lay entangled in ruined clothes, the pads of their fingertips gently touching, staring at each other through the motes of dust dancing in the sunbeams. The gate opened and closed, then the main door. Tera, from how quietly the door closed. Aven was a bit of a slammer. A carriage rolled by in the street. The city was waking up. But the apartment was still quiet. Except for the bubbling of the water, which was probably half boiled-out by now.

"I'm going to get some tea steeping, then wash up and put on a clean dress. I may have to start charging you for my laundry bills."

"I figure services rendered and all of that."

Avisse squeezed Lila's ass and gave her a quick peck on the lips. Lila pushed her away gently, then stood up and shed her dress, which was soaked and sticky, and her gaff, which was worse. She stood facing away from Avisse, then felt guilty about it and turned around, which she felt awkward about too. The way Avisse leered at her made her feel awkward in a different way. She grabbed a robe and pulled it around herself before things got even more awkward.

"Don't get dressed on my account."

"I'm going to go get washed up. Pick me out a dress."

"Ooh, okay! I love dressing you almost as much as undressing you." Avisse popped out of bed and ran over to Lila's wardrobe. Lila turned away quickly, as the sight of Avisse's ass in that nightgown was pushing her in the wrong direction. Tea, that was it. Set the tea to steep, then wash up and get dressed.

She made a pot of darkroot with cloves and went to the washroom to clean up and check her makeup. As she reapplied the smudged edges of her lipstick, she cocked her head toward the door. Something wasn't quite right. Something was missing. She quickly touched up her lipstick and opened the door, staring around the hallway to see what could possibly be nagging at her brain. A few pictures on the wall, a chest of drawers with a few knickknacks on it and a bowl of keys, a coat rack, and a crate of sample glass figurines she'd been mulling over for the shop. Her eyes returned to the chest of drawers and the bowl of keys, which was not as full as it should have been.

Most notably, the ring with the shop keys and the big brass key for the big bronze door in the back of the baths was missing.

Something about the way Avisse stood in the doorway to Theo's room made Lila's stomach drop. She looked smaller, her usually proud shoulders slumped in defeat. She picked at the door frame for a moment, then straightened and turned slowly around, her tear-streaked face hardening by the second.

"Sylvan better hope to all the ancient gods and the Thousand Worlds beyond that Theo is safe and sound right now because if he put his hands in that machine and—" She closed her eyes, clenching her fists so tight her knuckles cracked. Lila's heart felt like it was being squeezed inside one of those fists. Avisse pushed past her into the bedroom, and Lila followed, pulling on clothes and shoes in tense silence next to Avisse. They rushed past the steaming teapot and the bag of pastries and trampled down the stairs. Lila led them across the empty courtyard, propelled by the wave of Avisse's rage and her own sense of guilt.

"I'm sure it's—"

"Don't say you're sure when we don't know where my fucking son is!" Avisse snapped. Lila died a little inside, but she swallowed it and kept walking. She deserved that.

"I'm sorry, you didn't deserve that." Avisse caught her hand, and Lila gave it a quick squeeze.

"It's fine. Let's just go find Theo."

The lobby was quiet. The only sounds were the burble of the fountain and the twittering of the snowbird that had flown in and nested in one of the dome's windows. They dashed across the lobby, through the padded doors, and down the stairs to the still-silent baths. The bronze door gleamed in multiple reflections across the pools as they hurried toward it. Lila reached into her pocket for the key, which of course was missing. She tried the large, polished handle, but it wouldn't budge. Avisse shouldered her out of the way and yanked on the handle, putting all her weight into it, but it was as solid as the door and would not be moved. Avisse pounded her fists against the door, her shouts of guttural rage echoing through the long room. Lila wanted to touch her, tell her something to make it all right, but Avisse was a bomb ready to explode. She turned, the lines on her face jagged with fury.

"*Sylvan.*"

She brushed past Lila, stalking down the walkway between the baths. Lila hurried after, catching up as Avisse reached the stairs. Tera stood on the landing, worry etched on her face.

"What's wrong?"

"Theo's missing," Lila said, stepping forward. Avisse stood breathing through her nose, hands balled at her sides.

The faint pinkish tint blanched from Tera's face, and she glanced toward the bronze door. "You don't think..."

Lila closed her eyes and nodded, head swimming, trying to keep it together for Avisse. For Theo. "The key was missing this morning. Have you seen Sylvan?"

"Not since last night. He said he wouldn't be staying late. Said using the Well is quite taxing, so he can only do it once or twice before he has to sleep."

"Has Ferdie been in yet?"

"She should be checking in shortly."

"Have her get Sylvan right away. Tell him to get his ass over here right now or Avisse is going to rip it out and feed it to him. Is that clear?"

Tera covered her mouth, her face reddening a little. Lila wasn't sure, but Avisse's nose-breathing might have veered toward a snort just for a moment.

"Yes, ma'am."

"The baths will be closed until further notice. Please make the necessary arrangements. You might want to call Aven in early."

"Understood. They'll be here soon anyway."

"Meanwhile," Lila said, turning to Avisse and sliding her fingers into one of her fists, forcing her fingers to uncurl, "you and I are going to sit down and have a cup of tea and something to eat. This may be a very long day and we'll need to maintain our strength."

Avisse's hard eyes softened just a bit as tears flowed anew. She glanced back at the bronze door, gave a single nod, and let Lila lead her back up the stairs.

Avisse moved stiffly, holding Lila's hand, through the lobby and across the courtyard. Lila pulled out a chair at the kitchen table, and Avisse sank into it, staring blankly at the floor.

"Let me just pour out this tea and brew some fresh. It's bound to be bitter as death by now."

"No, pour me a cup. You always make it too weak." Avisse's lips twitched in the direction of a smile.

Lila smirked and poured a cup, which was so dark it made her tongue curl just to look at it.

"Extra honey, extra cream." She pulled the cream from the coolbox and mixed the tea, though she couldn't get it the color Avisse usually drank it.

"Mmm." Avisse raised her mug, wincing. "Just what my nerves need." She set the mug down, and her hands immediately began moving. They found the pastry bag and tore it open, revealing an unnecessarily large number of pastries. She plucked a sugar flower and studied it, eyes suddenly streaming with tears. Lila reached across the table and took her hand. Avisse clenched her fingers tight, covering her face with her other hand as she sobbed, a rumpled sugar flower dangling from her fingertips.

Lila's tears flowed along with Avisse's, and she scooted closer, holding her hand as she watched her lover fall apart.

In time, weeping was replaced with devouring pastries and making tea. They watched out the window for Sylvan's arrival, too on edge to do anything else. Lila felt the first nubs of stubble on her cheek, but it felt selfish to worry about shaving while Theo was missing and Sylvan could come rolling up any minute.

It seemed to take an eternity. Groups of would-be bathers had begun to show up and be politely turned away by Tera and Aven, who were kept more than busy dealing with the rather major inconvenience. The courtyard was more crowded than usual as a result, so when Sylvan's carriage finally did arrive, it took an excruciatingly long time for it to advance far enough for him to step out and come face to face with Avisse, who was vibrating like a top stuck in a divot.

He bowed his head, holding out the key. When he looked up at Avisse, his green eyes were shot through with red, and his gray paint was streaked with tears.

"Enough." Avisse snatched the key from his hand and stalked across the courtyard. Sylvan eyed Lila, who hurried after, motioning him to follow with her chin.

"I can't imagine him trying to actually use the Well," he whispered as he struggled to keep up with Lila's strides, a full five paces back from Avisse. "And even if he tried, I can't imagine—"

Avisse whirled around, eyes ablaze with fury, arms bowed at her sides. Sylvan wilted toward Lila, who kept her distance. He was on his own on this one.

"What you can't imagine, Sylvan," Avisse spat, "is what I'm going to do to you if Theo is not sitting there safe and sound in your little room." Tears rolled down Sylvan's cheeks, his mouth half-open in horror, though not, Lila thought, at what Avisse was threatening. "What you can't *imagine*, Sylvan Kirin, is what I'll do to you and your family if anything happens to my son because of what *you* did!" She stuck a finger in his chest, and he staggered backward, yelping in pain. Lila took a half-step toward Avisse, who cocked her head toward her, eyes still blazing hot.

"We need his help, baby," Lila said with all the cool her frazzled nerves could muster. "Sylvan fucked up, and Sylvan is going to fix it, aren't you, Sylvan?" She turned to Sylvan, who stared at his hands, shell-shocked, for a moment. "Sylvan?" Lila barked.

He snapped to attention, running a hand across his tear-smeared cheeks. "Yes, yes, of course. We have to get down there right away and see what's even happened. Maybe—"

"Maybe you live to see the sun set today." Avisse whirled back around and stormed through the door, which banged against the wall and hung open. The handful of clients in the lobby stared as Lila hustled Sylvan through the door and closed it gently behind her. It didn't want to close right; she had to lift it to keep it closed. Avisse had broken it in her rage.

Whatever. It would give Aven something to do. Avisse was already through the bath doors. Lila ran through the lobby, dragging Sylvan along with her, heedless of the gawking stares of the handful of people milling about.

They caught up with Avisse as she was trying to open the door. The lock turned in a peculiar way, which had taken Lila a few tries to get used to. Avisse was torquing the key too hard, and Lila was worried it might break, strong though it was.

"Would you let me..."

Avisse's stiff posture relaxed with a great huff. She stood aside, glaring poison daggers at Sylvan as Lila opened the door. Avisse stormed through it, down the hall, and to the other door, which was locked as well. Avisse stood with arms braced against her hips, her breath fast and shallow as she watched Lila fumble with the key. It had grown slippery with nervous sweat, and this lock was a little trickier than the other one.

"Come on come on *come on*," Avisse hissed, her voice rising with each utterance.

The lock clicked, and Lila turned the knob. She looked into Avisse's desperate, bloodshot eyes, gave what she hoped was a reassuring blink, and pulled the door open.

The round room was empty, except for the arch, the podium, and the work desk. A small stack of books sat on the desk, one of which Lila recognized from her library, a book of meditations on time and the Thousand Worlds. She'd bought it when she was in her philosophical phase, but she'd given up reading it a third of the way through. Avisse rushed to the podium and picked up a small object, which she studied with rounded, sagging shoulders. Lila approached cautiously, seeing now that Avisse was shaking with quiet sobs. She came around the side, so as not to alarm her, and saw that Avisse was holding a small picture frame with a painting of a woman. She had reddish-brown Naeili skin, long braids, and a warm smile that was matched by a twinkle in her dark brown eyes.

"Jillia," Avisse said softly.

"She was—" Lila's chest flooded with grief as she realized what this meant.

"He's gone looking for his dead mother."

A strange noise sounded from behind, like a sack of laundry being tossed down a set of stairs. Lila turned to see Sylvan crumpled on the floor, unconscious.

Sylvan stirred after the third time Avisse slapped him. He looked around, confused, his face twisting in horror as Avisse reared up and slapped him once again, extra hard.

"Ow!" he shrieked, scrabbling away from her and covering his face with his hands.

"You do *not* get to fucking pass out on me when it's *my* son who's disappeared into your fucking machine!"

Avisse held her arm half-cocked for another slap, easing it slowly as the anger flowed out of her face. Fatigue and deep sadness took its place. Lila put a tentative hand on her back, and Avisse leaned into her.

Sylvan pushed himself to standing, rubbing the back of his head and wincing. "So, I really just...passed out?"

"Dropped like a sack." Lila demonstrated with her arm.

He shook his head, wandering toward the well, where he crouched, shaking his head some more. "The water's completely uncharged. The Well must have been on for hours and just burned through its conductive capacity."

"Try saying that in Southish," Avisse snapped.

"I need to add some more minerals to re-balance it before we can turn it back on."

"And what happens then?"

"I don't know...In theory, he should be able to come back the same way he got in."

Avisse stepped closer to Sylvan, who tried to back away but bumped into the arch. "I don't need your theories, Sylvan. I need..." She jabbed a finger into his chest, pressing him against the arch, which swayed slightly at the pressure. "My son back." She released the finger, and Sylvan let out a long, shaky sigh. He swallowed, then nodded, gently at first, then more vigorously.

"If he doesn't come back right away, I'll go in and find him." He turned toward the podium, his eyes fixed on the crystal globe. "I've worked with him, talked scholarship with him.

We have a connection. I should be able to find his thread and follow him easily enough."

Avisse turned to Lila, biting her lip, eyes wet with worry. Lila looked at Sylvan, who was so focused on the crystal he hardly seemed to notice her.

"I should go." The words chilled her as she spoke them, but a warmth followed close behind at Avisse's trembling smile. "I've used the gloves, so I'm sure I can figure it out. We need Sylvan to fix the machine in case anything *else* goes wrong—" Lila stared Sylvan down, as his eyes showed he was ready to protest his machine's innocence. "And besides. I hope to someday be Theo's family. I like to think we have a bit of a connection."

Avisse flung herself at Lila, who staggered back as she caught her.

It took Sylvan nearly an hour to drain, re-fill, and balance the water using a variety of powders, tubes, and colored liquids. Avisse paced from the Well through the baths, up the stairs, and back, giving Sylvan increasingly impatient glares with each pass. Lila sat on the floor and tried to meditate, difficult as it was with Avisse storming in and out every couple of minutes. She used that rhythm to anchor herself as she sat facing the bronze arch, which had a pleasing symmetry. It made it easier to empty her mind of the worry of what she was about to do. The thought of entering the Thousand Worlds with her body and mind was more than a little terrifying, but what she'd seen through the Sooth Mirror gave her hope. She'd seen only pleasant things, only things she'd chosen. Surely the same would be true for Theo. She pictured his big, bright eyes, the ones he used on Avisse when he was trying to soften her up. Her mouth turned toward a smile. She would find him and bring him back.

"That's it!" Sylvan shouted as mist rose along the inside of the arch, forming a uniform sheen. Running footsteps approached, soles smacking stone, echoing down the hall. Avisse burst through the door and skittered down the steps, heaving and wide-eyed.

"The Well is ready," Sylvan said solemnly, gesturing toward a tube of pink water in a wooden stand as if that was supposed to mean something to them. He glanced at Lila, then at the podium. The three of them approached, staring at the gloves, the tubes, the crystal ball.

"What's happening?" Avisse said in a strained voice. "Where is he? Is he coming back?"

Sylvan winced, touching the lever, which was still in the *on* position.

"In theory, he should be able to come back now. I suspect he'd feel the tug on his tether and—"

"If my boy doesn't appear in the next ten seconds, you're going to feel more than—"

Lila raised a finger, taking a step forward, and Avisse stopped, still glaring at Sylvan. Lila's head was light as she approached the podium. Avisse took her hand and turned her sideways.

"Bring my baby home." She pulled Lila in for the briefest kiss, then released her and took a soft step back.

Lila turned to face the gloves, glowing golden in the room's oddly cozy array of lights. She salivated at the thought of them, the feel of her fingertips touching the pads, tapping into that power. She shook her head. *Theo.* What was it he'd said? *Wherever my mother goes, there's a part of her that's inside you, and you in her.* The same was true for her and Theo. On some level, he *was* family. And she was going to bring him home.

She stepped closer, lowering her fingers toward the gloves, whose dark interior looked cool and inviting. She glanced up at Sylvan, who stood frittering at his fingernails, eyeing her nervously.

"Anything different than before I need to know about?" Lila's stomach was a great yawning chasm threatening to suck her and the entire world into its endless void.

Sylvan cocked his head, and his hands stopped moving for a moment. He raised a hand, holding his thumb and index fingers close together.

"Right before you…go all the way in, you may feel a slight pinch on the back of your neck." He reached behind his head to demonstrate. "And you sort of…reel yourself back in by that point." He threw his hands up in the air. "It's the best way I can explain it. I don't even know if your experience will be the same as mine, but that's what it felt like for me. There was really nowhere to go *but* back once I'd reached the spot I'd projected into."

Lila rubbed the back of her neck. Her stomach roiled at the idea, acrid warmth rising up the back of her throat. She swallowed and shook her head.

"Okay. Okay." She took a deep breath and thought of Theo, the first time she'd seen him, hair blowing wild and free in the courtyard. She slid her fingers across the mesh of the gloves' palms, closing her eyes as her hands slid all the way in.

"Whenever you're ready," Sylvan said quietly from beside her.

Lila let Theo's face dance in her mind's eye and counted her heartbeats. One. Two. Three. Four. Five.

She slid her hands all the way in.

18

What surprised Lila most was the silence. It enveloped her like a duvet, keeping any tendrils of sound from sneaking in. Rather than the misty gray screen of the Sooth Mirror, she saw only darkness, pierced in the distance by a haze of stars. She was in the darkness, and the darkness was moving. Swirling. Flashing with coppery light, hidden strands revealing themselves for an instant before being buried again in clouds of inky void.

One strand did not hide from her. It rose from within her, piercing the murky nothingness, curving off into the distance, warm and familiar as the dawn.

Theo.

It pulled her along like a kite, buffeted by unseen winds. Soon she learned to make herself small, to lean into the invisible current. She flew along the thread as if on a rail, faster and faster, stars shooting by like fireworks. Light and darkness curved into a tunnel, and Lila spun out of time and mind, following a wisp of hair in the breeze, a pair of thin hands pressed together in greeting, a pondering frown.

Light overspread the darkness. The tunnel opened to a brilliant blue sky bejeweled with shards of white cloud. A warm, briny breeze flooded Lila's nose, but there were other smells too: pipe smoke, perfume, cinnamon, and fried bread. Wood creaked and flags flapped in the breeze as boats bobbed up and down along the docks. An army of seagulls massed overhead, splitting into groups and diving whenever they spotted a mark among the throngs of people milling about, many in blue and purple garb.

Rontaia.

It took Lila a moment to spot him; he was much smaller, no more than four, though with the same flyaway hair he made no effort to tame. He stood on tiptoes to take the cone of tri-fries from the vendor while a woman with long braids placed a coin in the tray. Lila recognized her immediately from the portrait: Jillia. Theo's mother, and Avisse's late wife.

Jillia lowered her hand instinctively as little Theo wavered with the cone, but he steadied it and plucked one out, tossing it in his hand until it was cool enough to bite off the corner. A seagull swooped low, testing his readiness. He shooed it away expertly, shielding the cone with his body. His eyes met Lila's as he turned, and his smile faded.

The gulls stopped mid-flight. His mother's dress hung half-twirled where she was turning to pluck a tri-fry from the cone. Her face was lit up in a smile that tugged at Lila's heart harder than the tether. Theo looked up at his mother, then back at Lila, begging with his eyes. She took a step toward him and crouched to his eye level, looking up at his mother again.

"She sure is beautiful," she said in a low voice.

"You think so? I can never tell. Her being my birth mother and all, I think I'm predisposed to find her so."

"I can tell she loved you a lot."

Theo squinted against the sun as he looked back up at his mother's face, frozen in that joyous smile. "I know. I just...I can't remember. I *know* it, rationally, but when I search in my heart, I can't feel it. Like she's slipping away. How can your own mother slip away from your memories? How can you forget what it feels like to know that she loves you?"

Theo's face stretched as his tears flowed. His body grew, still thin and knobbly, but taller now, like the Theo she knew, the one who was due back in Avisse's arms. How much time had passed back in that room? It could be seconds or hours or even days. There was no way to tell. She had to get them back.

"It's like you told me. There's always a part of her that's in you, and you in her. But you have another mother, Theo, and if you don't come back soon, I'm afraid she's going to kill Sylvan, and nobody wants that."

Theo's serious face quirked into a tiny smile. "I don't think she'd *actually* kill him."

"You should have seen her slap him around."

Theo winced, covering his mouth. "Gods, how long have I been gone? I figured I'd be back before anyone woke up." He stared down at the cone of tri-fries in his hand, which were still steaming, even though everything else in the scene remained frozen. He lifted one out and cracked the corner in his teeth, chewing thoughtfully. "I guess I should have known time would work differently here." He offered the bag to Lila, who waved it away. She wasn't going to push her luck. Theo sighed, setting the bag on the cart, where the vendor was frozen in the act of swiping the coin into her apron.

"There's never enough time." His words sounded small in the emptiness. He stared up at his mother for a long moment, tenting his fingers below his chin.

"Sylvan rebalanced the water in the Well, but I'm not sure how long we have." Lila tried to keep her voice level, but her tether was pulling on the back of her mind. She had only to let go and it would snap her back like a spring.

Theo nodded. "I feel it too. It was nice before, when it stopped. I felt like I could stay here forever, and it wouldn't matter. Nothing mattered except for my mother and me getting tri-fries on the dock." He touched his fingers to his lips, then pressed the fingers to his mother's lips.

"I love you too, Mama Jillia," he whispered.

When he turned to Lila, his eyes were wet, but he wasn't crying exactly. His face was brave, resigned, and maybe a little hopeful. The scene behind him faded away, leaving them in blackness punctuated by clusters of stars and the faint shimmering of twisted golden lines crisscrossing the dark.

"So, how do we get back?"

Lila watched Theo's face light up with surprise, distend into a golden streak, then vanish into the clouds of darkness. Her tether pulled taut, vibrating, then went slack. Her heart flooded with panic as she searched for the pressure on the back of her mind. It was there, but so weak, she couldn't grasp it. She tried expanding her mind's reach, as she did in her meditation, but found only emptiness all around and a feeble connection like a slack rope. She strained to tighten it, but neither she nor the tether would budge.

Lila floated, helpless, in the void, wondering if this was how she'd spend the rest of her days. Or perhaps days were not relevant here; eternity felt like a more appropriate concept. A sense of calm washed over her. There was no pressure here, no one to please, no one to worry about. It was like the quiet moments before sleep when anything was possible, the mind unfettered by responsibility.

A sharp tug at the back of her mind snapped her from her reverie. The Thousand Worlds folded in on themselves, and soon she was hurtling backward, stars and streaks flying away from her as if she were regurgitating the universe in her flight. Her mind and body hurtled together with the force of a thunderclap, and she stood, hands in the gloves, her vision spinning with colors and shapes she'd never imagined before. She couldn't breathe, couldn't hear, couldn't focus on anything other than the kaleidoscope of colors and the searing pain like lightning running through her bones. A sharp cry pierced her ears—her own, she realized—and her hands tore from the gloves as if they were on fire. She fell back into strong arms, which wrapped around her and carried her to the ground. Soft lips on her face, hot breath in her ear, the world slowly coming into focus. Two white orbs with dark centers, a mess of brown hair, the curve of reddish-warm skin.

"You did it." Avisse's kiss returned the breath to Lila's lungs. "You brought my baby boy back to me." Avisse's forehead was hot on hers, their tears mingling as they held each other on the hard stone floor. Another pair of hands joined them, another forehead, another pair of legs entangling with theirs.

"I'm not a baby," Theo said in a tremulous voice, his tears wetting Lila's cheek. "But I'm ready to admit I may not be ready for my early majority just yet."

Avisse's laughter quickly turned into sobs as she squeezed them both tight. Theo's thin arms reached around Avisse and Lila with surprising strength. Lila held still in the center, crying along with them, suddenly happier than she had been in her entire life.

Sylvan stood in the corner, insofar as there could be a corner in a completely round room. He leaned against the stairs, watching with his head half-turned toward them as Avisse lifted the glass globe, studying it under the light of several dozen tiny brightstones.

"And it won't work without this?"

Sylvan shook his head, eyes weak and watery.

Avisse tossed it in the air and caught it several times. Lila could almost hear Sylvan's heart skipping a beat each time.

"How much you think he paid for this thing?" she asked, turning to Lila.

"I wouldn't even know where to begin to guess. I'd say certainly north of—" Lila's breath caught as Avisse wound up like a horseball pitcher and hurled the crystal ball through the shining bronze arch. It exploded against the wall, sending a thousand slivers of glass skittering around the room. Sylvan slumped to the floor, covering his face. Avisse picked up a wrench that was lying on the table and advanced on the podium, every muscle in her wiry frame tense. She brought the wrench down again and again, smashing the fine tubes and wires, mangling the sophisticated metal flower into an unrecognizable tangle of bronze in a matter of seconds. She hurled the wrench at the wall, then threw her weight against the podium, which was bolted to the floor and didn't budge at first. She rocked it back and forth, moving it a little each time, until the wood splintered away from the bolts and the whole thing came crashing down. She picked it up, staggering against its weight, and slammed it against the arch, screaming at the top of her lungs, filling the room with her cries of rage as she battered the once-shiny metal into an increasingly bent and wrinkled shape.

On the last blow, the arch tore loose from its moorings and crashed into the table with all of Sylvan's jars of powders and liquids. Several of them shattered on the floor, dumping much of their contents into the well, which fizzed and bubbled and steamed as gods knew what mixture of chemicals raged in the water.

"Gods, no!" Sylvan scrambled to his feet, grabbing Theo by the elbow as steam billowed from the well. "We have to get out now!"

Avisse's eyes cleared in an instant, and she coughed against the steam. Lila covered her mouth with her sleeve, holding out a hand toward Avisse. Once she held those strong fingers in hers, they followed Theo and Sylvan out of the room as the well popped and hissed angrily through the thickening haze. Sylvan slammed the door closed, turning the key in the lock, then took off running down the hallway, dragging Theo behind him, with Lila and Avisse on their heels. A dull boom sounded behind them as they neared the big door to the baths. The ground shook for a moment, then all was still.

Sylvan leaned against the wall, closing his eyes. His gray paint was streaked with tears and dirt. Theo released his hand, sidling over to Avisse, who took him under her arm, sheltering him like a mother hen. Lila stepped toward Sylvan, whose eyes fluttered open as she approached.

"I'm so sorry," he said, eyes leaking fresh tears. "I ruined everything."

"Shhh." Lila pulled out her handkerchief, which was none too clean, and dried his tears. "Everyone is safe and sound now." She dabbed at his paint with her finger, smoothing out the lines made by his tears, like her mother used to do to her whenever they went out. She'd always hated it, but she'd kind of missed it when she'd outgrown it. "No one died, and I daresay we all learned a thing or two from your little experiment."

Sylvan took her hand and held it in his, a trembly smile forming on his lips.

"I think I'll do my scholarship in books from now on."

19

Avisse didn't kill Sylvan that day, nor the next. She didn't talk to him or let him see Theo, but when they passed each other in the courtyard, Avisse gave him a nod that wasn't entirely unfriendly. Avisse and Theo spent the day out walking their horses, and Lila pitched in at the shop as much as she was able, though she was still lightheaded from her adventure in the Thousand Worlds. She had a spread of dips and fish roe ready for dinner when Theo and Avisse returned, with enough extra flatbread to split Theo's face into an ear-to-ear smile.

"I think I like the little black roe best." Theo smacked his lips, having tried all three kinds over and over, clearly as an excuse to eat more bread. "We don't get roe like this down in Rontaia."

"*You* don't get roe like this down in Rontaia," Avisse quipped. "Lila's *spoiling* you."

Lila winked at Theo, holding her thumb and forefinger close together. "I'm just really glad to have you back. Both of you." She stretched her arms to take their hands. "For however long you're staying." She glanced hopefully at Avisse, who squeezed her hand tightly.

"Well, I don't have any deliveries scheduled in..." She glanced up at the ceiling, as if doing mental calculations. "Ever." She smirked at Lila, who shook her head in confusion.

"What do you mean, *ever*?"

"I told Antonia this would be my last delivery. I was waiting for the perfect moment to mention it, but..." She shrugged, wincing a smile at Lila.

"Mother!" Theo stood from the table, almost knocking his chair over. Lila's mind spun trying to comprehend what was happening.

"What...what will you do?"

"Well, I figure a woman with my talents can surely find work in the biggest city on the continent. And I was hoping, that is, in the short term at least..." She bit her lip, glancing up at Lila with her big, brown eyes.

"I—" Lila choked on her words, clutching Avisse's hot, damp hand in hers. She glanced at Theo through her tears, saw his toothy little smile and bright eyes, and a laugh burst out of her. "Yes, yes, YES!" She stood, yanking Avisse out of her chair and into a tight hug, which grew even tighter as Theo piled on.

"I promise I'll get better about making up the sofa in the morning." Theo's voice was muffled by her hair. "And I'll stack my books all nice and neat on the bookshelf. I won't be any bother, I promise!"

Lila pulled back, touching foreheads with Theo. "You couldn't bother me if you tried."

"I did though, the other night. I worried you both sick." He slunk out of their arms, standing up straight but looking down, composing his face. When he looked back up, his eyes were as serious as if he were about to launch into a lecture on the history of the languages of the Time Before.

"It's the most selfish, irresponsible thing I've ever done in my life, except when I was a baby, and that doesn't really count. Mother, I lied to you directly, which I've never done before, and to Sylvan. And I know it will be hard for you to believe me, but I swear on every star in the Thousand Worlds, I never will again." A tear rolled down his cheek, followed by another on the other side, but he kept going.

"And Lila, you took me in, showed me nothing but kindness—you *listened* to me, more than my mother does sometimes—sorry, mother, I just swore I would never lie to you—and I betrayed your trust. I took your keys, I trespassed on your property, and I put you both in a very dangerous situation. I am truly sorry." He paused, and Lila wanted to scoop him up in her arms, tell him it was okay, everything would be okay, but she could tell he wasn't finished yet.

"And even after that, even after all I did, you came for me. You risked your life, put your hands in the gloves, and traveled into the Thousand Worlds for me. That is a debt that will take a lifetime to repay."

Lila glanced at Avisse, whose eyes were as full and wet as Lila's. Avisse opened her arms, and Theo stepped into them, landing between Lila and Avisse, clutching them both with his thin but freakishly strong arms.

"There are no debts in family," Avisse said. "Only the daily promise to be there for each other and to ask for help when we need it."

Lila buried her face in Theo's long, fluffy hair to muffle her sobs. Her own family was nothing like this; asking for help was a sign of weakness. They were only there for each other when they had to be. When Lila had needed them, they'd kicked her out in the most ruthless way possible. And now Avisse had used the word to describe the three of them.

Family.

Lila's heart swelled to fill the space between them, growing larger still until it enveloped them like a bubble. A few months ago, she'd never known these people existed, and now she couldn't imagine the next day or the next minute without them.

As they disentangled awkwardly from the group hug, Lila dabbed around her eyes and blew her nose discreetly. Avisse and Theo were in similar shape, all puffy-faced smiles and runny noses.

Avisse's eyebrows lifted, and she clapped her hands together.

"What do you say we head down to the canal for some ice toads?"

Theo held both of their hands as they walked along the canal, jerking his hands away to point whenever a fish surfaced, which was often. They could see the glowing green frog-shaped paper lanterns atop the ice toad carts from half a mile away. It was just as Lila remembered it from her childhood, but instead of one cart selling the freshly toasted cones of half-frozen green glop, there were three of them. It tasted exactly the same, creamy and overly sweet with a sharp bite of greenorange and two preserved cherries on top, which were supposed to be the eyes.

"I could get used to this whole Anari thing." Theo licked a stray streak of green from the side of his cone.

"We'll see how you feel once winter comes." Avisse bumped his hip, sending him careening into Lila, who bumped his floppy body back to Avisse.

"But at least you have snow!"

"A couple of times a year, if we're lucky."

"Sounds like a couple of times too many to me." Avisse shivered. Lila scooted closer, wrapping an arm around her.

"That's what snuggling tight under the blankets is for."

"I guess winter doesn't sound *all* bad." She leaned her head on Lila's shoulder, watching Theo bite the bottom off his cone and suck the green liquid out. He lost quite a bit of it to the gravel and his fingers and face, but he didn't mind a bit if his smile was any indication.

Theo's enthusiasm gave way to yawns as they made their way back along the canal and through the gate to the second ring. By the time they reached the carriage house, Lila was ready to carry him up the stairs, but Avisse pushed him forward with a sharp finger between the shoulder blades.

"Up, up, up, like a pup!"

"Puppy's tired." Theo slumped up the stairs and into the washroom. Avisse leaned into Lila at the kitchen table, brushing the hair away from her neck and planting a small, wet kiss on her windpipe. Why was that the sexiest thing she'd ever done? Avisse's hand rested on Lila's stomach, rubbing in slow circles as she kissed her way up to Lila's chin, pulling it down with her lips. Lila held onto the table for support as Avisse climbed halfway onto her thigh and her lips made contact, filling Lila's mouth with the tang of citrus and desire. She moaned as Avisse's fingers slid down between her legs, feathering over her cleft, which swelled at this faint touch.

The washroom door opened, and Avisse slid off Lila as casually as she could. If Theo noticed through his slitted eyelids, he made no show of it. He shuffled down the hall toward his bedroom, formerly known as the study. It wasn't as if Lila studied there anymore, or even read. At least someone was using it for its intended purpose. Avisse slipped from her arms and followed Theo down the hall. She stopped in the doorway and motioned Lila over with her head.

Lila's heart leapt, and her feet followed. Theo had already slipped between the covers, and Avisse was kissing his forehead.

"Good night, sweet boy," she cooed.

"Good night, Mother," he said, kissing the air. "Good night, Lila."

"Good night, Theo," Lila managed, though she was too choked up to speak above a whisper.

Avisse patted his shoulder, turned off the lamp, and padded out of the room. Lila made way, closing the door behind her.

"Good kid," Lila whispered.

Avisse closed her eyes, nodding.

"Real good kid."

20

Avisse's expression was difficult to read as she returned from the washroom in her sleeveless shirt and briefs. Her eyes were hard and soft at the same time as if she were giving something a lot of thought and wasn't sure how she felt about it.

Her actions were easier to interpret.

She grabbed Lila by the shoulders and unlaced her dress, pulling it over her head in a flurry of deft movements. Lila dropped the brush she'd been holding as Avisse seized her hips and spun her around. Before Lila could catch her breath, Avisse had her pinned against the dresser, tongue down her throat, strong hands everywhere at once. Lila let out a little whine as Avisse's hand slid between her legs, fingering her cleft through the thin silk of her gaff. Avisse's kiss softened, her touch so gentle it made Lila light-headed. She wanted to lean into it, but the delicate edge Avisse kept her on was so delicious that Lila was frozen in place.

Avisse broke from the kiss, lips wet and eyes glossy, hands sliding to grip Lila's hips.

"Go sit on the bed," Avisse said over her shoulder as she bent over to retrieve something from her pack, offering a tantalizing view of her backside. Lila backed up to the bed and sat, watching Avisse, whose eyes sparkled as she knelt and set a foot-long rectangular package on the bed.

It was professionally wrapped in sturdy lavender-colored paper and tied with a black ribbon into a knot like an elaborate flower. Lila picked up the box, which was heavier than it looked, and set it on her lap. She glanced up at Avisse, who was biting her lip, face flushed and eyes aglow with anticipation. Lila tugged on the long tail of the ribbon, and the flower unfurled itself gracefully. She found the seam of the paper and peeled it apart without ripping it; it was such a pretty color, and she might find a use for it. The box inside was made of polished darkwood, with the familiar dripping S.D. of the Silver Dock logo in silver inlay.

"Avisse, this is..." It had to be an olli, and their prices were astronomically high. Lila had wanted to buy one for Avisse, but even at wholesale, it seemed like a foolish luxury.

"It was a going away present from Gilli, from Silver Dock." She bit her lip harder, gesturing toward the box. "Go ahead, open it!"

Lila slid the top off the box, revealing a red flameglass olli with a gently bulbed and curved tip, a generous handle at the other end, and a mechanism inside unlike any of the others she had in the shop. She picked it up, marveling at the glasswork, alternating ribbons of rich red and a softer pinkish hue. Inside, she could make out springs and wires like the other vibrating ollis, but also something like clockwork, intricate interlocking wheels in a dense array spiraling the length of the olli. On the handle were a set of six metal buttons and a slot like the alchemical ollis had for blackpowder pellets. She scanned the box and saw two rows of pellets nestled in neat velvet trays.

"This is a new model?"

Avisse nodded, gesturing to the olli. "It has six different settings, and you can change it with these buttons here." Her fingers brushed over Lila's as she touched the buttons, sending a fresh round of shivers across her skin. "The highest setting is supposed to be twice as strong as the old ones."

Lila thought back to the demonstration, the feel of the olli in her hands, how it had stirred her. She hefted the device, which was nicely contoured, easy to grip. She'd pleasured women with ollis before, but she swelled against her gaff at the thought of using this on Avisse. What the vibration would add. All the things she could do with it. The sounds Avisse would make. How hard she would come.

She looked up just in time to see Avisse's lips closing on hers. Avisse pushed her back onto the bed, taking the olli from her and laying it between her legs, where it lay, heavy and still. Avisse stripped her tank and briefs in seconds, then crouched over Lila, breasts brushing against her chest, ineffably soft and warm. Her tongue explored Lila's mouth, tenderly at first as their bodies slowly connected, skin against hot skin.

Avisse's fingers ran through her hair, nails grazing her scalp as they kissed. Avisse's weight pressed the olli between Lila's legs, and even without vibration, its hard length was intoxicating. Avisse began moving against it, pressing it into Lila's cleft as her tongue delved deep. Lila wrapped her arms around Avisse's strong back and held on for dear life, willing herself not to spill as Avisse slid slowly back and forth along the olli's length.

Avisse pulled back from the kiss, breathing heavily, and leaned back, taking the pressure off and saving Lila from certain doom. Avisse reached down to fiddle with the olli for a moment, and the bed began humming with vibrations that traveled through the mattress, sending shivers throughout her body. Avisse leaned over to grab the oil from the bedside table, breasts swaying above Lila's face, then returned to kneel between Lila's legs. She locked eyes with Lila as she picked up the olli, whose vibrations were nearly silent, but she could almost feel them in the air. Avisse drizzled a thin stream of oil from the nozzle onto the olli, which she twisted as the oil hit it. When the olli was glistening with oozing streaks of oil, she returned the bottle to the bedside table, then straddled Lila's stomach, holding the olli in the air as her fingers smoothed the oil all over.

"Do you want?" she asked in a voice far too innocent for someone holding a vibrating olli covered in oil.

"I need," Lila moaned.

The touch of the olli on Lila's chest sent a shock through her entire body, which grew into a seismic wave as Avisse trailed it around one nipple, then the other. Each time it brushed against her buds was like a lightning strike, and when Avisse held it in place above one nipple, barely touching, Lila thought she might levitate out of her body and dissipate into the sky. She gasped as Avisse moved the olli away, trailing it along her stomach, scooching her body down. She spread Lila's legs wide, caressing her cleft gently with oil-soaked fingers. Lila made sounds then that she wasn't proud of, low, animalistic sounds that grew higher as Avisse lifted the waistband of her gaff and slid the olli down her cleft. Lila's voice trailed off as her breath left her. All she could do was pant in desperation as the vibration filled her with sizzling need.

Avisse adjusted the olli with careful fingers; the gaff held it firmly in place, and it protruded by an inch or so. She crawled atop Lila, licking and sucking on her neck, then lowering her chest first, then her belly before wriggling into place. Avisse took in a sharp breath as she made contact, teeth sinking into Lila's neck for a sharp, hot moment. Her strong thighs pushed Lila's wider, then she began moving.

She gripped Lila's shoulders, her breath hot and heavy, eyes dark and deep. Lila wrapped her arms around Avisse's tight body, which moved like crashing waves, sending vibrations deep within Lila's core with each thrust. Avisse's breath grew hoarse, and the bed began to creak as she hammered away, dislodging the olli, but by now it didn't matter. Avisse's breath was like a racehorse as she rode Lila with the power and fury of a thunderstorm, fucking her into a state of helpless euphoria. Lila's arms and legs flailed to the sides as she came, Avisse's fingers digging deep bruises around her collarbones as she trembled, her sweat-slicked face twisted in an almost pained oval, and collapsed in a heap atop Lila.

The silence that followed was broken only by the slow clip-clop of a solitary carriage somewhere in the distance. It seemed they'd managed not to awaken Theo with their noise; Avisse had said he seemed to sleep better here than anywhere else.

Avisse was much heavier in this position than in any other, but Lila lay happily crushed beneath her. The vibration of the olli ran through the mattress, stirring almost painful twinges between her legs. She managed to grab it without dislodging Avisse and fumbled with the buttons until it turned off. Lila smiled up at the ceiling as Avisse's faint snore sounded in her ear. Avisse was warm when she slept, and though Lila was wet and sticky and her feet were a little cold, she was happy in a way she'd never thought possible.

21

A strange tinkling sound roused Lila from her slumber. She pulled on her robe, tucking her hair behind her ears as she eased open the door and padded into the kitchen. Theo stood at the table, measuring porridge flakes into a bowl. He flashed her a quiet smile and waved with two fingers.

"Is it okay if I heat some water?" he said in a low voice.

"Of course, sweetie." Lila touched him absently on the shoulder as she passed, filling the kettle and setting it gently on the stove. "I'll give you a hand since I've got to get tea going."

"You don't need to whisper. My mother sleeps like a turtle."

"So I've noticed."

Theo put the lid back on the porridge flakes and studied her array of tins and jars.

"Dried fruits in the red one, nuts in the brown one. Honey's in the jar over there."

Theo pulled out the tins and the honey and lined them up on the table.

"You feeling all right?" she asked him.

"Of course! Why wouldn't I be?" His voice was as bright and chipper.

"I don't know, with everything that happened, and with all the big changes…"

Theo sat down, folding his hands together and furrowing his brow. "I guess it's a lot to take in, but we've always traveled. I haven't been in regular school for over five years. It's not like I have many friends in Rontaia anyway."

Lila's heart ached for the boy. Did he even have friends his own age at all? Or was he just one of those kids who only related to adults?

"You could enroll at the university here if you want. There's no age limit, as long as you can pass the entrance exam."

"I know," Theo said as if it were the most obvious thing in the world. "I've completed all but one of my prerequisites, and I'll have that done in a few weeks. I'm just not sure if a traditional diploma is what's best for my scholarly career at this point."

Lila covered her mouth to hide her smile. The boy was not even thirteen years old and already talking about his scholarly career. A little mini-Sylvan in the making, minus the painted skin.

Lila had her tea and Theo his porridge, then Lila washed up, shaved, and put on her makeup. She couldn't get dressed for another hour, when Avisse finally stumbled out of the bedroom, adorably rumpled, hair sticking out in every direction.

She kissed Theo on the head and Lila on the lips, then padded to the washroom, yawning and scratching her behind.

The clear chime on the High Tower sounded middle morn. Low voices rose from the courtyard as the first bathers filtered in. Lila sighed contentedly into her tea. Tera and Aven had forbidden her from setting foot in the shop for another two days, so whatever problems arose were theirs to deal with. She poured and mixed Avisse's tea, handing it to her as she emerged from the washroom, accepting a grateful kiss in return.

"So, what shall we do today, mother?" Theo asked, looking up from his book.

"Nothing, Theo. Absolutely nothing."

'Nothing' turned out to involve a visit to the market for provisions, which they did on foot. Thankfully, the sun stayed at bay, and the summery heat had finally fled, leaving in its place a pleasantly cool and cloudy day. Lila and Avisse walked hand in hand, with Theo trailing behind them. Lila played the game she always played in her mind as she walked through public spaces, studying women's outfits and crowning the best dressed among them with a mental award. Sometimes she got ideas for her own wardrobe from the game. Other times, there were looks that would never work for her, but she appreciated them nonetheless. Occasionally, she saw someone who reminded her of the woman in the paisley dress from her childhood, which sometimes made her a little melancholy.

On this day, she saw a woman who looked devilishly familiar, but Lila couldn't get close enough to see her face. Avisse had stopped to examine some bloodroots, and Theo had his nose in a book he'd brought with him. Lila watched the woman, who stood in profile, talking to a friend and laughing, gesturing with her hands. It was the shape of her that was so familiar, the slope of her shoulders, the curve of her bust. Lila got that hollow feeling in her chest again, and she realized who the woman reminded her of. Other-Lila. The one she'd seen in the Sooth Mirror.

Was she out there, in some other world or dimension, living her life as a painted face? Was she arranged to be married to some strange man, prized for her skin tone, the shape of her face, the heft of her family's fortune? Lila would never have been happy in such a life. She was sure her sister Jaeni wasn't happy. Nor her mother, for that matter. But Other-Lila had smiled so earnestly...maybe she was happy after all. Maybe...

"Let's see if they have some nice mudcrawlers." Avisse's cheery voice pulled Lila from her reverie. "I haven't had those in a while, and the freshwater ones always taste a little sweeter."

"Yes, of course!" Lila wasn't a fan; she'd been raised to think of them as outer-ring food, and her fingers always got shredded from picking the shells. "I think...over there?"

The woman was gone when she looked back. Lila didn't see her again, but she hovered on the periphery of Lila's mind, and the empty feeling in her chest grew as they finished their shopping and schlepped their provisions back to the carriage house.

"I don't know about you, but I could use a nap." Avisse looked genuinely sleepy, rather than seductive, though if Lila joined her in bed, all bets were off.

"You go ahead. I need to go talk to Tera for a moment."

"Hey!" Avisse grabbed her chin, pulling her close and frowning. "No work until the day after tomorrow. You promised!"

"This isn't work, I swear." Lila kissed the frown from Avisse's lips. "You go lie down and I'll be back before you know it."

"Take too long, and I might fall asleep," Avisse murmured, her hands slipping over Lila's hips, stirring her desire with a simple touch.

"I promise."

Aven rushed toward her as she slipped through the door, wagging their finger at her.

"No, no, nope! Absolutely not. You are forbidden from entering!"

"It's not for work, Aven. I'm here to see Tera."

They stopped, hand moving to their chin, which they rubbed in suspicion. "She's in the office." They pointed, sticking their arm out rather dramatically. "And you better make it quick. She's quite busy, I assure you."

"Well, as it happens, I'm here on business, but not"—she raised a finger to stop their obvious objection—"not as owner. I'm here as a customer."

Aven's arm fell gently to their side, and their eyebrows raised slightly.

"Then I'm sure she'll be most happy to see you," they said, warmth creeping back into their tone.

Lila's stomach roiled as she approached the door, though the smell of citrus tea calmed her somewhat. She peered in and saw Tera writing in a ledger, the desk neater and less cluttered than it ever was when Lila was present. Tera looked up and huffed a sigh, glancing toward the half-open door.

"Aven was supposed to stop you before you got this far. I'm afraid I must insist, Lila. You need your time off!"

"I'm not here for work, Tera."

Tera's face softened as Lila approached and settled into the chair opposite the desk. Tera poured her a cup of tea, which Lila picked up to have something to do with her hands.

"Is everything all right?" Tera's voice was so gentle, Lila let out a silent laugh.

"Yes, yes, everything's just perfect. We went to the market this morning, and Avisse and Theo are napping. It feels like...it feels so *normal*. Like it was always meant to be this way."

Tera nodded slightly, eyebrows dipping with concern. She didn't say anything, gave Lila the space to continue.

"Things are great between us, between Avisse and me, and with Theo, and the shop is doing so well. I feel like I've been working so long to get out from under something, to build something new, and now that it's here..." She took a deep breath as tears came streaming down her cheeks. Gods, why was this so hard? She dabbed her face with her handkerchief, forcing a little laugh as she looked up into Tera's piercing hazel eyes. Tera would understand. Tera surely understood already. With eyes like that, she saw through everything.

"The reason I'm here is..." Lila took another deep breath and kept the tears at bay this time. "I want to book an appointment in the Lavender Room."

Tera came around the desk and took Lila in her arms, holding onto her with soft, steady strength. Lila's tears flowed again, with the warmth of pure release. She clung to Tera, who held her for a long time, never wavering, never speaking, just being there for a friend.

"It is *such* a pleasure to have you." Sera's voice was rich and mellifluous, her tone oozing warmth. "You are an inspiration to so many of us, and such a natural beauty to boot."

"I don't know about that." Lila felt the flush spread across her face and neck.

"Look," said Sera, leaning forward in her seat, showing a peek of her generous cleavage, "there's more beauty in all of us waiting to be unlocked, but you've got a ten-mile head start, is all I'm saying."

Lila was sure her entire head was crimson by now. "Thanks, I guess."

Sera smiled indulgently.

"Why don't you tell me a little bit about your history, then we can talk about your goals and what we can do to get you there."

Lila forced a giggle. "I see these teenagers coming in with their parents, and I think, what would it have been like, what would *I* be like, if only…"

Sera waved a finger in the air.

"We have only one rule in the Lavender Room. No regrets about the past. We're here to focus on the future."

Lila nodded, smiling, biting back tears.

"The future."

Sera nodded, her face lit up with a warm smile.

"That's right. It's never too late to take the next step."

Also By Dani Finn

The Maer Cycle (*Hollow Road*, *The Archive*, and *The Place Below*), a classic fantasy trilogy with LGBTQ characters. It tells the story of the encounter between humans and the legendary hairy humanoids called the Maer and the struggle for the two peoples to reconcile their history and their future.

The Weirdwater Confluence duology (*The Living Waters* and *The Isle of a Thousand Worlds*) are a pair of romantic fantasy books with meditation magic. They are independent of the trilogy, but there are little connections. Both books are sword-free and death-free, in sharp contrast to the Maer Cycle. *Unpainted* is a standalone arranged marriage fantasy romance set in the same universe.

The Time Before: *The Delve*, *Jagged Shard*, *Wings so Soft*, and *Cloti's Song*, a group of linked romantic fantasy standalones set 2,000 years before the Maer Cycle. Meant to be read before or after the other books, they tell the story of the fall of the great Maer civilization of old.

Scrublands: A new series set in a Switzerland-inspired fantasy world. *They of the West* is a novel of friendship and self-discovery about two teens who go chasing after treasure in forbidden canyons.

Acknowledgements

This book would not have been possible without May Peterson's inspiration, encouragement, advice, sensitivity reading, and moral support. She helped me gain the courage to write this story, which is so close to my heart, when I'd all but written it off. *I* wasn't the one to write Lila's story, my brain weasels said. I was an *imposter*. May helped shoo away the weasels, and the rest is history. Any issues with representation or handling of sensitive material are mine and mine alone, of course.

I'd also like to thank the many brilliant writers who pushed and prodded me behind the scenes, helped me think through some tough ideas, gave me cover advice, and generally formed the support group I needed to write this, including, but not limited to: Krystle Matar, Fiona West, and Steve Westenra, among others.

Huge thanks to Beth Blaufuss, my alpha reader and long-time critique partner, for her helpful suggestions and for pushing me to make this the absolute best it could be.

Thanks to Chris Zable, whose careful and thoughtful copyediting has ensured that this will be my cleanest and most coherent manuscript yet. Any errors you find were surely introduced by me changing something at the last minute.

My most heartfelt thanks to the trans community, especially the inspiring transfem writers who show me time and again what books with trans women as main characters can look like. Y'all are kicking so much ass right now.

And thanks to my readers, whoever you are. It means the world to me that you joined me on this journey.

About the Author

Dani Finn (they/them) is a nonbinary fantasy romance author who occasionally writes fantasy without romance as well.

They favor high-steam love stories that crisscross the gender spectrum, from swords and sorcery to sword-free fantasy with meditation magic and everything in between.

Made in United States
Cleveland, OH
06 April 2025